white flames:
erotic dreams

Also by Cecilia Tan

Telepaths Don't Need Safewords
Black Feathers
The Velderet
Edge Plays

white flames:
erotic dreams

by Cecilia Tan

RUNNING PRESS
PHILADELPHIA • LONDON

9 8 7 6 5 4 3 2 1
Digit on the right indicates the number of this printing
Library of Congress Control Number: 2007943026
ISBN 978-0-78672-080-4

Cover design by Scott Idleman
Interior design by Alicia Freile
Typography: Sabon and Type Embellishments

Running Press Book Publishers
2300 Chestnut Street
Philadelphia, PA 19103-4371

Visit us on the web!
www.runningpress.com

CONTENTS

INTRODUCTION

SUCH A FRAUGHT WORD: "fantasy." It seems to carry two distinct connotations. When someone "fantasizes" it's assumed we are talking about sexual fantasies. But "fantasy" in the bookstore is the shelf where the elves and wizards sit, as well as the science fiction, robots, and spaceships.

The stories I write seem to inhabit the space where fantasy meets reality. Sometimes that means the erotic fantasy that would never "really" happen. Other times that means a story that uncovers the magical world that intersects the "real world," or a glimpse into the future. But when I tend to do that, eroticism tends to leak through. If I had to make a stab at a lit-crit explanation, I'd say my subconscious thinks the "normal" state of sexual repression in real life needs cracking open, and sometimes the cracks come in the erotic lives of the characters, sometimes in the "reality" they inhabit, and sometimes both.

So this book has stories like "Thought So," where a pickup in a bookstore happens entirely too easily for "real life" though we later find out the less-than-mundane reason why. It has stories like "Dragon's Daughter," where the eroticism is sublimated into a story of yearning and coming of age, and at the other end of the spectrum has "encounter story" romps like "Halloween" and "Drumbeat." How funny, "encounter" is another of those words. Some people will immediately think of alien abduction, while the erotica enthusiasts know it's a term for a story where the premise is simple: two people meet, they have sex. Granted, in my stories, an "encounter" could be both, though there are very few spaceships in this book (two, in fact).

The unadorned truth is that I wrote every story in here because the idea "turned me on." And yes, I do mean that phrase to have both its general vernacular meaning and its specific erotic one. Some of them, like "Bodies of Water," came from dreams, others, like "Lip Service," from real life experiences of mine.

I hope you "enjoy" them as much as I did.

Cecilia Tan
Cambridge, MA

FLARES

Stories that leave a flash behind your eyelids

love's year

IT BEGAN IN APRIL, because she said that was when she began, and it was a time for new things. She taught me more than one new thing, like how to kiss her and fondle her at the same time without fumbling either one. She said my kiss resurrected her, and hers made me bloom. In May we discovered sex out of doors, long hours in the rope hammock, each with one of the other's hands tucked between our legs, until we were both satisfied and the Goddess had played tic-tac-toe upon our backs. But our moment in the sun was yet to come. June was a month of true summer, when I learned to lick the sweat from her back, when we would soak the sheets with our wetness—so slick we were like seals or mermaids as we slid against each other. The intensity of July sent us to the mountains, to laze in a cabin by the lakeshore, but by evening when the mosquitoes came out, we would have already spent the afternoon biting one another. By August the heat became too much for me and I struggled to hold her at arm's length. But I was too torpid to move that fast, as she licked at me like I was ice cream. With September came first day classroom feelings as she sensed my unease and began to instruct me in new endeavors: how to hold her gently afterward, what to talk about when the sweating and sucking is over. In October she declared it the season for indoor sports, and so I held her like a bowling ball—thumb in one hole, fingers in the other—and she ping-ponged me from wistful to wanton and back again.

November was the month of the turkey baster.

Snow came in December, and long mornings spent in bed after office closings; her hand sliding between the blanket and my stomach, her hair around her head like a wreath on the pillow. But somehow I knew her heart was no longer a gift. January we celebrated with a kiss at midnight, but it would be a winter of discontent. By February the cold was bitter. And in March that is exactly what I did.

always

MORGAN WAS always the one who wanted a child. Even when I first met her, before we got involved, before we got engaged; always the talk of motherhood with her, of empowering Earth-mother stuff and of making widdle baby booties. I, on the other hand, had always said I would never have children, was sure somehow that I would never decide to bear a child, and yet I had always thought about it, secretly. So when I fell in love with Morgan, and she fell in love with me, and we had a hilltop wedding where we both wore white dresses and two out of our four parents looked on happily; I figured I was off the hook on the parenting issue.

This was, of course, before John, and way before Jillian. But I'm getting ahead of myself.

Back up to the summer of 1989. New England. Cape Cod. Morgan and I are in a hammock in the screened-in porch of her aunt's summerhouse. The night is turning smoothly damp after a muggy day, cars hiss by on pavement, still wet from the afternoon's rainshower, the slight breeze rocks us just enough to make me feel weightless as I drowse. I am on my back with one foot hanging out each side of the hammock; Morgan rests in the wide space between my legs, her spill of brown curls spread on my stomach and her knees drawn up close to her chest. The hammock is the nice, cloth kind, with a wide wooden bar at either end to keep it from squeezing us like seeds in a lemon wedge, not the white rope type that leaves you looking like a bondage experiment gone wrong. Morgan's hands travel up my thighs like they come out of a dream. It never occurs to me to stop her. Sex with Morgan is as easy and natural as saying yes to a bite of chocolate from the proffered bar of a friend. Before her fingers even reach the elastic edge of my panties I am already shifting my hips, already breathing deeper, already thinking about the way her fingers will touch and tease me, how one slim finger will slide deep into me once I am wet, how good it feels to play with her hair on my belly, how much I want her. With Morgan, I always come.

Imagine afterwards, lying now side by side, holding each other and sharing each other's heat as the beach breeze turns chilly. When I decide to propose to her, I am gifted with a sudden and utter clarity—this is the right thing to do. It has been six years since I came out as bisexual, three years since I began dating women, but something like ten years of getting into relationships with men and constantly trying to disentangle myself from them. It's not that I don't like men. I like them, and love them, a-proverbial-lot. But I've never been able to explain why it is I've always felt the need to put up resistance, to define myself separately, to have my foot on the brake of our sex lives. With a man, I always do.

But here, with Morgan, the urge to resist is not even present. Maybe it has nothing to do with men versus women, I think, and maybe it has everything to do with her. She's the right one. And she says yes.

So we got married, that part you knew. Marriage for us did not mean monogamy, of course—rather we defined it as "managed faithfulness." We had our boundaries, our limits, our promises, and our outside dalliances were allowed. But when you're happily married, who has time or energy for all the flirting and courting and negotiating with someone new? Neither of us did for several years. And that's when John came into the picture.

Morgan always toasts the bread a little before she makes cinnamon toast. Always two ticks on our toaster oven's dial, then on goes the butter and sugar and cinnamon, and back in for the full six ticks. I've tried making it without the pre-toasting and can't tell the difference, but she insists.

A raw spring day in Somerville, me in galoshes and a pair of my father's old painting pants with a snow shovel, cursing and trying to lift a cinderblock-sized (and -weighted) chunk of wet packed snow off the walkway of our three-decker. On the first floor lives our landlady, one frail but observant old Irishwoman, Mrs. Donnell; on the second a new tenant we haven't yet met, a single guy we hear walking around late at night and never see in the morning. Hence me trying to shovel the late-season fall, two April-Fool's feet of it, because I'm pretty sure no one else will. Morgan inside; rushing to get ready for work, emerging soap-scented and loosely bundled to plant a kiss on my cheek as she steps over the last foot of unshoveled snow onto the sidewalk (cleared by a neighbor who loves to use his snowblower). She's off to catch the bus to her job downtown as facilities coordinator at the Theater Arts Foundation. I heave on the remaining block of snow with a loud grunt and perhaps it is my grunt that keeps me from hearing the noise my back must surely have made when it cracked, popped, "went out" as they say.

I am hunched over in pain, cursing louder now and not caring if Mrs. Donnell hears it, when another person is there, asking if I'm all right. His hands are on my shoulders and he slowly straightens me upright. It is the new tenant, wearing an unzipped parka and peering into my face with worry. I tell him I'll be all right; he says are you sure? I say yes but I'm clearly not sure—it goes back and forth the way those things will until it ends up somehow with me in his apartment, drinking some kind of herbal tea and then lying face down on his Formica counter with my shirt on the floor while his thumbs and palms map out the terrain of my back.

In the theater world, a backrub is a euphemism for sex. ("Hey, come upstairs, I'll give you a backrub" or "Oh, those two, they've been rubbing each other's backs for years.") So you'd think I'd know. But no, there's no way obviously that he could have planned that I'd try to lift too much snow. No, it was an honest case of one thing led to another. Maybe a couple of resistance-free years with Morgan had dulled my old repeller reflexes, and we... well, in specific, after they had done their magic with my spine, his hands strayed down to my ribs, and he left a line of warm kisses down my back. He had longer-than-average guy hair, straight and tickly like a tassel as it touched my skin. I moaned to encourage him, my body knowing what I wanted before my mind had a chance to change the plan.

Morgan always says I plan too much.

My father's oversize pants slid to the floor and kisses fell like snowflakes onto the curve of my buttocks, feather light, and then a moist tongue probed along the center where it went from hard spine to softness. We got civilized after that, and went to the bedroom and it wasn't until we were lying back having one of those post-coital really-get-to-know-you talks that Morgan came and knocked on the door. "No bus, saw your galoshes on the second floor landing," she explained at her seeming clairvoyance, to which I replied, "This is John."

John always says, "How do you do," and bows while he shakes two-handed when he's formally introduced.

Our first threesome happened right away, that night after dinner—fetched on foot from the Chinese restaurant on the corner. On our living room floor, the white waxy boxes and drink cups scattered at the edges like spectators, the elegant curve of our bay windows standing witness to his hand between my legs, Morgan's mouth on his nipple, my lips on Morgan's ear, John's penis sheathed between us, my chest against his back while he buried himself in her, her tongue on my clit, his nose in my neck, my fingers in her hair, our voices saying whatever they always said, mmm, and ahh, and yes. I didn't know if this was going to be one of Morgan's experiments in excitement, or one of my few dalliances, or one of John's fantasies come true. What it was, which I didn't expect, was the beginning of something more solid, more intricate, and more satisfying than any twosome I had known.

John always buys two dozen roses on Valentine's Day, which he gives to Morgan and me one rose at a time.

When was it, maybe a year later, when Morgan became director at TAF and John, who was in computers, had a discussion with Mrs. Donnell about buying the building? Morgan always loved housewares; I've always loved renovation and design. The idea hit us at Christmas dinner, Morgan's parents' house in Illinois; her mother on one side of her, me on the other, John on my other side, and all manner of relatives near and far spread down the two long tables from the dining room into the ranch house living room (in folding chairs brought for the occasion in minivans and hatchbacks). Turkey so moist the gravy wasn't needed, and gravy so rich that we used it anyway. Wild rice and nut stuffing heaped high on John's plate, shored up by mashed potatoes, his vegetarian principles only mildly compromised by the addition of imitation bacon bits on green salad. Family chatter and laughter, Morgan's father sometimes directing men's talk at John. And somehow the discussion turning to Mrs. Donnell and her plans to sell the house, and somehow our three hands linked in my lap, under the table, and John announcing to everyone, suddenly, that the three of us would buy the house together, voicing the thought that was at that moment in all three of our heads, even though until that moment we'd never contemplated the idea.

I always clean the toilets and the sinks but I hate cleaning the shower and bathtub. John, who has a slight paranoia about foot fungi, loves to do the shower and tub. If only we could convince Morgan to do the kitchen floors.

If my life seems like a series of sudden revelations, that's because it is. The most recent one was watching Jillian walk her stiff-legged toddler's walk from one side of our living room to the other. I knew then what Morgan looked like as a child, what her exploratory spirit and her bright smile must have been like when she was knee high.

The night we made Jillian we had a plan. We didn't always

sleep together, or even have three-way sex together, but we knew all three of us had to have a hand in her creation. For months we had charted Morgan's period, her temperature. We cleared a room to be a new bedroom and put a futon on the floor, lit the candles and incense (we're so old-fashioned that way), and made ready. Imagine Morgan—her long brown curls foaming over her shoulders, her back against the pillowed wall, her knees bent, framing her already seemingly round Earth-mother belly—watching us. John kneels in front of me, naked and somber-faced. I will not let him stay that way for long.

I begin it with a kiss. I kiss Morgan on the lips and then John and we pull away from her. I take his tongue deep into my mouth, my hands roaming over his head and neck, and he responds with a moan. My hard nipples brush against his—my hands on his shoulders I continue to kiss and wag my breasts from side to side, our nipples brush again and again. Then I am licking them, my teeth nipping, my hands sliding down to his hips, one hand between his legs, lifting his balls. He gasps and throws his head back. My mouth is now hovering over his penis, hardening in my hand. I reach out my tongue to tease. Instinct begins to overtake the plan, his hands are reaching for me, he pushes me back, his mouth on mine, his tongue on my nipples, his fingers seeking out my hottest, wettest places and finding them. He knows my body well, he slides two fingers in while his thumb rests on my clit.

Morgan watches, her belly taut, her hands clenched in the sheets.

He is slicking his hand, wet with my juices, up and down his penis, and then he climbs over me. My legs lock behind his back, and he settles in. Tonight there are no barriers between us. I let go with my legs and let him pump freely. If I let him I know he will grant me my secret wish, to make me come from the fucking, from the friction and rhythm and pressure and slap and grind. I am sinking down into a deep well of pleasure, his sweat dripping onto me, as he becomes harder, hotter, faster, tighter, his jaw clenched, and I become looser, and further away. The turning point comes though with a ripple in my pelvis, and then every thrust is suddenly bringing me closer to the surface, up and up again, drawing me in tighter, closer, until my wish comes true. I break the surface screaming and crying, and calling out his name, and thinking how good it is to have learned not to resist this....

His eyes flicker with candlelight as he strokes my hair and jerks from me—the plan is not forgotten after all. His penis stands out proud and red and wet and the strain of holding back is evident in his bit lip. Morgan's nostrils flare and she slides low on her pillows. I go to her, my fingers seeking out her cunt, which is already dripping, my mouth smothering hers, our tongues slipping in and out as I confirm what we all already know. She is ready.

And I put myself behind her, my hands cupping her breasts, my legs on either side of her, as John lies down between her legs. My fingers sneak down to spread her wider, to circle her clit and pinch her where she likes it, while he thrusts slickly, my teeth in her neck, her hair in our faces, the three of us humping like one animal, all of us ready.

Morgan always comes twice.

There's nothing like a grandchild to bring parents around. So Jillian has six grandparents and none of them mind enough to complain about it. We always have them here for Christmas now; we've got the most bedrooms and the most chairs. Jillian will always be my daughter. John always shovels the snow. And Morgan always says we could make Jillian a sibling—that it could be my turn if I want. I don't know. I just know that I love them always.

MODERN
LOVE

*The vagaries and complications of desire
in millennial America*

the hard sell

LOVE IS HARD on people without unassailable
self-esteem, she thought, as she looked herself over in the
mirror and tried very hard not to wonder if she was in any
way physically inadequate. She wasn't—she was the right
height, the right weight, her hair had bounce, she didn't
yet have crow's feet, she didn't have zits. She was pretty
sure she didn't smell. Steam was rising off her shower-
damp skin as she stood in front of the sink and raised an
eyebrow with practiced skepticism. You Too Can Have a
Body Like Mine.

On an average day in her average life, she would never
even consider these kinds of things. Prole-thoughts, she and
Gerald called them. Gerald had started calling the consumer
audience "proles" one day in jest, and ever since then the
whole graphic design department at Fitch & Zellwiger had
been doing it. Proles were the people advertising was aimed
at, or, more specifically, the ones that advertising was
supposed to be effective on. Have a Coke And a Smile!

Being in the industry herself, Linda didn't think of herself as susceptible. Which was why it was so weird to be standing there, wondering if her deodorant really worked or if maybe she should try Jenny Craig.

She shivered. Was it love?

She pulled on her bathrobe and began combing out her wet, dark hair. Without a doubt, it was no fun to fret over this body-image crap, especially when she was supposed to be immune to it. Then she thought about Kyle, which was much more fun.

It was because of Kyle, of course, that she was having these thoughts at all. She wished he was there, at that moment, as she stood wet and naked in the bathroom, the cat pawing at the door and the tinny blare of her clock radio seeping through the crack where the door didn't quite close. She wished for his hands encircling her from behind, leaning back into him as into the shade of a tree on a hot summer day, his fingers making their rough but tender way over her skin, puckering her nipples and teasing her ribs. How Do You Spell Relief?

But then she would really be late for work. As she probably would be tomorrow, if he stayed at her place tonight. If she saw him. And if he stayed the night. If.

Kyle had a random life, it seemed, working odd jobs between acting gigs, living sometimes with his mom on Long Island, sometimes with a friend in Hoboken, that is, when he wasn't on the road with a show. He was off the road now, but it had been over a week since she had seen him. She could still smell his shampoo and she wondered what brand it was. She shivered again, pulled her hair up into an artistic twist, and went to get dressed.

The cat, a Roseanne-Barr-voiced Siamese, followed her back to the bedroom and hopped into the bed with a hopeful look on her face. But when it became clear Linda was dressing for work, the cat settled herself on top of the comforter for her day-long snooze.

Linda pulled a silk tank top over her head, her heart beating harder than she felt it had a right to. No wonder the ancients thought the heart was where love was kept. It was beating a lot harder recently and she didn't think it was because she was slacking off on the Stairmaster (though she was). She gave in to a prole-thought about whether her thighs were too chunky. Behold the power of cheese, indeed.

As she was grabbing her keys on the way out the door she realized that a basic tenet of the ad biz was wrong. Thousands of ad campaigns ran every year on the assumption that single people anxious to find love were the ones most likely to be concerned every waking moment about their breath, their hair, their choice of clothes, their cologne. But, if she was to accept her personal experience as having any validity, well, the whole thing was backwards. When she was unattached she couldn't care less about those things. It was when she was hooked up that she suddenly couldn't keep those prole-thoughts out of her head. Calgon, Take Me Away!

She could hear Gerald cackling to himself over the wall of his cubicle before she even reached hers. She hung her Armani raincoat (her brother's actually, a gift from her father that didn't fit his ever-bigger shoulders so it had become hers—it was definitely a man's coat, but hey, *Armani...*) on a hook and settled into her ergonomically correct chair. While her computer flared to life she yelled over the cubicle wall, "Now what?"

Gerald appeared a moment later with a piece of paper in his hands. He was only twenty-seven but already balding, so he had taken to shaving his head down to pretty much nothing, and had grown a goatee to prove he could. With his white shirt rolled up to his elbows and a smudge of Xerox toner on his face, he looked, as he might say, quite the graphique artiste today.

The paper showed a bottle of some kind of booze, two glasses, and an ice bucket on a marble table. The label hadn't been designed in yet but Linda guessed it would be another HiBall Swingin' Liquors Ad. Gerald had been working on their campaign for the better part of a year.

She looked hard at the paper. "I don't see anything," she said, scrutinizing the ice cubes.

"Not the ice," Gerald sniggered. "The marble."

"Ah." As he'd said it, the smoky finger-lickin' good figures copulating in the tabletop seemed to come to the surface before her eyes. She nodded. "It's a fine line between too subtle and too obvious," she said.

"Tell me about it." Still, he seemed very pleased with himself, and retreated to his own computer. The folks at HiBall rode the crest of the retro-lounge revival wave. Remember the to-do in the seventies and eighties when it was revealed that advertisers were hiding subliminal sexual messages in booze and cigarette ads? Not the ultra-penile Joe Camel character, before that, when there were words airbrushed into the mountain range behind the Marlboro Man and all manner of suggestive shapes floated in every glass of Smirnoff? The folks at HiBall, in trying to recapture some mythic "swinging" lounge era of the past, were using Esquivel in their TV ads and purposefully playing up the "subliminal" parts of their print campaign. According to Gerald, if the public seemed indifferent to, or maybe oblivious to, the subliminals, HiBall's next step would be to ignite a publicity campaign about the ads themselves. As in, like, how cool.

Linda thought, Pop truly does Eat Itself. She pushed a stack of WottaCards aside on her desk and logged in.

Reach Out and Touch Someone. There was email from Kyle. He had an audition in the morning, early, downtown, could he stay at her place tonight?

She left him a message at his mother's: sure, did he want to have dinner?

He left her a voice mail while she was out to lunch: he'd be over at 7:30.

Her heart beat hard as she listened to his voice on the fuzzy, digital message. Just the sound of his voice! She felt herself blushing as she sat there. You'd think I was thirteen, not thirty, she thought. Such an unusual feeling, or it was for someone who hadn't dated in a few years. Had she felt like this about the others? She remembered the ends of relationships better than the beginnings, it seemed. You've Come A Long Way, Baby.

She put potentially depressing musings out of her mind and turned her attention to the WottaCards. Her specialty at F&Z was redesigning, rejiggering, and redoing advertisers' magazine and billboard campaigns to fit the freebie postcard format. Yeah, boring, but it sure beat welfare.

So here's the state he found her in when he came to the door at 7:45 or so. She had worked as late as she possibly could, then tried to rush home through the public transit system, nearly lost her bag on the subway, and then ran up the street when she saw the bank on the corner's time and temp sign flashing 7:31. He wasn't there when she got up the stairs, and though relieved that she hadn't been late to meet him yet after all, she had hung up her coat and then begun to fret about why he might be late. She was halfway out of her work clothes when the thought struck her that he might have been there and then left when she wasn't there—no that was silly, why would he do that? And did she have time for a quick shower before he did arrive, or should she just put her clothes back on and wait for him? Would he want to take a shower for two? Would it be too suggestive and weird to be in a bathrobe when he came to the door? As it was, then, she was half undressed and frowning when the knock came on the door.

She opened it. "How did you get up here?"

"Someone was coming out as I came in," he said. He was wearing a leather aviator's jacket, a white scarf around his neck and his helmet and goggles hung over one arm. His hair flipped rakishly over his eyes where it had escaped the helmet and been tugged by the wind. He flashed a smile. "Is something wrong?"

She let him in, stalking back to the bed alcove still in her nylons and silk tank top, trying to think of what to say. "It's not fair," she began.

Kyle placed his helmet on the floor and petted the cat. Then he sat cross-legged on the throw rug and let the cat knead his lap. His pants were leather, too, worn and cracked like they'd been through a lot. "We can talk about it now, if you want, or do you want to do it over dinner?"

"It's not fair that you're always perfect and poised and I want you so much sometimes my heart hurts." She sat on the bed and closed her eyes. That wasn't really what she meant to say, or maybe it was, and that was the problem. "And I'm all...." She threw up her hands.

He pushed the cat off his lap, slid the jacket onto the floor, and went to sit next to her. It was a high old bed, and her feet didn't reach the floor if she sat back. "Hey."

It doesn't make any sense for me to be angry or upset right now, she thought, but that didn't stop her face from being hot or her throat from being tight. He took her hand in his. He touched her chin.

Obey Your Thirst. In a moment she was kissing him, hard, her arms around his neck like a drowning victim. When she came up for air, she felt better.

"Miss me?" he said with an Errol Flynn grin.

She let out a long breath. "Yep."

"So, when I came in," he said, his breath soft on her bare neck, "were you just getting dressed, or...undressed?" Two fingers had slid under the tank top and were sending chills up her spine.

She closed her eyes and let him caress her, melting in his mouth or in his hand.

"Well?"

"Um...." She leaned into his chest as he ran his knuckles over the silk that covered her breasts. "I don't know why, but

I can't seem to answer the simplest questions with you around."

"Just a simple question," he said, and kissed her again, then let his lips trail over her chin and neck. Like Visa, he was everywhere she wanted him to be.

"But it isn't, Kyle," she said as she lay back. "It's not just a question. It... you're trying to seduce me with it."

"That's true." She raised her hands over her head as he slid his hands under the silk and over her breasts again. But he did not pull it over her head. He let his fingers graze her nipples as they floated up and down under the shirt.

"Well, then, how I answer might determine what you do, how you act, mightn't it?"

He leaned over her now, and let his tongue flick her now-hard nipple right through the silk. "You know," he said, between flicks, "if you want it to go a certain way, you can just say so."

But that's just it, she thought. I don't want to mess it up.... "It's going just fine, from what I can tell."

He sucked her nipple through the cloth and she sucked in her breath. She pressed her knees together as her arousal spread from her bosom down to her midsection. She gripped the comforter with her fingers as he went from one nipple to the other, sucking, nipping lightly with his teeth, fluttering his tongue. The silk was wet and whichever one he was not attending to stood up even harder in the slight chill.

At last he peeled her out of the tank top and rolled her gently over, his lips and rakish hair soft on her back and shoulders. It was like ballroom dancing or something, the way he could just turn her with a slight cue. She wondered if he could dance and figured he probably could. You're In Good Hands.

His hands slid around her from behind, following the valleys of her hips into her panties and playing with her fur. She moaned, all doubt and drama swept away by desire for the moment. She knew what would happen in the next several minutes, maybe not the exact moves or the exact order, but she knew what was coming. A few beats later and the nylons and panties were gone, and she was naked in her bed, and he was still fully clothed. He raised himself above her and she ran her hands over the worn cotton of his shirt. It was a white linen dress shirt, or it had been once, that had been worn so much it felt like sheets in an old hotel, smooth and soft. She pulled it out of the pants and ran her hands over his chest as he'd done to her. He shuddered as she did so, but held himself up. Actor's body, dancer's body, had she ever been with someone so strong, so lithe?

"Kyle," she said then, and the question did not come out at all the way she meant it: "what are you?"

He answered without pause. "Your lover."

Her hands trembled as she ran them down the hairs of his chest and on past his stomach to his belt. "Is that what you are?"

He could do accents, too, a poncy British one: "I think we have established that fact quite well, madam."

"But is that all you are?"

He slid to the side as she opened his belt and the bed bounced and creaked as he let himself fall back. She tugged at the leather jeans for a few moments until he lifted his hips and pushed them off himself. "Is that all..." he mused. "That, I think, is for madam to decide."

Her fingers wrapped around his shaft then, which, freed from the confines of his pants, was quite hard. "What do you mean, that's for me to decide?"

He had bedroom eyes, for godsake, brilliant and sultry at the same time, predatory and vulnerable, hypnotic. Very Brad Pitt. She looked into them as he said, one slow word at a time, "I mean, what, do, you, want?"

Sucking him was a convenient way to avoid answering and give herself time to think. He shuddered and gripped the bedcovers. That, at least, she felt sure was a genuine reaction and not an act. What did she want? Funny—sitcoms, soaps, dramedies, they all assumed it was the man who thought with his genitalia. But at that moment she really could only seem to get one thought to come clear in answer to that question. She let him out of her mouth with a pop. "I want you inside me."

"What a happy coincide...."

"No acting!" She shushed him with a fierce finger on his lips. "I want you, not Errol Flynn, not...Brad Pitt...."

He was rolling her onto her back and burying his face between her legs. In a short while he'd be burying something else. She felt her insides spasm in anticipation. So strange. The animal human that was her body wanted him no matter what role he played or what she called him, lover, boyfriend, fling. The arousal was like some kind of miracle every time it happened.

Now was not the time to be thinking about exes. Not with Kyle's tongue drawing circles between her legs. But that was something Andrew, for example, never really wanted to do, and which Jared had never done well. Jared, for whom sex was a recreational activity couples did together like playing tennis and weekly gourmet cooking classes, and so she had, long after it had ceased to be arousing or fulfilling. Diamonds may be forever, but desire was not.

Why was she always the one who stopped wanting them first? One day, the arousal wouldn't work, it would just stop, like the flow had been dammed upstream somewhere. It had been so long... no wonder it felt like a miracle.

Kyle's fingers were inside her now, while his tongue kept lapping, and she felt herself rising, like mercury in a thermometer slowly creeping up into critical temperatures, as her arousal built. She hadn't told him yet how very much she liked it when he did that, when he licked her and put his fingers inside her. Maybe she didn't have to, though, maybe the moans and screams and sighs were enough. He seemed to relish it himself. She'd have to ask, later, when she could speak again, if he liked it as much as he seemed to.

She blinked as a prole-thought came to her, as she realized what all those prole-thoughts really were underneath it all. All the worries about shampoo and clothes and image were really just safe ways of wondering if he was going to keep liking her, keep wanting her. Here she had just wondered why it was that she was always the one in relationships to stop wanting sex first. But on the other hand she'd been worrying about the exact opposite all day. When would he tire of her?

She started to cry out just about then. As he increased the pressure of his tongue just enough, as he crooked his finger in just the right way, as she began to come. Orgasm distracted her from all thoughts as she clung onto him, as he continued his motions until, some minutes later, she stopped twitching and seemed done. Good To The Last Drop.

"What are you thinking?" he asked, as she stared at the ceiling.

She began to laugh. "I can't explain."

"So don't." He was on his knees on the bed, his erection standing out at an angle. It was long enough that it had a noticeable bend to the left, which she liked even though she couldn't say why. He had a soft smile on his face. "I think we should get some dinner before it gets too late."

"But you...."

"Can wait." He stepped off the bed, and pulled his pants up, turning away from her to settle himself somehow, despite his protruding state. "You'll be a grouch if you don't eat."

This was true. And she'd had a stupid carob-covered diet bar and a fruit smoothie for lunch, which had meant she was starved by four o'clock. The clock now read nine. "We've been in bed for an hour?"

"Happens. Want to make it to vindaloo?"

So they had been together enough times that they now had habits and preferences. The Indian restaurant around the corner would probably still seat them if they hurried. They had eaten there twice before already. Was this how relationships started? Her labia was still slick with juices, but somehow it felt right when he helped her into her panties and kissed her on the back of the neck.

Over dinner, she began trying to untangle some of her thoughts for him. With hot mulligatawny soup in her stomach and her legs still rubbery from orgasm, it seemed easier to focus, somehow. Never Underestimate the Power of Soup. She traced circles on the white tablecloth with her finger as she spoke. "So, I have these two totally opposite fears."

He sipped sweet yogurt and then offered the glass and its frothy straw to her. The drink was cool and shockingly sweet going down.

"See, on the one hand, I'm afraid you're going to lose interest in me, and I also fear that by telling you this, I'm going to somehow either hasten the process, or guilt you into not telling me you've lost interest, and I wouldn't want you to think I was trying to manipulate you like that." She took a deep breath. "But that wasn't the other fear, that was more like a digression. The other fear, besides the one that you're going to lose interest, is that *I'm* going to lose interest."

His fingers intersected hers on the tablecloth. "I don't think either of these things has to be a problem if we're honest about how we feel. If you lose interest in me, you gotta tell me, Linda, that's all."

"Lose interest sounds like you're some kind of a hobby or something... that's not the way I mean it." As she sat up straighter, she felt her wet crotch tighten again. "I don't know why I stop wanting people, almost like my body stops suddenly, when sometimes my emotions aren't ready to."

He nodded with a silent "ah" and took another sip of his drink. "What are your emotions ready for right now?"

"I'm not sure." She looked at his chiseled, actor face. "We're not really boyfriend/girlfriend, are we?"

He shook his head slowly and kissed her hand.

She went on. "But we're not like a casual recreational thing, either."

"No."

"So, we make love, and you make my body feel ways it hasn't felt since I was a teenager, and I think about you all the time, wondering when...." She lowered her voice as the waiter placed steaming metal dishes of fragrant stewed lamb in front of them. "You're going to do it again."

"Yes." He made no move toward the food, his eyes fixed on her.

"Are you afraid to use the word love?"

"No."

"Then what are we?"

"I said it before. Lovers."

"And what's that mean?"

"It means we are what we are. We enjoy each other. And we will, until one of us no longer enjoys it. Any other limits or obligations we've never really discussed."

They both reached for the food at the same time. He spooned rice onto their plates while she picked up the curry.

After they had taken a few bites, he asked, "Do you want more limits or obligations?"

She chewed her lamb for a moment; then laughed as she realized she was, literally, ruminating. "You know, I don't think I do."

"Then everything's OK?"

"Situation normal." She felt surprised at how calm she was.

"Excellent." They ate in silence for a while, then talked about inconsequential things, and then returned to the apartment.

He kissed her right inside the door, his hunger evident in his touch on her back, the bend of his neck over hers. She sucked in a breath. It felt almost like the more he wanted her, the more her body responded. Her heart skipped a beat and she stood back.

"You all right?" He let his jacket fall to the floor, and she ran her fingers up his bedsheet-smooth shirt, before putting one hand over her chest, pledge-of-allegiance style.

"How does anyone tell the difference between being excited and having a panic attack?" She took a deliberate breath. "It's like I'm too out of shape for love."

"Maybe you are," he said softly. "You said it's been a couple of years before me."

She nodded. "Maybe I just don't remember how hard it can be on the body." She laughed. "Or maybe I need Jack LaLanne."

"Or maybe you just need more practice." He kissed her again then, taking her face in his hands.

They didn't fool around with disrobing, each of them stripping to nothing once they broke apart. She slid under the covers and held them open for him.

As he slid in next to her, she felt the velvet steel of his erection draw a line down her body. Their lips met again and she wrapped a leg over his hip. She ran the V of her fingers over his hardness and felt herself gush a little in anticipation. "I'm afraid of not feeling like this," she whispered. "I want to feel like this forever."

She kept condoms in a box on the bedside table, and retrieved one. "Please make me stop processing," she said, handing it to him.

"I'll do my best," he said, as he ripped open the package.

She tucked her knees up as he knelt back to roll the condom on. He then lay it gently along her labia. She rocked her hips, coating it with her juices, then hooked her feet behind him and pulled him forward.

He held himself above her in that way that still amazed

her, then tucked his crotch into hers, slipping into her by inches. She kept her eyes on his face and was rewarded by the sight of his eyes rolling back into his head. His eyelids flickered and then it was he who gasped.

For a while she played with the hairs on his chest, with his nipples, with the long hair behind his ears. But then, as his rhythm changed, she found her arms going limp, then her head lolled back, and soon she was moaning as the arousal mercury began to rise again.

He just kept going and going. He reared back, still pumping with forceful strokes, while his thumb insinuated itself between them. Linda began to come almost before she realized it, she was so lost in the sensation of his ever quickening pace. She cried out and grabbed him by the elbow to make sure he knew she was coming, and suddenly he panted and broke out in a sweat. He went rigid above her; then collapsed, the bedsprings creaking happily as they settled down again to stillness. Such a simple thing, such a basic thing, yet so important.

"So," she said, when she could, "what will we be after one of us no longer wants the other, assuming that that happens someday?"

"Friends," Kyle said. "I believe that's called friends." He caressed a damp strand of her hair away from her eyes. "Does that seem likely to happen soon?"

She let a yawn creep up. "No, it sure doesn't."

In the morning he was out of bed before she was. He was in the shower as she brushed her teeth. "So Kyle," she said, when she had rinsed, "what kind of shampoo do you use?"

"No idea," he replied, sticking a soapy hand and small bottle through the slit in the shower curtain. "Picked up a bunch of bottles of it at the hotel when I did that show in Arizona."

She climbed into the tub, sealing the curtain behind her with a handful of water. "Let me have some of that."

He circled her into the hot water and squeezed some of the shampoo into his hand. She closed her eyes as his fingers worked their way into her hair. The sweet scent of the no-name brand swirled in the steam and she pulled him close, wet skin to wet skin, and let the water run.

thought so

I HAVE NEWS FOR YOU, boys: there are horny women out there. There are women walking the streets, in bookstore aisles, riding trains; who are practically crying inside because they want it so bad. Either that, or I'm the only one. But I would put money on the fact that I am not the only one. Especially given what Jason has told me. It's because of Jason that I don't have to prowl those aisles, those trains, anymore.

I first noticed him in Walpenny's, in the cookbook section. I was thumbing through a spiral bound volume on Thai cookery when I caught him looking at me. Or maybe it was he who caught me. By that point, I was frustrated. It was a summer evening, cool and breezy, and though I wore a brief, swishy dress, and had arranged my hair suggestively, I had not had good luck. The only mild interest I'd gotten was from people I had no interest in. And while I was starting to think I'd hump an aardvark if I had to, I knew better.

I was biting my lip and trying to decide if I should give

up and go home, the book open in my hands but my eyes unfocused, when Jason stepped out from behind a tall bookcase. My eyes flickered up and then back down to the book. He was tall, a little underfed, blue eyes, light brown hair... and was he looking at me?

He was. I gave him a longer look, and a smile. He returned the smile in a knowing way. Thank goodness. The hook was baited. I put the book down on the table, and let my head fall back, some of my curls brushing my bare shoulders. I saw him gulp—hook swallowed.

He came toward me and said, "Hi."

"Hi," I said, lowering my eyes with a shyness that wasn't entirely unreal. I was accustomed to being the cute one, the desirable one—but Jason would have turned my head even if I hadn't been having one of my horniest nights. Suddenly I wasn't sure what to say to him.

He saved me by speaking first. "I've been following you for a while."

"How long is a while?" He blushed, but kept talking.

"Since Alton Station." He reached his hand toward mine, and brushed his fingertips against my arm. I had to stifle an audible intake of breath. "Would you like to go somewhere?" he asked.

I nodded. "My place, if that would be all right with you."

There was that smile again. "Lead the way."

He orbited me with a crooked arm as I turned toward the door, but he did not touch me.

He waited until we were sitting on a bench at the station to do that. I was almost shivering by then, fantasizing his arm around me, waiting for it to happen—and then he slid close, his blue-jeaned leg touching mine, and his arm slid across my shoulders. His breath was warm in my hair, against my ear, in the air-conditioned coolness of the station. If I had an engine, it would have revved.

I didn't want to wait until we got home. It would be twenty minutes on the train, and then a five-minute walk, and I was so hot and ready that I was afraid I would slip off the peak and lose my edge. The frustration and need of the long evening made my jaw stiffen; the ache in my belly only intensified by the proximity of our bodies.

His lips nibbled at my ear and tears almost sprang to my eyes.

He smoothed my dress down over my legs. I wished I could just lie down on the concrete bench, put up my legs and let him root around to his heart's content (and mine). Another pass with his hand....

I hadn't felt so hungry-frustrated since junior high, when I used to sit backstage during drama club rehearsal, on Daniel Pera's lap. We were too young for sex, and knew it I guess, because we never took our clothes off. But he used to trace every line or design on the cloth of my shirt, with just his fingertip, roaming feather-light over my chest and up and down my neck. Sometimes he would trace the seams of my jeans. We'd sit like that for hours, while rehearsals were going on, in the dark of the wings, until we were needed. Sometimes I went onstage flushed and dizzy, unsure of where my feet were, unsure even of who I was, which character I was to play, what words I was supposed to say. I went home every night dying to masturbate the minute I got to my room. Jason's fingertip began to trace the flowery vines on my dress. I shuddered a breath in and out. I wanted to murmur sweet nothings in his ear, to give him a taste of the painful anticipation I was riding—but I could not speak. His finger slid along the center seam of the dress and came to rest at the crook of my hip. Then he turned my chin toward him, and as I was about to say something, smothered my unspoken words with a kiss.

His fingers were drumming now, like a piano arpeggio, closer and closer to where my clit throbbed under layers of cloth. Yes, I wore panties, even when out on the prowl. The gentle tapping made the longing even worse. I didn't dare open my eyes, afraid people were staring at us. He kept his rhythm even, his touch light, as if there were no urgency in him at all. It was all inside me, making my shoulders tighten under his arm, my breath shallow, my jaw clench.

And then came the train. He held my hand and pulled me into the car. There were only four or five other people within earshot and none of them paid us any attention. Jason pulled me down into a seat—onto his lap.

That finger was busy again, this time deep under my dress, pushing aside my cotton panties, then nosing back and forth in my wetness. More liquid was forthcoming, and I licked my mouth as if to match it.

When his finger slid into me, I started to cry. You ninny, I was thinking, you're going to ruin it, he's going to freak and run away on you. But I couldn't help it. His slow, gentle touch was going somewhere deep inside of me, somewhere I needed to be touched so much, that the relief triggered tears. I clung to his neck and sobbed softly, my face hidden by drifts of my own hair, as his finger went in and out, soon joined by a second one. He could barely move his hand, jammed between my legs like that, but it was enough, just rocking. Then his thumb perked up and rubbed against my overlubricated clit, and my crying intensified.

"It's okay," he said into my ear. "I know."

Like those moments of confusion, stumbling from the curtains in the wings, unsure where to stand or where to go, I found myself being carried from the train. He had me in his arms and whispered in my ear and nibbled my neck, and the next thing I knew we were at my door and he was asking for my keys. He set me down on my feet and I opened the apartment door and we climbed the dark stairs.

At the time I didn't think it odd that he knew where to go. I was too grateful to be there, mere steps from the bedroom, where we soon were, me kneeling on the bed, him standing while I unbuttoned his white cotton shirt, unbuttoned his jeans, and revealed him. His silky red erection came free and I sighed. I cupped his balls with my hand and let my lips fall around him. Ahh. Mmm.

He sensed I didn't want to waste much time, but let me swallow him deep a few times before he pushed forward onto the bed, flattening me in the process. The rest of our clothes were shed at that point, while I pulled a condom out of the side table drawer. I kicked off my socks while he put it on. I wrapped my legs around his back and pulled him into me.

With every thrust I felt like sparks flew down to my toes and from the tips of my fingers. I thought again of junior high, a trip to the beach—baking in the sun for an hour and then running headlong down the sand and plunging into the cool water. An intensely pleasurable shock. A shockingly intense pleasure. And Jason gave it to me again and again.

I thrust my hips up to meet him, trying to match rhythm to get an almost violent crash of bodies. It's hard to admit, but I wanted him to fuck me so hard that it would hurt. It was one of the reasons I liked picking up strangers—they were unlikely to worry much about whether I was in pain or not. Anonymous encounters tended to fuck with abandon. Of course, sometimes that meant that I would end up abandoned, if he'd come before me or if he couldn't keep it up. But somehow Jason was hanging in there, giving it to me and giving it to me.

When I'm that wet and when I've wanted it for so long, I can fuck for a long time. I started to worry that he wouldn't last, but I didn't want to say anything. Just when my worrying began to distract me from the pleasure, he whispered, "It's okay. I can do it." And he began to dunk harder, and I lost myself.

The orgasm was coming—but if I followed my usual pattern, I would need a tad more clit stimulation. I tried to slide my hand along my stomach, but bumped into his hand, beating me to it. He had turned his long arm partway over and slid his thumb down over the very slippery, sensitive bump. The ripples in my midsection started that instant. My legs shook and my heels drummed on his back as I quaked with the power of coming. I wondered if this would make him go off, too, but when I settled back into the bed, he was still lodged deep in me, fucking me slowly and contentedly.

Wash, rinse, repeat. After a while, he sped up, my muscles started to contract, he would rub my clit, and... insert sound effects like Fourth of July fireworks here. And again. And maybe again.... I can't do math when I'm like that. I kept thinking, oh, this time he'll go off, too. But he didn't. And then I started to feel like I'd had enough and I feared that he hadn't, and I was going to end up having to go through the ordeal of letting him fuck me when I didn't want to anymore. It would not be fair, after all, to get what I wanted and leave him unsatisfied.

Suddenly he pulled out, and lay back next to me, and smiled.

"You didn't come," I said.

"Are you sure?" he asked.

"Yes." I put my hand on his chest and felt his heart beating hard. "I'm sure of it."

"You're right."

"Do you want me to go down on you?" I could not move, at that point, as I lay there, thoroughly screwed, but I figured I'd be able to sit up in a few minutes.

"No, that's okay," he said, sounding sleepy, or maybe I was projecting my feelings onto him. "You just rest."

We lay there in the semi-dark of the street light and after a short nap, my brain began to perk up. That's when I realized that I had never told him where I lived, nor how to get there. He had been following me all evening, by his own admission. I didn't think I would feel so comfortable snuggling up to a psycho. Did I have a stalker?

"No," he said, stroking my hair. "I can read your mind."

"What do you mean, you can read my mind?" I guess I thought it was some mushy romantic thing he was trying to say. But I was wrong. He meant it in the most literal sense.

"In the bookstore, you picked up that cookbook because you thought the cover image looked phallic."

"Spring rolls and bananas."

"Then you watched that clerk, the one with the nose ring, walk by, and decided you really didn't like the way he smelled." His voice was soothing in the dark. "That's the smell of patchouli, by the way."

"And what was I thinking about when we were in the train station?"

"The Man Who Came To Dinner."

"Holy shit." That was the play we'd done in drama club. That convinced me that he really could read my mind. "So you were following me around all night, and knew how horny I was the whole time."

"Yes."

I propped myself up on an elbow and slapped him on the shoulder. "That's for making me wait so long." Then I kissed him, long and deep, until we were both breathless.

He started to get up and I thought, aha, now he'll want to come. But he made a quick trip to the bathroom, and when he returned, began to get dressed.

I asked him if he wanted to come and he smiled that sweet smile at me. "Yes, very much. But I'm going to wait."

I wasn't sure what to think about that. "Why?"

"You wanted me to experience the exquisite pain you had gone through. I figured I'd try it." He leaned over me and kissed me on the lips, then on the forehead.

It struck me then that I couldn't just let him walk away, like any other anonymous encounter. "Will you come back tomorrow?"

"If you want me to."

"You have to." I told him I wouldn't feel complete until he came, too.

And he said: "I know."

baseball fever

THIS IS MY FANTASY about Derek Jeter. For those of you who are saying "who?" you obviously haven't watched much post-season baseball. This guy's in his fifth year of his major league career and has been to the World Series with the Yankees three out of four years already, won Rookie of the Year, and almost won the batting title. I heard as a kid he was voted "Most Likely to Play Shortstop for the New York Yankees" by his junior high class in Michigan. And you know what? That's exactly what he is. This guy's got destiny. He fits in great in multi-ethnic New York too—half-black, half-white, cannily polite with the media but cocky as hell when he gets on the field.

You know, I think I started fantasizing about him when a crotchety old neighbor of mine and I were watching a Yankees/Red Sox game—the neighbor rooting for the Sox. I had made a pilgrimage to Yankee Stadium earlier in the year, and I remarked to this neighbor how when Jeter came up to bat you could hear every teenage girl in the stadium scream. It was like "Chuck Knoblauch," cheer, "Derek Jeter," CHEER!—way up in both pitch and volume. To this, the neighbor said: "Well, of course, look at him, with that cafe-au-lait skin..." in a kind of disparaging tone. Apparently for teenagers and for me (now 33 years old and counting...) the disapproval of the older generation may be an important part of what it takes to make someone cute and famous into a real serious crush object. Mmm, anyway, I was going to tell you my fantasy about him.

It's Spring Training in Florida and the Yankees are coming out of their winter hibernation. Things are relaxed, days of practice are intercut by barbecues and stuff... OK, I admit, I lifted this background right out of the most recent Kevin Costner baseball movie. Anyway. It's not hard to make myself a fixture in the neighborhood. I figure if I'm going to have any chance with a hunk like Jeter I better give him a lot of good looks. This is the guy who went out with Mariah Carey, after all, and I can't really impress him by telling him I'm a somewhat famous (or maybe infamous) erotic writer. (Trust me, it doesn't work.)

So here's what happens. I'm riding a bicycle along the waterfront. I'm wearing shorts and a bikini top, and I'm that nice half-Asian golden brown that I get. Jeter is, uh, fishing off the pier with Bernie Williams (Yankee Centerfielder and four-time Gold Glove award winner, who also happens to be cute as hell). It's Williams who notices me. He kind of waves as I go by—just a friendly wave, but I take it as an opportunity to stop. I say something like, "Catching anything?" and Jeter, not looking at me, replies something like "Only with a glove."

Hey, if the scintillating dialogue doesn't do it for you, fill in your own exciting chitchat here. It's a fantasy after all.

Bernie and I exchange some banter about the upcoming

season while I'm watching a bead of sweat slide down Jeter's temple. The seat of the bike is hard between my thighs and I'm trying not to squirm. The sun will set in about an hour and the breeze is full of salt smell and I'm wishing I could lick that bead of sweat off his sandpaper stubble face.

The next time we meet is in a swank restaurant in Tampa, which is very lucky because I look great in a black evening dress. I'm there actually, with a friend who has just sold a screenplay—this is a fantasy after all—and she and I are celebrating like it's Oscar® night. I'm drinking a Shirley Temple, but I've got one Kahlua and cream in my crepe de chine already, and so I have no restraint whatsoever when I run into him by the restrooms. The place is dimly lit with tiny jewel-eyed track lights, and my neighbor is right, that cafe-au-lait skin does look irresistible.

I walk right up to him and say, "Hey, Derek Jeter."

"Hey," he says back, a quizzical smirk on his face. I tell him my name and shake his hand. Then I hang onto his hand just a little too long as I, looking over my shoulder, walk away.

You know, in the old days of baseball, shortstops were short, but not anymore. Jeter stands six feet in his socks. But now I'm getting ahead of myself.

Third time's the charm. This time it's a... let's see... charity golf tournament, where Jeter and some other sports celebrities are playing to cure leukemia or some other poster-child type malady. Most of the fans at this thing are golf fans—even Arnold Palmer's there, and Jeter can't golf for shit it turns out, so the pack following him around the links is mostly New York media and me. The Nike golf hat he's wearing looks weirdly small compared to the baseball hat he wears on the field—I'd never known there was a difference before. Anyway, when the tournament's over, he just casually walks up to me, his golf shoes still shiny and new, and says, "You want to get a drink?"

And I say, "Sure."

We go to the country club bar, and he does that ultra-male thing of letting the woman, me, sit in the bar stool, while he stands with one arm over the back of the stool, one foot on the rung while he talks to the bartender. I order a Shirley Temple and he cracks up, and gets one, too.

OK, here's where I have to pause to apologize to Derek Jeter, because we're about to go way deep into my fantasy land, and the chances of what follows being any kind of accurate or reasonable representation of what he is really like are incredibly slim. So, on the off chance that we ever do meet, please understand, this story was written in a sex-hungry daze on the day of Game One of the '99 World Series purely to get me off, and I am really sorry if this wouldn't be like you at all.

We laugh, chitchat, and of course end up in the hotel suite upstairs that the tournament organizers have provided.

Shit, this guy's tall. Once I kick out of my shoes I really have to reach up to get my hands around his neck. Of course, one of the things shortstops do a lot of is bending over. Good thing. His lips are sun-soft and warm, and under the slight chill of the soda he drank downstairs he tastes like...well, like someone delicious tastes. He smells like Florida sun and summer grass and salt air and I'm breathing it all in as we kiss. Wow.

I want to touch every part of him and see what color he is all over, but there are clothes to be dealt with. He's kicking off his shoes while still holding me by the shoulders, when he winces.

"New shoes?" I ask. "Let me see."

He sits back onto the bed and I peel off his socks. His feet aren't in bad shape—there's a spot that might blister on the back of one heel. He lies back as I start to rub his feet, and groans out loud as I find the crunchy spots in his arch. I'm getting my thumbs in there good when he jokingly says, "Oh god, that feels good. Is it too early to tell you I love you?"

"Mm, definitely. You have to be naked first."

"That can be arranged." He pulls off his polo shirt in one gymnastic lunge and then falls back on the bed again. I crawl up him to admire God and a professional trainer's handiwork. What can I say? Nice. I can't resist the urge to lick. He doesn't seem to mind. I can feel his hands on the back of my sundress, trying to find a zipper or something. But it's a tube dress. I rear up and let him push the fabric down, his thumbs hooked over the top. My nipple is hanging in his face as his long arms work the dress all the way down, and he can't resist the urge to lick. I don't seem to mind.

We roll over then—his idea, I think—me now completely naked and pressed back into the cushy bedspread, but him still in his golf pants. A chino-covered knee insinuates itself between my legs.

"So are we really going to do this thing?" he asks, his eyes startlingly light-colored in the afternoon sun through the window.

"I'm going to root for the Red Sox if we don't," I say.

"I guess I better come through in the clutch," he says, levering himself up on his arms and settling his face between my knees.

I start to crack up before I can even say anything in response.

"What's so funny?"

"Nothing. Ignore me."

"I sure don't intend to do that."

"No really, I just laugh at dumb things is all. Really dumb."

He props himself on one elbow and starts playing with my pubic hair with his fingers. "Now you have to tell me."

"It's really bad."

He lets one finger come to rest at the tip of my pubic bone. "Tell me."

"Okay. As you were going down, I heard this voice in my head. What's the name of the announcer who says, 'th-e-e-e-e-e Yankees win!' at the end of games?"

"John Sterling." Wow, are his eyes green or blue or what?

"I heard John Sterling's voice say 'And Jeter steps up to the mound....'"

"That *is* bad," he says.

"Told you," I answer, as he dips his tongue into the folds of my labia. Uh, in a word, nice. Jeter then—and you know you have to refer to sports figures by last name, no matter how intimate you may be at the moment—reaches up with those long arms of his and, without stopping the languid lingual action below, puts a hand on either breast.

As he applies pressure with his fingers, his head suddenly pops up and he says, "Squeeze play," at which point I clamp my thighs over his ears and flip us both over—hey, he's not the only athlete in this bed.

"Jeter's holding at third," I say as I'm grinding my hips up and down while he eats me. That sandpaper stubble feels electric on my clit as I run back and forth. Then, as he starts to suck the hard tip, I feel his fingers circling the wet center of my cunt.

He slides one finger in and I'm digging my hands into the fluffed hotel pillow and trying not to meow like a cat. Then a second finger and I'm making some kind of hungry noise in my throat, unable to say anything for a moment. Then he stands up and I look over my shoulder and say, "Let's see that Louisville Slugger, shall we?" He might be blushing as he drops trou, or maybe he's just flushed. I pull him back down on top of me, kissing him messily and tasting sex and salt and musk.

"Going to make a play for home?" I ask.

"I feel like I should make a joke about being safe or something," he replies, his thick lashes blinking as he glances down.

"It's okay," I say, "It's a fantasy."

He takes his time coming inside, his clearwater eyes staring out of his suntanned face into mine. His lips move once or twice as if he might say something as he slides in a half inch at a time.

Seventh inning stretch, dig it out, curve ball, on the warning track, soft hands, Gold Glove, base on balls, in the dirt, in the seats, into the upper deck, clear the bench, double play, strike zone, outside corner, middle reliever, switch hitter, screw ball, batter's box, long ball....

His neck becomes slick with sweat—I run my fingers up into the short-sheared hair there. Is it good? Yeah, it's good. He opens his eyes and it's like the sun shines. It goes on and on, but I won't.

When we're finished, he goes soft and one last spasm of my orgasm squeezes him right out of me. "Force out," I whisper.

He gasps out a laugh as he lies back on the bedspread. "You are something else."

"Wait 'til you hear what I do for a living."

Then the phone rings. Jeter reaches over me to pick it up. "Yo." Yeah, in my fantasy, he talks like a jock sometimes. Hence: "Yo." And also, "Hey, yeah, we're having a little party up here." 'Party' means sex in jock speak. "Come on up."

I'm still emerging from my post-coital haze when there's a knock at the door. Jeter, tall, naked, and rangy, bounds over and opens it.

In walks Tiger Woods. I'm blinking my eyes in disbelief as Jeter walks up to him with the same insouciant nonchalance he shows when he approaches the plate, and starts to unbuckle Tiger's belt.

"Whoa, now," Tiger says. "What's going on here?"

Jeter shrugs, thumbing in my direction. "Her fantasy, man. I think you're here to make sure it's not 100 percent heterosexual."

"Well, all right, then." Tiger smiles and runs his hands over Jeter's damp shoulders....

All right, all right, now I've really gone too far. But what the hell, it's my fantasy. I mean, come on, don't tell me it doesn't get your blood racing just a little to imagine Woods' hand on Jeter's cock, making him hard again before going down on him? And wouldn't I love to do them both at once! But I better stop before I start making puns about holes-in-one and putters.

Some people say a fantasy is better than reality. Well, I don't know about that. There's really only one way to know for sure. So, how about it, Jeter? Are you out there? I know fantasy and reality aren't the same—sometimes reality's better. If you want proof, call me. I'm not kidding.

III

MYTHIC

Fairy tales and legends make echoes in
the archetypes of my eroticism

the little mermaid

WHEN I WAS young, a wise old sea cow told me of the four elements: water, earth, fire, and air. At the time I had laughed, for I had never known a world other than the watery kingdom my father ruled, the softness of kelp beds and the caresses of the currents. I could not imagine what she described, her great green eyes focused on a place far away: the hardness of earth, the burning of fire, the lightness of air.

All that changed on the day I came of age. On that day I swam to the surface, as every mermaid must do when she seeks her heart's desire. I thought it a joyous day, and yet I could taste the salt of my father's tears in the water as my tail swept me from him, far and fast.

When I came upon the surface the first time, I saw the spray fly up into the moonlight like pearls. The Moon! I called out to her with a sea song, having heard so much about her as a child. She smiled down on me and I swam on my back, feeling the rush of foam over my skin. So this was air! Air tickled and made my nipples pucker where they broke the surface. Air caressed and teased as it blew this way and that.

In the moonlight I saw a great shape across the flat surface of the sea. It groaned and I swam closer to it. From my place in the water I could see its shape, so similar to one my sisters and I had found, cracked open at the bottom, a ship. And then I heard another sound, shouts and voices.

Far above me, leaning on a railing, was one of the most beautiful creatures I had ever seen. He had a face like a comely merman, only his hair shimmered gold in the moonlight. He wore a white shirt with a circle of gold across his brow. He stood back from the railing then, tall and upright, and shook back his shoulders, as if he had leaned there too long. He walked then, on back flippers long and stalky, along the edge of the ship.

I waved, but he did not see me, his eyes fixed in the direction of a far-off shore.

I followed the ship as they continued toward that shore, as the clouds gathered and covered the moon, and as the storm began. As a daughter of the sea I had nothing to fear from the waves, but as the storm built, the ship was tossed. And as sea and sky battled, the ship split apart, and men spilled into the water like sand from an overturned shell. I could save but one, and I found him struggling for the surface. I calmed him with a sea song and buoyed his body with mine until the storm passed and a rosy dawn lit the sky.

When he woke, we floated near his destined shore. I lay on my back in the water, his head cradled between my breasts, humming softly to myself.

"I'm dead and gone to heaven," he said to himself as he opened his eyes. "And you're an angel."

His hands crept along my ribs and caressed my nipples as

gently as the breeze. His legs hung into the water, one on either side of my tail. He blinked as if he expected to wake up at any moment. Then he leaned his head toward mine, and kissed me.

If his touch was like air, his kiss must have been fire. It started like a current of warm water, flowing down my body from my mouth to the tip of my tail. But as his lips and mine moved across each other, the warmth became almost unbearable, until I knew what I felt was burning. The sun rose then, a ball of hot fire into the sky, and I cried out with an ecstasy so intense it hurt.

"Is this a dream?" he said, then, brushing his fingers along my cheek. His arms circled my shoulders and I felt his body then, against mine, where my tail met my torso. He pulled his legs together as I turned us in a slow circle and he pressed firm against me, as a part of him became tall and upright and as hard as I imagined the earth to be. I wanted to feel him press harder, but in the water we slid past each other too easily. I locked my arms over his spine and took us in to shore.

The waves obliged and carried us up onto the sand, where I felt the weight of his body settle onto me. We kissed again, and as the sun blazed hot on my skin I held him tight. I had never felt such pleasure or agony as the way I burned for him. His eyes were closed now as his hips rocked like a boat on the waves, groaning like the ship with each sway. But this wasn't right, and I knew it. The burning was deep inside me now, where neither of us could touch. We rolled in the edge of the surf and I looked at the part of him that stood now like the mast on the ship. The yearning part of me knew I wanted to have him inside me, and I knew of no other way than to open my mouth and drink him in. He gasped as I slid my wet mouth over the hardness that was his essence, and I nursed upon him like a hungry calf at a sea cow's teat. Then came a wave of saltiness that was the taste of home.

He gasped and blinked then, and looked up into my face, then hastily down at the rest of me. He stifled a cry and then rolled to one side, hands clutching at the wet sand. "You, you're a...."

He said no more as a voice from up the beach came to us then. "What, ho! Who's there?"

More people on stalky legs were up on the dunes, and they began shouting as he stood. I dove into the water, then, knowing somehow that I should not be seen there on the sand. I was still full of the burning, but knew I could not stay. Does not water quench fire? I dove deep, but still I burned.

I came after a time to the cave of a sea witch, an old mermaid who had spent so much of her life at the bottom of the sea that her hair was green like kelp and her skin glowed like a jellyfish. And I asked her if there was anything she could do to ease the pain I was feeling.

"Pain, is it?" gurgled the sea witch. "What sort of pain?"

I described to her as best I could, how it felt like hunger, only it wasn't in my stomach, it was lower down, how it felt like fire, only it didn't harm me.

"And does it ever feel better?"

Here I hesitated. For I knew the one time it felt like pleasure was when I was with him. So there was nothing else I could do but to tell her of my golden-haired man from the ship.

"Man from a ship!" She cackled and schools of small fish darted away from her. "Oh, you poor thing, there be only one thing to ease your pain then." She dove into her cave and came up with a shell. She carefully pried it open to reveal a tiny blue pearl. "Swallow this," she said, rolling it into my hand.

I asked what it was, but all she would say was, "The Pearl of Desire. When you find what you most desire, you will have it. But in trade you will give up the two things that made you one of us, your tail, and your sea song."

But of course I swallowed the Pearl, because I could not know then what a price it was to pay. I swam back to the shore where I had left the man from the ship but of him there was no sign. I went along the coast then, until I came to a cliffside. In the moon's light I could see the palace built above the water, and see the flickering of firelight, dancing bright like my desire. I swam into a calm lagoon toward the sound of voices.

I watched from the water as a man and a woman emerged from the darkness of the trees. It was he, and my heart leaped in my chest to see him. He had a crown of flowers upon his head and his white shirt had been replaced by a patterned cloth around his waist. He pulled the woman down to the sand and pushed the cloth aside and I could see then what I had wanted so inexplicably before. The hard part of him, rising like a finger of coral. "Come here," he said to the woman.

"My prince, we should not," the woman replied. "If the princess finds out...."

"The princess is busy just now," he said, his voice liquid and low. "And I am on fire."

So he too burned. My breath came in quick gasps, the air seemed to fill my head as I watched him turn her body over, as I watched her legs spread.

I pulled myself up out of the water then, and as my body emerged from the shore I felt as though a sword were cleaving me in two. I bit back my cry of pain though, as I felt the breeze in the space where my tail had been, in the space between my legs where now there was a hungry, burning mouth.

Up the beach I heard the sound of sand as someone ran. And then a soft curse.

He was sitting alone, his arms on his knees, his jaw as hard and set as a stone.

I opened my mouth only to find I could not speak. I had no sea song to seduce him with this time. So instead I crawled toward him.

He looked up to see me and his eyebrows knit together as I came near.

I tried to remind him of the sunrise—I touched my nipples as he had, gentle like the breeze. I rolled onto my back and opened my legs to feel the cool air fanning the burning need there.

He did not ask any questions then, did not even pause to kiss me. Instead he heaved his body over mine and sank that long finger of his flesh into me, pinning me to the sand. It felt like a sword cleaving me in two, but then water flowed from somewhere in me, and the fire melted into warm pleasure, and he dove and plunged into me until we were both quenched.

While we lay upon the sand I marveled at the creation of man. Hard like the earth, burning like fire, gasping for air, and then leaking the water of the sea through his skin. He looked at me looking at him and laughed. "What is it, my darling? Are you going to scold me, too?"

I shook my head.

"No? I finally escape the cold and chill of the mountains, my father's sour temper, and the admonitions of the priests, to be married to an island princess so my father can rule the shipping lanes, and what do I find? Her people may not wear much, but they are just as afraid of lust as mine. Maybe more."

He paused, as if waiting for me to say something. When I did not, he went on. "You look familiar. Have we met before?" He squinted at me in the light of the moon, then said to himself, "Must have been a dream."

I touched him on the shoulder to prove to him I was real. He laughed again. "Can you believe I was rescued from a shipwreck? I thought I was dead, but I had this dream...." He looked over his shoulder toward the flickers of torches beyond the trees. "A lustful dream...."

He pulled me to my feet and it felt as though pins and needles were being driven through my skin. But I smiled and took a step to follow him, to be with him.

"Can you speak?" he asked then. I shook my head. He nodded to me then, smiling, and his smile made me as warm as the sunrise.

I followed him through the trees, up the hill, to a wide terrace of hard stone. "Look, everyone!" he cried. "Look what I've found!"

People came running from inside the palace bearing more torches, all of them dressed as he was, with bright cloth wrapped around their bodies. "My prince!" one of the men said, "where did she come from?"

A woman came out of the crowd and wrapped a cloth around my bare skin. "She must have been in the shipwreck also, the poor thing. What is your name?"

I could not say a thing.

"She's still in shock from being half-drowned," said a man.

"So beautiful!" said another.

Finally the prince quieted them with a gesture of his hands. "Yes, yes, she was on the ship with me. In fact, she was my maidservant, and I'd thought her lost with the rest of the hands. She will be my maidservant again, once she regains her speech. Isn't that right... Emerald?"

I nodded, not knowing of what he spoke, only knowing that he seemed to want me near him. And to be near him was all I wanted then.

He came to me again in the morning. The prince had his own quarters, a wing of the palace all his own. I had slept in a bed as soft as any kelp but as light as air, and then had gone to the bathhouse, where hot water sprang up from within the earth. Again I was amazed to find water, earth, fire, and air, all in one place. And again my prince came to me, and I tasted his salt with my tongue, and took him deep inside me. I could wrap my legs around the trunk of his body, and then even if we slid into the steaming water—which we did—I could still have him inside me. "My salvation," he breathed into my ear, as his flesh spear plunged into me and out, as I squeezed him hard. "And so you rescue me yet again, from my own burning need."

I wanted to tell him what pleasure he brought me. I wanted to ask him about this land. I wanted to tell him that everything was new to me and to ask him his name. He lifted me out of the bath onto the wet stone and I felt the roughness of his beard like sand between my legs. His tongue wriggled like a fish as it nestled into the soft spaces there and sparked the fire of my desire again and again. With another sudden rush of pleasure like a plunge into deep water, I clamped my knees around his head. But I had no voice to cry out with.

That afternoon I was taken to see the princess. Women came and dressed me and braided my sea-tossed hair. They were very grave as they led me to her chamber, or perhaps they did not wish to speak and remind me I was mute.

The guard there was about to open the door when my prince came running up to us.

"You must not enter, my lord," the guard said, stepping in front of the door, his arms crossed over his chest. "You must not lay eyes on the princess until the day of the wedding."

"Where are you taking Emerald?" he asked.

One of the women who had dressed me looked up with dark eyes. I wondered if this was the woman he had tried to take on the beach last night, for she fixed him with a hard stare. "She will not be harmed," she said. "The princess merely wishes to... inspect her."

My prince stepped back, then, and went back down the hall toward his rooms.

The princess sat upon a throne of fine polished wood, worked with gold and silver, and wore elaborate layers of cloth. The throne room was round like a cave, the slatted windows letting a sea breeze blow through. She looked over my white skin, which had only seen the sun once in my life, yesterday, and nodded. She turned to the woman who had spoken to my prince.

"She cannot speak?"

"No, not a word," the woman replied.

"She can tell no secrets, then." The princess sat back in her chair, her eyes on the far edge of the room.

"So it would seem, my lady."

The princess waved her hand, still not looking at me. "If the barbarian cannot wait a week, let him plant his seeds here. No one shall speak of it."

And then I was returned to him.

And so it went, for seven days and seven nights, during which I spent most of my time either in the bathhouse or in the air-light bed, waiting for my prince to quicken, waiting to have my newly empty spaces filled in a manner so intimate I would never have imagined it possible before. The household was busy, preparing for the wedding. The cool white halls were filled with the scent of meats being roasted on the beach, and servants with heaping baskets of fruit went back and forth. From the prince's window I could see men were erecting a roof where the wedding would take place. But my prince had no role in these preparations, and we spent long hours, lying in the bed cloths, as he would slide a finger over my shoulders, down my arm, or use a small palm frond to brush and tickle my newest and most sensitive skin, between my thighs.

On the seventh night, he came to the room bearing a basket with food for me as he always did, but he did not feed it to me as he had before. He put the basket down and took me in his arms immediately. The torchlight flickered in his gold-spun hair, and his kiss ranged down from my lips to my neck, then to my breasts as he pulled the cloth away from me, as his lips and tongue moved hungrily over my skin. My hunger for food was forgotten as I drank in his touch instead. He lifted me off my feet then, and brought me to the bed. I lay there a moment watching him emerge from his clothing like a crab from his shell. Naked and new again he came to me then, his skin on fire and his eagerness for me making his breath shallow. I matched his hunger with mine, gobbling up his maleness as I had that day on the beach, the hard pole of him going deep into my mouth. But soon he pulled me away with a shudder, before the salt spray could come. He hooked one of my legs over each shoulder, folding me up so that the burning slot between my legs was lifted for him.

He plunged a finger into me and I gasped. "You know," he said to me then, "I had not known many women before you. I had dreamed of them, desired them, hungered for them, but had tasted so few." Here he bent his head to lick at me and I tensed with pleasure. "And the few who would give in, desperate serving wenches looking for a way to better their position. Dirty sluts. I feared their diseases and their plots for my bastards." His finger returned to the empty place in me, and burrowed there. "But then there you were, delivered to me by a magic prayer. A virgin, clean as the sea water running off your skin, and you took me in." Now he heaved himself up to lay his manhood onto my mound. I felt it there, heavy and hot, and it twitched like a fish. He seemed to have no more to say, and into me he dove. How many times had he been inside me since that first night on the beach? More times than I had digits to count. And yet I lived for that moment, when we were as close together as two bodies could be. Even as my arms clutched at his back, I held him tight inside, and he cried out. I felt the salty flow that always reminded me of home.

He slept, then, and I would have, too, but I heard a song then borne on the sea breeze through the window. I heard my sisters singing down in the lagoon, and walking on my pins and needles feet, I made my way down to the water. There they bobbed, their heads just far enough above the water that I could hear them.

"Sister, sister, come back to us!" they cried.

I shook my head, unable to say anything else.

"We spoke to the sea witch," Mara, the oldest told me. "And she told us what she had done."

"But she did not tell you everything," Lara, the youngest said, salt tears welling in her eyes. "She said you would lose everything of us if you joined with him."

"Your tail, your voice..." said Sara, my closest sister.

"But she did not tell you what would happen if you lost him!" Mara swam closer to the shore. "Only while he is yours will you live. If he gives his heart to another, you will die."

Lara wailed. "We begged her that it not be so. She should have told you."

Sara held something out of the water. "So she told us there is one way you might be saved." She tossed the thing and it flew slickly through the night air to land in the sand near my aching feet. "Take the knife. If you cut out his heart, you will live. Let his blood drip over your legs and you will grow a tail again. Swallow his blood and you will regain your voice. And then you can come back to us."

"Emerald?" The prince's voice came from above me on the terrace. And my sisters disappeared with a quiet splash.

"Here you are," he said, as he approached. The tips of his fingers brushed my cheek and I leaned my face into the dry smoothness of his hand. I took a deep breath of his salty scent, and licked his palm. "Hungry again, are we?" he whispered. My lips found his neck then, and the soft place behind his ear, and I felt the fire in him begin to burn again. The breeze itself was a caress on my bare flesh, the rush of the waves a seductive song of its own.

He slid his fingers into my hair and it felt as if I dove into a clear lagoon, my hair swept back from my face and my body tingling with his touch. Our lips met then, and it was like the moment when I broke the surface for the first time, his breath mingling with mine. I could feel his heart beat everywhere along his skin.

We let gravity take its course, as it so easily did on land, and soon our legs were entwined on the sand. I could feel the hard barb of him, the stone that I hungered for, sliding back and forth trying to find its way inside me. And I knew, somehow, that my sisters were wrong. In that first fateful moment when we had kissed, in that first spark of fire inside me, in the first breath of air we shared that fanned the spark to a flame, in that first embrace of the weight of the earth, I had lost the purity of the water. I could not go back. I could no longer live without air and earth and fire.

I cried out as he sank into me, salt tears tracking my face, my feeble feet drumming on his back as I tried to drive him deeper and deeper in. Tomorrow he would marry the princess and I knew, if I did not have his stone to hold me, I would float away into the air. If I did not have the salt of his come, I would burn away to ash. If I did not have his breath to fill my lungs, I would be buried alive. If I did not have his burning desire to draw me up again and again, I would drown. Tomorrow he would marry the princess, but for tonight, I was whole.

rite of spring

I KNEW HE had the magic in him when I first saw his eyes. How could I not? How could anyone not? Adram Gyrien Hastor, Blood of Tarasco, was reputed to be the first king successor in generations for whom the magic flowed freely. Some, including Arnissa, said it was all talk, all politics to bolster his position. But that day in the courtyard when he met all the daughters for the first time, I stopped doubting.

We, the daughters, were dressed in our finest. Arnissa was next to me: her gown blue, her lily-white skin and her red hair glowing in the sun bathing the courtyard. My dress was red, my father's colors of course, my black hair hidden inside the hat they made me wear to keep my skin—which browned as easily as a chicken's in a fire—out of the sun. The garden was filled with flowers, criss-crossed with flagstones, and I wanted to walk among them and admire them. But at that moment, we were made to stand still, all twenty of us in a pretty line, as various officials and ministers looked us over before Adram's arrival.

At last we were free to wander the garden, and I used the flowers as the shroud for my nervousness. I was by far the youngest of all the daughters there. Arnissa's father and mine were close, and she had grown up like an elder sister to me. She, like all the others, was in her twenties. I was not, and I was apprehensive about what was going to happen those weeks we were in the castle. Perhaps if I kept my head down, with my hat shielding my eyes, he'd never notice me.

Once I could get a closer look at them, I could see many of the flowers were suffering from lack of water, their petals curled or their leaves drooping. I was standing in a shady corner with Arnissa, telling her about the brookflower which needed more water than any of the others, when Adram was suddenly there in front of us. He had not been announced and he was wearing the same plain green tunic and brown boots he would wear to go riding. But I knew it was he all the same, as he approached Arnissa and the serene expression on his face turned to a smile.

Those eyes! As blue as the brookflower with reflections of green in them, but it wasn't their color that startled me. It was their intensity, something in his gaze that made me suck in my breath, and I could see it, sense it, the magic boiling behind those eyes. He had broad shoulders but gentle-looking hands as he took Arnissa's fingers in his own, and planted a soft kiss on her knuckles before turning away and moving on down the path.

I could barely speak, but I tried. "Arnissa! Did you see the way he looked at you?"

But Arnissa did not match my breathless excitement. She clucked her tongue once. "He's just a man, Melinne."

That was all we said about it then. There were others

around and voices carry in a stone courtyard. But I was now sorry that I had gotten my wish. He had walked past me without even a glance, and now my wish was different. I wished desperately that he would turn that gaze on me.

That night in the women's quarters I sat upon my bed in the room I shared with Arnissa and tried to explain myself.

Arnissa sat at the mirror, the candles all around her, brushing out her hair which shimmered in the candlelight. Arnissa was, in my opinion, the most beautiful of all the daughters, and given Adram's reaction to her this afternoon, I thought he would choose her, and I told her so.

"And what if he does? In a few weeks it won't matter."

"No, Arnissa, I think you could be the one."

She hissed through her teeth. "Not likely. More likely he'll bed me a few times while he has the opportunity and then move on."

"Why do you say that?" She sounded so disdainful and I didn't understand. "You're... did you see the way he looked at you today?"

"Like a hungry hunting dog? Of course." She hissed again.

I hugged my knees to my chest, bunching my plain cotton sleeping shift around my ankles. "I think he really liked you."

"He liked my low-cut gown and what was in it."

"But didn't you see the...." I wiggled my toes in frustration. "He's going to be the king, Arniss'. Doesn't that mean anything to you?"

She put the brush down and turned to face me. "Oh,

Melinne, you're still so young. Adram may be the next king of Tarasco, but until he is, he's just another courtier. One who happens to have a privileged opportunity to poke his finger into all of our pies."

I blushed when she said that and hoped the candlelight wouldn't show it. "They say the king successor sometimes just goes with one...."

"Not since Meldinor, I believe." She looked almost sad as she leaned toward me and whispered. "Adram's father, they say, put off making his choice until the very last day, and had each of the daughters into his chamber a dozen times."

I shivered a bit at that thought, that a man who was not my husband could have me again and again at will. When we were sent off to the choosing, our mothers invariably told us that some of us would likely never see the successor's bed, and we could return home with our duty fulfilled and our maidenheads intact. Even if we were among those he decided to try, the expectation was that it would be once—one night for the sake of the country, for the sake of the kingship, for the health of the nation and what keeps us strong. And no man could turn away a woman who had been blessed with the king's seed. His own sons would grow up strong as a result, his animals and crops, too... which raised a question in my mind.

"You mean, King Hastor bedded"—here I blushed again—"them all?"

"Multiple times."

"But then, why weren't there more children?"

Arnissa wrinkled her nose. "Because the magic in Hastor's blood is thin. And I expect his son is going to be the same."

I shook my head—I wanted to argue. I was sure Adram was different. But I didn't know what to say or how to explain it.

We both jumped at the knock on the door. A moment later it opened, and an old man in a white robe stuck his head in. He was blind but not mute, and he called out Arnissa's name. We exchanged glances. So it was the first night, and Arnissa had already been chosen. As she took the arm of the blind old man, he led her along the corridor with one hand on a golden rope that threaded along one wall. I had never thought much about the rope until then, and I stood in the hallway watching him lead her to the end, where they turned and disappeared out of sight.

I lay down on the bed and knew that I should sleep. But I could not. I let the candles burn low and sputter out one by one, but no darkness came behind my eyes, as I lay there trying to imagine what was occurring in the sacred chambers. Would she lie down upon the bed, looking up at him? I pictured her lying back upon the platform. He would kneel at her feet and say a brief prayer before pushing her shift up to her belly and spreading her knees apart. He would lie between her legs then, moving himself up and down until he found the right place, and then he would be inside her. She would have the Blood of Tarasco inside her and she would be blessed.

I rolled over and I was surprised by the wetness between my own legs. I could feel the slipperiness in my crotch and reached down to touch it. I bunched my shift between my legs, pulled up my blanket and tried to sleep, with the vision of Adram's eyes still burning in my head.

Some time later I was woken by the sound of the door opening. Moonlight came through our window and I knew some hours must have passed. Arnissa came in, and the attendant closed the door behind her. She sat down onto her bed.

I sat up and stared at her. Her hair was more disheveled

than before and she made no move to brush it out before lying down. She lay back upon her pillow like she was very tired.

"Well?" I squeaked.

Arnissa gave a quiet laugh. "It was what it was, Melinne. Nothing to be afraid of."

"Aren't you going to tell me about it?"

"What is there to tell? His thorn pricked my rose." Her words were tough but I could tell by her voice that she was not. She was crying very softly.

"But don't you feel blessed? Didn't you feel...?"

"The magic? Please Melinne," she said, her voice growing harsh. "Grow up. Magic is for children's stories. If my husband thinks I'm going to bring him something special because the king-to-be plowed the furrow before him, then all the more fool him."

Her crying was making me cry, too, as it always did. "Was it..." I didn't understand what could have made her so upset. "Did it hurt?"

She came over to my bed and hugged me. "Oh, poor little Melinne. Don't be afraid. No, it didn't hurt. He was very gentle. I'm just tired is all." She kissed me on the forehead and then climbed back into her bed. "Have a good night, now."

She still thought I was afraid of him, and maybe I was in a way, but with her words ringing in my ears I wanted even more to be chosen. He was very gentle....

But time went on and I was not chosen. The choosing goes on until the king successor chooses his queen, or until all the daughters have had their menses. If none are chosen at the end of that period of time, then none were suitable and everyone must wait until the following spring. As I understood it, no king successor ever wanted to have to wait another year to ascend the throne, and so someone suitable was always chosen.

I still thought Arnissa would be the one, though. She went again and again to Adram's chamber, until she no longer cried when she came back to our room. She would just climb into bed and go to sleep, or pretend to, and I gave up trying to ask her about what had happened.

But there was gossip and talk among the daughters, as we would sit to do needlework in the afternoons or as we would eat. Soon I began to feel I was the only one Adram had not taken to his bed, and when the attendant would come for Arnissa, my heart would leap, hoping that this time it would be me, and after she would leave it would be me that lay in bed and cried.

We would see him every few days, either all eating together in the grand hall, him seated to his father's right at the table above ours, or in the gardens. He shone, his hair brown and straight and gleaming, cut short for a helm, and those eyes, always those eyes. I wished I had a way to catch the attention of those eyes and more than once almost reached out to touch his sleeve. But I did not.

In our room one night, Arnissa returned and as soon as the door closed, flung herself down on the bed.

"What's wrong?" I asked, sitting up.

"He's a pig," she answered, "just like his father."

"I... I thought you said he was gentle...."

"I told you before, Melinne. He just wants to poke his finger into all of our pies, that's all."

I sighed. I wanted to tell her how much I wished it was me he called. I almost told her again, of what I saw in his eyes that very first day, but it was as if I could already hear her voice replying to me. She would tell me I was just a silly girl, too young to really know, young enough to fall for a handsome face. "If you dislike it so much, why does he keep asking for you?"

Arnissa sat up and stared at me in the light of the sputtering candles I had let burn down as always. "Melinne, I don't let him know I don't like it."

"Why?"

She shook her head. "There's just no explaining anything to you, is there." She sighed. "I shouldn't seem as if I'm ungrateful for the so-called blessing, should I? I mustn't make trouble for my father at court, isn't that right?"

"Yes, yes I suppose...."

"So no one knows how much I hate being taken to Adram's bedchamber, except you." She lay back and seemed disinclined to talk any further.

But what she did not know was that I had let it slip to one of the other daughters already, a few days before. Some of them, I knew, wanted very much to be queen, but did not seem to be enjoying the act itself. Others, like Arnissa, wanted to go back to the lives that they knew, but they were not unhappy about Adram's attentions. Surely, I thought, there were others like Arnissa who neither wanted the queenship nor his attentions? What was the harm in admitting that to one another? But as I lay there I went through the list of daughters in my head, thinking of the whispers I had exchanged with each of them over the weeks that had passed... it seemed upon my tally that Arnissa was the only one who wanted nothing to do with Adram at all. I was ashamed then of what I had done:

whenever the women put their heads together to whisper, I had talked about Arnissa and not about myself. They would have pitied me, or poked fun at me, the runt of the litter who wanted to be queen, that's the way they would have seen it. But I could not have cared less about the throne. All I wanted was for him to look into my eyes, to touch me, for our lips to meet. That was not something I could say to the other daughters, so I kept my feelings hidden, and had ransomed Arnissa's feelings in their place. I knew then that trouble was coming.

It arrived the next day when a cleric, one of the Keepers of the Magic, addressed the daughters as we were gathered together in a windowless meeting chamber deep in the center of the castle. It seemed an odd place for us, quite different from the usual audience chamber, but when we heard what he had to say, I realized why we were there.

"It has come to our attention," he said, his deep blue robes making him almost invisible in the ill-lit room, "that one of you is reluctant to perform her duties." Like the court-trained ladies that we are, we sat straight and did not look around at one another. That room was cut off from other areas of the castle, impossible to eavesdrop on, and the only place for such an admission to be made aloud. The cleric droned on, then, telling us again what we had heard so many times, that in order for the magic to manifest we had to believe in it, we had to surrender ourselves to it. We were half of what was needed, the rain that makes the seed blossom, and so on. For some reason, listening to him tell the tale then, it sounded less convincing than when my own father had explained it to me. Perhaps it was the tone of his voice, almost mocking us, as if he himself did not believe a word of it.

When he came to the end of his speech, though, we all sat up to take notice. "We know which one of you it is. She will be called tonight. If her resistance is not broken, then the choosing will fail, so it is of tantamount importance that she surrender herself utterly to our king successor." He went on, about how a drought would come, the cattle would fall ill, and so on, if the choosing failed, but I was barely listening. My heart beat hard in my chest and I wanted so much to look up at Arnissa, but I could not.

Instead I looked around the room again. The torches had been hastily lit when we had first entered, but now they were burning steadily and I could now see into the corners where before my sun-dazzled eyes could not. There were chains on the walls.

"Her resistance will be broken," the cleric said with finality, as if this were one thing he truly had faith in.

It was a long, long day. After the speech they pretended as if nothing had happened, and we ate, and practiced our dancing, and did our needlework just as we did on any other day, and so it was not until that night that I finally had a moment alone with Arnissa.

I immediately told her it was my fault that they knew. "I'm so sorry, Arniss'! I never dreamed...."

"Hush, it's done with now."

"But they're going to do something horrible to you, I know it."

She sat on her bed in her white shift, shaking her head slowly. A few tears fell into her lap. "There's nothing you can do, Melinne."

Just then the knock came at the door, and suddenly I knew what to do. "Yes, there is," I told her.

Before she could argue, I took the arm of the blind attendant and it was me he led out of the room.

The castle is large and full of twisting stairways and corridors, and yet the blind man knew his way around them. We went through areas where there were no torches at all and I had to cling to his arm to keep from stumbling. But of course, I realized—a blind man needs no torches. They did not want the daughters to know where Adram's chamber was, so that we could not visit him unannounced, and thereby influence his decision. As we stepped through the pitch blackness, though, I sensed we were heading back to the room where the cleric had spoken to us that day.

My heart thumped and felt like it was trying to climb up out of my throat. So at last I was taking the walk to Adram's chamber that I had dreamed of every night since coming to the castle, but this time it would not be to his bed. What was I thinking?

We reached the door of the chamber and I walked in of my own accord. The cleric was there with his back to me, and I was unsure what to do. Adram was nowhere in sight. My plan had been to tell Adram that I had lied, that when I had said Arnissa had not wanted to go, I had been talking about myself and trying to deflect the blame. But faced with the dour cleric, I found I could not say anything at all.

He turned to face me and frowned as he looked me up and down. "So, you are the one? Come here."

I stepped forward and he seemed to get taller with each step I took. He then pulled a hood over my head and I could see nothing more. Behind me he tightened the hood so that it was snug against my eyes, covering my hair and my ears, but leaving my mouth and chin free so I could breathe. He led me over to the wall and pushed my back against it. I heard the clank of chain and then he wrapped my wrists in leather that creaked like a horse's saddle as he lifted my arms up over my head. I guess that he had attached the leather to a metal ring set in the wall. I was trembling. This was not the night as I had imagined it, with the gentle, loving Adram planting his seed in me while we gazed into each other's eyes.

The hood covered my ears but I could still hear. Someone else came into the room, the door closed heavily behind him, and I heard Adram's voice. "Is all in readiness?"

"Yes, your highness," the cleric answered. "I have brought the book in case you would like me to refer to it."

"Do you think that will be necessary?"

"With all respect, your highness, you have no experience in breaking the will of a human being and may need some advice."

"And what would you advise me to do now?"

"You must assert yourself over her, prove to her that she is utterly and completely within your control. Remember, it is surrender we are seeking, ultimately. She must feel as though she has not a shred of her own will left." The cleric cleared his throat. "You could begin by tearing her clothes off."

I heard Adram's boots on the stone as he approached me. How could I not feel as if I was utterly and completely within his control? I was chained to a wall, helpless. I felt his hands take hold of the cloth around my neck and then his muscles strain, his breath warm on my lips for a moment before the seam gave way and tore down the middle. He jerked the cloth a few more times and then the shift was rent all the way to my feet.

I felt his hand caress my chin and I shivered. He leaned close and I was expecting a kiss, but then I heard the cleric's voice. "A slap would do better than that, my lord."

Adram hissed. "Not on her face."

"You are supposed to be showing her no respect, my lord."

"Not on her face, Keeper," he repeated.

"Then turn her."

I felt his hands on me then, as he turned me under the ring so that my face was to the stone. I felt then the edge of a blade against my neck as he slipped his knife into my sleeve and swiftly cut the rest of the shift away. Now I was naked against the stone and I felt one of his hands on my shoulder. His other hand slid down my back and between my buttocks. I sucked in my breath. How many times had I lain in bed, dreaming about him doing just that? One finger insinuated itself into the slippery folds and I could not help but push back into him.

"Keeper, she is wet."

"And of what concern is that to us, your highness?"

Adram's voice crackled with suppressed anger. I almost felt I could see his face through the hood. "Does that not indicate that her body is ready for me?"

"Perhaps, but it is her body only, my lord."

His hand drew back then, and through the hand that was still on my shoulder I felt him tense as he drew back for the blow. His hand fell upon my bare buttocks with a loud smack and I cried out. At what point, I wondered, would the Keeper decide it was enough, and allow Adram to plant his seed? I held the leather between my hands and squeezed it hard as the next blow came, and the next, and the next. Sometimes I was able to hold back my cry, but mostly I was not. I counted ten, then twenty, and then I lost count, gritting my teeth and wailing and waiting for it to be over.

And then came Adram's hand, soothing the sore skin. I trembled hard, sobbing against the stone. Such a gentle touch! I craved it again, and pressed back into him. I could feel the rough cloth of his tunic against my skin, and then bone of his hip. No, not his hip. I sucked in a breath as I realized what I was rubbing against. Adram was eager for me and his finger again slid down into the cleft between my legs. I was dripping with honey, now.

"Keeper, she is ready. She's never done that before."

"You know perfectly well, your highness, that a wild horse may feign tameness."

Adram hissed, but softly. "And what does your book suggest we do next?"

I heard the leaves of a book being turned. "Why your highness, we've barely begun."

Adram left me then, and I surmised he was looking at the book as well.

The cleric's voice continued. "We have all of these means at your disposal. Whips, flails, needles, candles, braided rope...."

The next thing I heard I can only describe as a growl, and then the sound of the book hitting the floor. "I'll not ruin her and I'll not perform for you like a trained animal."

"Your highness...."

"Your title may be Keeper, but who is it who holds the power here?"

"My lord, I meant only...." Then all was silent for a few moments, and I heard the cleric gasp. "My lord, your eyes...!"

Adram's voice was soft again. "Are you surprised?"

"I, I..." the cleric stammered into a silent wonder.

"Did you think the power would not manifest in me?" I heard Adram's boots as he walked back and forth. "Did you not believe?"

"I never dared to hope that...." The cleric cleared his throat. "Clearly the ritual has worked. She must be ready to give herself to you or...."

His voice sounded like he could barely contain himself. "I am not like my father. My blood is not so thin. Now, go."

I heard the rustle of cloth and then the door opened, and shut.

And then Adram's hands were running down my back. I tingled everywhere he touched and I moaned out loud. He turned me again, so that my back was to the stone and my lips could meet his. We chewed hungrily at one another's mouths, and I almost thought I would cry for joy. His body pressed against mine, the roughness of his clothes against my bare skin, the hardness of him pressing into the softness of me. I wrapped my legs around him and pulled him in tight.

"Slowly, slowly," he admonished.

I thrashed and tried to squeeze him harder with my legs.

He chuckled. "I suppose it is a blessing that you are tied there." He caressed my cheek. "I know, I feel it, too. But do you know what would happen if I were to plunge into you this instant, my dear?"

"What?" I whispered back.

"All the power we feel, all the magic we've gathered, you and I, would dissipate in an instant. And we haven't gathered nearly enough." Adram brushed his lips past mine. "The Keepers know only what is in their books. I know what is in a king's heart."

I felt him pull back then. "Don't go!"

"Do not fear, my sweet, I am right here." And then I could hear the sounds of him disrobing.

The next thing I felt was his fingers along my ribs, and then his tongue wrapped itself around one of my nipples, and the tingling I felt in my body grew. He lapped at the other then, as his fingers cupped the mound of my crotch, one finger making its slow way toward the center like the blind man to the dungeon. I let out another cry as he slid it back and forth, and shook my arms, trying to free myself so I could hold him, pull him to me.

"Calmly, calmly, my sweet," he whispered, as his sliding finger moved faster in the wetness there, and I thought perhaps I would faint from the hard beating of my heart and the feeling surging through me. Then he slowed and I could breathe again.

"Please," I managed to choke out, once my breathing slowed. "Please Adram, let me see your eyes."

He pressed himself against me then, his chest to my chest, his lips to my lips, and reached behind me to fumble with the ties of the hood. It came loose, and I felt my hair slide down my neck, even as his hands slid it from me. He cupped my face in his hands then as we kissed. I opened my eyes first, in time to see him open his.

It was not my imagination. His eyes glowed. Then they widened in surprise. "Melinne, daughter of Gilliman?"

"Yes, your highness." I could not get my voice above a whisper.

"But how could you be the one who...?"

I put one of my legs around one of his and pulled him

closer. "As you have seen, the Keepers are not right about everything."

He kissed me again then, letting the kiss move southwards, over my neck and down to the hollow between my breasts. His hands followed his mouth, and he caressed my nipples with his thumbs, making me cry out again. "Adram..." I said, unable to say anything more. "Adram...."

When he came up for air he said, "Can you see your reflection in my eyes?"

I shook my head. The candles and torches were not strong enough, and their inner light burned brightly.

"Your eyes burn like mine," he said into my ear. "You are the one."

"Adram, please...." What could I say? "Please, I don't think I can wait any longer."

He looked at the straps of leather above my head. "When the time is right, my sweet." But he began parting my legs with his and I felt the hard length of him against my mound. With one hand, he swept it back and forth in the wetness, and I whimpered. Then he put one of his hands under one of my buttocks, and lifted me a few inches, just enough so that the head of him slid between my legs into the wetness. He slicked it well and then pressed me into the wall, his thorn only then settling against the center of my rose.

He came into me an inch at a time, and my legs shook and I cried out as every part of me wanted him at that moment. He crept in, and then backed himself slowly out. He repeated it with excruciating slowness, again and again. But when I looked up into his eyes, I saw that they burned brighter than ever. He was trembling also now, sweat beading on his forehead as he struggled to hold himself back.

And then he began to increase his pace, bit by bit. He had both hands planted on my buttocks and pulled me onto him with increasing speed. Energy was pouring into me then, and I strained toward him. I heard a snap then and my arms came free—I had broken the leather strap and we tumbled to the floor, but did not separate. Now I hooked my legs behind his, and held him to me with my arms, and he drove me into the floor with the force of his thrusts. The energy just built and built and built until, as they describe it in the legends, we were both consumed by it. We were both screaming as we hit the release point, clinging to one another as the dam burst. I felt as though I could see across the country, a cow giving birth in one of my father's paddocks, a wolf mounting his mate, Arnissa's sister Hellenne suckling her first born son. The magic raced out from us to everywhere in the kingdom.

Arnissa told me later that a thundercloud had gathered that night, its rumblings growing louder and louder until the whole castle was suddenly shaken by a tremendous clap, and then it began to rain. Down in the dungeon we could hear none of it, but the next day the brookflower in the garden had grown as high as the second story. The daughters wove countless blossoms into my hair for the bonding ceremony, and when my father's retinue arrived, there were petals aplenty strewn in his path, for he was now the father of a queen.

bodies of water

HER SKIN IS more sensitive now, she's sure of it. As the water trickles over her back, she can feel every drop, each rivulet tracing a line down her back like a fingertip caress. Water never felt like this before, not even in the most luxurious shower.

She remembers the shower at Argyropoulos's palazzo. One of Steve's rich investors, taken in by the adventure of treasure hunting, he had not only bought in to the expedition company but insisted the team stay at his palatial home while they were landside. She barely remembers what the bathroom looked like, only that the shower was such a luxury—hot water, dry towels—after three weeks on the ship sifting through sand-covered artifacts and always being damp.

It was one morning when getting out of that shower she had seen the blue speck on her skin, just glimpsed it in the mirror on the underside of her arm. *No, no it can't be...* she thought to herself. It was blue like a spot of spilled ink, just like Jackie's, just like Karros's. She refused to believe it. In a few hours she would be back on the ship, and they would be that much closer to solving the mystery of the wreck. The fact that Karros was in a hospital in Athens and Jackie was on her way to the CDC in Georgia affected her only slightly. *Not when we are this close*, she thought. She felt sure they were on the verge of a breakthrough.

The wreck was a mystery, and that was what mattered most to Lydia. When she had gone into archaeology she had thought she would be sifting dust in an Egyptian desert or hacking through the Yucatan jungle. But there was pioneering work being done in undersea archaeology, and her fiancé Ambrose had hooked them up with Steve to do a few voyages. No matter how much he claimed he wasn't a treasure hunter, Steve still hoped for a large haul of gold to pay back his stockholders with. Ambrose hoped for prestige and fame. But Lydia just wanted the answers to questions history had left for them.

Her arms are crossed over her chest, but the water flowing down her back feels so good she wants to reach up into the stream. She lowers her hands, her fingers sliding over her skin, and she shivers in delight. She has never been comfortable in nakedness, but now she forgets modesty as she leans back to let the water spatter onto her breasts. She reaches up and spreads the water between her breasts, over her nipples, her neck and lips.

She had argued with Ambrose over the origin of the wreck. That morning at Argie's, before they had set sail again, he had picked a fight with the other archaeologist, a young man named Tomson, Will Tomson, who had speculated that if they couldn't find evidence for a Mediterranean culture who whaled, who was to say the cargo came from the same place as the ship? Ambrose had practically bellowed at the man, "What sort of twisted logic is that? You'll never get anywhere with thinking like that, my boy. You'll spend your life on one wild goose chase after another. Simplify!"

Lydia had been pretending not to hear the exchange, putting sugar into her coffee with slow deliberate spoonfuls, and stirring so that the spoon did not clink against the side of the mug. But when it had come to that she had stood up, and approached their table.

Ambrose had put his hand around her hip as she came over, proprietary. But he took it away again when she said, "It very well may be that our explanation is going to be a complicated one. Where did the whale oil come from? Where did the ship come from? They may well be two different answers." As she walked away, she could feel Ambrose's usual daggers in her back. She would pay for defying him later, she was sure of it. But no matter the consequence, Lydia could not allow an incorrect or foolish statement to stand.

And they certainly had to consider every option. This wasn't like the Spanish galleon they had recovered off the continental shelf last year, doubloons and rare artifacts and a diary clearly revealing the date of her voyage. No, this wreck was older than any ever found, probably three thousand years or more, and nothing they had brought up yet had matched their body of knowledge. There were amphorae and other jars they expected to be full of olive oil. But some were found with their seals still intact, and when opened they were found to be whale oil. Some of them were strangely fragrant, as if perfumed to last over centuries, millennia. Staggering.

Almost as staggering as the news that came to them after the ship had set out to sea once again. Lydia had been standing on the deck of the ship, her hands gripping the railing. The sun was hot but the spray was cold and damp as they headed back to the deep water where the wreck lay. She barely felt the pitching and yawing of the converted trawler as it sliced through the waves, her eyes fixed on a far spot on the horizon. The answer was out there, somewhere.

Tomson disturbed her reverie with a hand on her elbow. "Jackie just radioed in."

He sounded like he was choking as he said it. Lydia turned and saw the distress on his face. "What is it? Is it the blue fever? What did they find?"

"Karros died in the hospital, some kind of pneumonia-like symptoms, but they weren't sure if it was related to the skin condition or not. But the CDC thinks it's some kind of infectious agent. They've got Jackie in a bubble."

For a moment, pure human emotion took over. "Oh, poor Karros...." She crumbled and he put his arm around her, held her for a moment. She coughed up a few tears, though she mostly held them back. But then she straightened up and looked into Tomson's eyes. Like the ocean, their blue was brighter in the sun. "What do they want us to do?"

"For now, stay out here, and tell them if we have any more cases of it. We shouldn't try to land anywhere, that's for sure."

She watched as his eyes roved the horizon like hers, and she felt their hips touch as they both leaned on the railing. "It's just lucky we were out here when the news came," she said.

"Why do you say that?"

"Because now we have no reason to stop operations," Lydia said. "We can keep digging."

Tomson nodded and a relieved almost-smile warmed his face. "I'm so glad you feel that way about it. Steve wants to keep going, too."

"Who doesn't?" Lydia asked, already suspecting the answer.

"Your partner," Tomson answered. "Ambrose thinks we should head straight for the mainland and all get ourselves into a hospital right away."

"A hospital didn't do Karros any good." Lydia stared back into the blue. "Do you feel it, Will? We've barely begun to investigate, but we're on the verge of something quite extraordinary."

"You sound quite sure of yourself."

"It's rare I find something so totally outside of my knowledge base. Whatever we find, they'll be rewriting the history books, I'm sure of it."

Will Tomson nodded then, and they both watched the sea roll under the ship for long minutes.

She opens her mouth to let the water dribble in, letting it run down her chin and over her closed eyelids. Her lips tingle where it touches, and she lets the tip of her tongue emerge. She touches her wet cheeks with her hands and then brings them together in front of her mouth—she looks like she is praying. She has never felt anything quite like this before. It must be the fever. Her chest heaves as she breathes, the water falling faster now, over her face, her breasts, and down her belly. Water, who would have thought water would be the key to it all?

Ambrose had fought her bitterly that night in their cabin. "You'll get us all killed. Crazy woman...."

She had held her ground as much as she could. "They've

ordered us to stay in quarantine. And no one else is sick. There's no reason to stop the expedition. For all we know, Karros's pneumonia wasn't even related."

Ambrose rumbled like gathering thunder. "It's still too dangerous. I'm not handling anything that comes up from the wreck and neither are you."

"What do you mean...?"

"You're my wife-to-be and you're mine to protect. You're not going near it. Let little Willie do it."

She tried to deflect him by teasing, but it was a mistake. "You sound like those old Egyptologists, running from the curse of the mummy."

"I'll have to tell the others that you're not feeling well, that you have a headache." He left then, and she realized what he meant, as he bolted the door from the outside. The converted trawler was all steel—there wasn't even a porthole for her to shout through.

She licks the water from her lips. They had been chapped from sun and wind but now they feel like rose petals, the water droplets beading on her face like dew. She cranes her neck down to lick the water from her breasts, and leans back again to let the water rain down her midsection, pooling in the triangle of her crotch, her bush half-wet like a shore plant in a tidepool.

That night Ambrose had brought her dinner, canned stew heated in the galley with some crackers. He unbolted the door and swept in with the bowl in front of him, placing it on one corner of the bed with a flourish. The ship rocked slightly, but the seas were calm and there was little danger of spilling. "I thought you might be hungry," he said.

"Not really," she replied, just to annoy him. His face said

he was expecting praise, as if he had forgotten she wasn't really ill, forgotten that was a lie he had invented.

But then, she thought, she really was ill. While he had been gone she had examined the underside of her arm—the spot had grown bigger. There was another spot in the small of her back, as well.

He shrugged off the annoyance and came over to sit next to her. He took her hand in his. "Lydia, my dove, please don't be angry. You have to realize how irrational you can be sometimes. It's better this way—you'll see how it will all work out. You'll be glad...." He was leaning toward her, to kiss her. She pulled back almost involuntarily, as if he were the one with the contagion. He pressed forward more, his eyes closing, until their lips met.

She allowed him to kiss her for long moments, until she broke away saying, "That stew smells good."

He straightened, remembering his pretense for being there. "Of course. Here you are." He stood up and she gathered the bowl to her. Then he left, and bolted the door behind him.

She ate the stew, but didn't taste it. She ate it because she supposed it was better to be fortified than hungry, but her mind was elsewhere. What was Tomson doing right now? He might be opening a basket brought up by a remote right this minute. The wreck was so deep human divers, even in submersibles, couldn't reach it. But machines, guided from the deck with video monitors, could go anywhere. She felt sometimes that it was her hands, not the robot's, picking through the wreckage, lifting an ancient astrolabe out of the silt, peeling apart the remnants of a wooden carton to find whatever lay inside.

She hesitates a moment, the rapture frightens her a bit, and she questions what is happening. But pleasure is a reassuring thing, it feels right rather than wrong, and she gradually separates her knees. Pooled water cascades between her legs, and her mouth quivers as the trickle touches a place she has only let Ambrose touch when he fumbles to insert himself in her. Unlike his hard knuckles, the caress of the water opens her, and she feels an outflow of her own juices come forth to meet the cascade of water.

Lydia was asleep when someone had come to the door. The knock woke her. "Lydia? Are you all right?"

"Open the door!" she shouted, her voice hoarse from sleeping. That sounded like Tomson.

With a clank the door came open, and he stepped in with a wrench in his hand and a puzzled look on his face.

She grabbed him by the hand and pulled him down the corridor to the dark, empty galley, and insisted he tell her everything that they had found. The room was lit only with the orange emergency light above the door and they blinked at each other.

"Lydia, wait a minute, were you trapped in there?"

"That's not important right now. Please Will, what's been going on?"

"That's why I came looking for you. I found something you're not going to believe." He shifted the sack on his back to the table, opened it carefully to reveal what looked to Lydia rather like a book. It looked to be some kind of leather, and Tomson folded it open once, then again like a roadmap, to reveal several sheafs of skin.

"How could something like this survive in the water all that time?" she asked, even as she began to take in the drawings and symbols.

"Have a look at this," he said, taking out his flashlight and flooding the table with white light. The pages were blue. "Tell me, please, Lydia, did Ambrose lock you away because you've been infected?"

She shook her head. "No, rather to keep me from being infected. But Ambrose be damned, do you realize this is a map?" In human measure of time, the coastline of Spain and Portugal looked essentially the same. But this showed some land one did not see in the modern era. The drawing detailed a tiny map-size city, and a route from the mainland to it—a route that they had followed to arrive at the site of the wreck.

He nodded and turned the sheaf over. "And it looks like an instruction manual, as well." On the other side were drawings of a man and a woman, the odd-shaped whale oil jars, and more. Lydia was reminded of the safety instruction cards in airplanes. The final picture in the sequence, if they were reading the correct direction, was of the two humans swimming with two dolphins.

The other page also had a sequence of pictures on it. Lydia felt almost dizzy as she looked at them. *Can I be interpreting these correctly?* she thought. It appeared to tell a story of a city being engulfed by the sea, the same drawing of the city as on the facing sheaf, with the water level going up and up and up.

"It's not possible," she said, her voice so low Tomson was not sure she spoke. "A lost civilization? Who had the know-how to make a book that would not decay after thousands of years under water?"

Tomson put his hand on hers. "That's not all. We got word from Georgia."

"Oh no, not Jackie."

"She's alive. They said she's almost completely blue now, though. Antibiotics, anti-virals, they aren't effective. They are assuming now if it's an organism, it's something like a prion, something they haven't seen before. They say her cellular structure is changing. Not just on her skin. They are seeing changes in her brain."

"What sorts of changes?"

"Cognitively she still appears the same, but they are seeing increases in activity in some very unlikely areas...." Tomson was blushing red again. "I have some theories...." He shook himself a little. "But this is the important thing. They're keeping her alive by keeping her wet."

Lydia's hand went to the small of her back of its own accord. "Oh my."

Tomson grimaced as he saw it. "Lydia, there's something else you should know."

She heard the tremble in his voice and looked up from the diagrams. He was unbuttoning his shirt, his head down, his blond curls hanging over his eyes as he pulled the garment out of his pants and opened it.

Lydia could see the blue creeping up out of his waistband, climbing his stomach and up his chest.

"I won't be able to hide it from the others much longer," he said. "It's spreading upward and outward."

Almost without thinking, she reached a hand toward him and touched the skin of his stomach. It felt smooth, hairless, soft. He gasped and she pulled back. "Did that hurt?"

"No, no... it's just, very, very sensitive." He quivered then, as if her touch reverberated throughout his body.

She rubs the water on her thighs, splashing up handfuls

of it from the puddle around her. The pleasure is unlike any-
thing she has felt before. She rolls over now, letting the water
run over her back, then rolls over again and letting it bounce
off her stomach. She lets her knees fall apart and invites the
droplets to fall there, as well. She is soaked now, wet over
every inch of her skin, and she reaches for the jar.

We must keep away from Ambrose. That was her only
thought as she and Tomson made their way to the hold where
the recovered objects were prepped. If she was reading the
diagrams correctly, then what Tomson needed to survive was
there. She located one of the jars with the curlicue top as
shown in the drawings, and opened it. The scent of some
extinct flower filled the small room, and the slight motion of
the ship made her grip the jar tighter.

Tomson pulled his shirt completely off and Lydia stood
close to him. She dipped two fingers into the jar and came up
with a dab of something with the consistency of honey. She
smeared it into his back where the blue part of his flesh met
the pink, and began slathering it upward. As she watched, she
could see the blue edge beginning to spread. "It's working,"
she said to him. "The ointment is encouraging the blue to
grow."

He trembled under her touch and when she tried to come
around the front of him he shied away. "Let me do it," he
said, holding his hand out for the jar.

She knitted her brows in puzzlement, but then saw the
embarrassment on his face. She turned away as his trousers
dropped, but she could still hear the sounds he made in his
throat. He could not stop himself as he covered his legs and
private parts, and then huddled away from her, hiding his
crotch with his hands.

"Now we need to wet you down," Lydia said, her eyes still averted by studying the diagrams. There were hoses with small nozzles here, made for rinsing away sediment on artifacts. She turned the spigot on one and brought it over to where he was sitting in a ball.

He cried out as the water hit his back. "Not too hard!"

She reduced the flow to a dribble and let the droplets spatter softly over him. He moaned and then sighed, the tension seeming to go out of his body as she wet him. He let her run the water down his chest, and she saw that he had been hiding a rampant state of turgidity from her. His eyes were closed now, and she watched his penis curiously. It was thoroughly blue, standing up like a finger of coral, and he whimpered a bit when the water sprayed it.

"Will," she said in a hushed voice. "What do you know about dolphins?"

He lay back into the puddle and let out a long breath, his shyness gone. "A bit. Why?"

"Do you think it's possible that the transformation taking place here is to make us more like them?" Lydia began to untuck her own shirt. "To survive the day when our home is overrun by water?"

Will sat up and blinked water from his eyes. The blueness was creeping up toward his neck and she wondered if they would remain the same color when it reached them. "No one will ever believe it."

She shook her head. "I believe it." She turned to show him the spreading patch of blue on her back, her shirt hiked up. His wet fingers traced the edges of it and she knew then why he had moaned. His hands reached around her then, and she felt his cheek pressed against the small of her back.

"I'm sorry, Lydia, I just can't help it...."

"It's all right, Will." *Dolphins*, she thought. "Help me with it, now."

He helped her to shed her clothes and then handed her the jar, so she could slather herself. But then she came to her back, and he helped her with that as she had with his. And then she tilted her head back and waited for the water to come down.

She opens her eyes to see him standing above her, the hose still in his hand. She reaches up and pulls him down to her, wanting the feeling of his water-slick skin against hers. Their still-red lips meet, and she feels like they are drinking each other. She laps at his mouth, her hands buried in his curls, as his hands run up and down her back. She wraps a leg around him and almost before either of them realizes it, he mounts her. Every part of her is slick, both inside and out, and she sucks in a breath, a tiny part of her mind realizing that it was never like this with Ambrose. She reaches a hand between their pumping bodies, curious to feel if something in her anatomy has changed. The breath keeps getting deeper, and her fingers slide over her clitoris, fundamentally unchanged and yet....

The intensity of it makes her want to cry out, and yet she does not want to exhale. Breathing has become a secondary thing to the urgent need between her legs, and she clings to him hard with three limbs, the fourth a moving blur between them even as he speeds up the rhythm of his own motion.

And then suddenly she feels him break loose, she feels the burst of hot salt liquid inside her, and her own pleasure cascades throughout her body, rippling from one end to the other. They cling together as the spasms quake through their muscles, and then, as one, they exhale.

They sit up slowly in the puddle on the floor, the hose still running, and look around them. Lydia looks down at her own body—the blue is everywhere their bodies touched, and spreading. She clasps Will's hand in her own. "Do you feel like you are coming down with pneumonia?"

"Actually, my lungs never felt better."

She nods. "Care to go for a swim?"

Before he can answer, the door swings open to reveal Ambrose. There is not even a moment for anger to register on his face before horror and fear set in. "Get me out of here!" he shouts, as he runs down the corridor. Some time after that, Steve calls them on the intercom and they explain what they've learned about the contagion, and everything else. There's still a lot of work to be done, there are so many more questions to answer, so much more to learn. But later, Will and Lydia will have plenty of time to swim.

dragon's daughter

THIS IS A STORY that began in ancient times, so it is hard to know where to begin the telling. Perhaps at the beginning of the end, although even the end is a beginning, just as the end of the night is the start of the day, and the end of the day the start of the night.

Let us start then with sunset, with summer heat shimmering on the streets poured with copper light, as the fire eye of sun burned away a late-day thundercloud. Jin Jin stood in the window staring into the street, one hand holding the other against her fine silk dress. I start the tale here because it was the first time I saw her, placid and still like a statue brought from some dynastic museum and installed there as decoration for the restaurant. Which, in a way, I suppose was true.

I was rushing up the stairs, all sneakers and blue jeans, while Skinny Dou cursed in Cantonese and English from the bottom of the steps to hurry myself up. Imagine me, a bundle of sweaty energy bursting into that room, where the window burned with gold and she stood in cool silhouette, like an empress. The new world and the old colliding, my questions piled one atop the other: who was she, would I find clothes up here, why would no one explain anything to me, ever? Maybe Uncle Charlie would change his mind about this job. My mind was so busy, but my body went suddenly still when faced with her image and one last question: why did she stare out the window so, and for what or whom did she look?

And then the moment broke and she came toward me, speaking accented but understandable Mandarin. I could understand her! She said hello, asked if I was lost. I said hello back, but then couldn't find any more words. This is the ignominy of the American educational system: that to speak the tongue of my ancestors I had to fight to be enrolled in a special college class and trudge to it every morning at 8:00. I didn't think I knew the words to explain what I was doing there, anyway—how to explain the complicated relationship of favors and feelings and resentments that had led me to this, especially when I was only dimly aware of them myself.

My mother was thoroughly against my being here, embarrassed at the existence of the "restaurant" side of her family, as if somehow she was failing as an adoptive mother to keep me from falling back into the Mainland sordidness she thought she rescued me from. She and my father were both born in the States. My father's society brother, whose real brother was Skinny Dou, needed someone with good English and a Chinese face. Then there was my own insistence on providing for myself, a stubborn youthful rebellion in the only way I knew: I turned away the things my parents would give me in the same way I yearned to turn away their attitudes about all things Chinese. No, these things I could not articulate then. We exchanged names instead. Jin Jin Tsu, hers; Mary Yip, mine.

But she could not say "Mary" and pronounced it "Mei" instead. So on that day, in that place, Mei is who I became.

Skinny Dou came into the room with his rapid-fire Cantonese, and Jin Jin herself was transformed from empress into seamstress in the instant she shooed him out and opened the wardrobe. As the sun dipped below the horizon, the glare turned to glow and I could see the room clearly. It was full of dark furniture, much of it lacquered wood upholstered with faded silk, chairs with carved feet and small tables at the edges of the room, a larger table in the center where four people could sit, and a surprisingly mundane-looking single bed pushed against the far corner wall, its white and yellow flowered bedspread looking like it could have been stolen from a cheap motel in Illinois. Maybe it was.

From the wardrobe Jin Jin pulled dress after dress, some large, some small, and held them up one by one, measuring them and me in a quick glance. She handed me a blue, high-collared cheongsam and urged me with gestures and a few rapid words to try it. My eyes flicked to the doorway through which Skinny Dou could charge at any moment, but that was another thing I could not yet express in my textbook vocabulary. I could talk about baby things—pencil and car and tree and food, mother and father and brother and sister, house and shoe and cat and dog. But I had no words yet for worry or conflict or secret or dream. And so I changed my clothes, there in the middle of Jin Jin's room, while she hung up the unneeded dresses. No one came through the door. And once I was dressed, and the loose button at the shoulder mended, and my hair tamed and shaped into a compact bun held in place by two black lacquered sticks with tiny dragons on the ends, Skinny Dou came back. We easily heard his heavy footsteps on the stairs (for he was not at all skinny, no matter what his name) and his bellowing about how he would only pay me half for the night if I did not hurry. And then he opened the door and saw us, two little empresses, and he gave a nod and went back down.

Thus began my first evening working in the bar, trying to milk as much money as possible out of white men who had crossed the line from the financial district or downtown for cheap drinks and deep-fried dumplings. It was not, technically speaking, a hard job. My title was hostess—not really a waitress, not really a bartender, but something of both and more. What made it hard was my unfamiliarity with the workings of the restaurant, and the seeming unwillingness of any of the cooks or waiters to aid me in learning about it.

At the slow point of the evening, just before midnight when the dinner crowd was gone, but before the late night crowd came in, everyone ate dinner. Cooks and busboys in stained whites emerged from the kitchen and joined waiters in ill-fitting bowties at a round table in the back. Some sat while others ate standing up, sitting as soon as another would leave, all of them digging in hand-sized bowls of rice with chopsticks and chattering on about what I couldn't be sure. They were probably talking about me, from the looks and occasional words I could guess at. Too put off to vie for a seat, but not too timid to do something about it, I took a plate of greens and stir-fried fish and two bowls of rice and a pair of chopsticks in my hands, and before any of them could quite figure what comment to make, I marched upstairs to Jin Jin's room.

So, you see, that night was the beginning of many things, my first quiet meal with her, the first time she told me a story, the first time I earned money that my mother did not approve of, my first step into a world of Chinese Americans that was so unlike the one of violin lessons and tennis that I had known. I could not have guessed how far it would take me, at that time my mind on graduation a year away, with decisions to be made all too soon about careers and where to live and other things I did not yet know. Things that were easy enough to forget once I went up the stairs to Jin Jin's room, where she made me look proper, she said.

Every night I came upstairs to find her watching the sunset, even in winter when gray flakes clouded the sky. And we would sit at the mah-jongg table (for that's what that little table was, of course); her East, me South; sharing siao bao and trading stories. I decided not to start taking the Mandarin class again in the fall, not when I was spending late nights in her room listening to fairy tales and rhymes meant for children's ears, only now I was the child again, learning anew. She insisted that I tell her stories, too, as she learned English a word at a time, urging me on like an empress to an ambassador from a strange and faraway place. I traded her "The Old Woman Who Lived In a Shoe" for the tale of seven brothers who all looked alike and fooled an evil emperor who thought that it was but one man coming back again and again.

But now it is me that comes back again, looking the same, but never the same again.

I should tell you of another first, the first night I knew there was more to fairy tales than whimsy. I had always assumed that some of the stories she told me were made up inventions, while others were based upon real people and events. I swapped "The Three Billy Goats Gruff" for the story of a fishseller to whom the Immortals gave a pill of life to keep his fish fresh. One day he swallowed it accidentally when hiding the pill from jealous rivals, and so became immortal himself. I told her the story of Cinderella when she told me of a pair of young lovers who cheated the gods. The gods banished the woman to the moon, and her sad face peers down forever at her lonely partner on the Earth. And when it came to people who became legends, like Robin Hood and King Arthur, I heard the stories of a princess who became a warrior, of a scholar who saved the city from demons, of the emperor's concubine who became immortal. You cannot know what a treasure these stories were to me, whose mother had only told her Mother Goose and Hans Christian Andersen, and never the story of the seven lucky gods or of the dragon's daughter who could travel anywhere that the sky touched. But imagine me one evening, this maybe four months into my time at the restaurant, autumn air carrying the smell of hot oil over a crisp, cool breeze and night coming on early, climbing the steps above the dining room and finding the door to Jin Jin's room closed, locked. Through the door my ear detected a muffled, rhythmic sound.

I was naive, I suppose. Twenty-one years old, I was supposed to be a decadent American, raised on violent television and subliminal sexual advertising. But what did I really know? Some experimental fumbling with well-meaning boys, a passing knowledge of "stag" videotapes. It had never occurred to me to think why Jin Jin was there at the restaurant, whether she was a relative of Skinny's (no, of course not, she would speak Cantonese then), or a boarder (where were her possessions? her pictures of home?), or what. Nor had I ever given a second thought to the Chinese men who often sat and drank tea with Skinny Dou at the back table, and sometimes went upstairs to play mah-jongg. If I had tried to consider it at that moment, I might have explained it to myself by saying that she had a suitor and that she was a wealthy renter who had no work. But maybe some things I had heard said that had not made sense at the time finally filtered in, or maybe I wasn't as naive as all that, because as Skinny Dou came up the stairs like a determined elephant, I knew that Jin Jin was not entertaining a suitor, and that she was not renting that room. How can this be possible, I was asking myself, that a man can keep a whore above his restaurant like it was the 1850s, here in America at the dawn of the twenty-first century? But no, I thought, as Skinny pushed me away from the door while hushing me with loud words, this is not America, this is not the same place and time. This is Chinatown.

I reeled back from Skinny, suddenly dizzy, as if I could not quite breathe. I clattered down the steps, not looking behind me, listening to the heavy clang of utensils against woks as I neared the kitchen, knowing that downstairs it would be as it had always been.

But it was not as it had always been. The room was bigger, a live fish tank bubbled in one corner, and familiar-looking yet unknown waiters stared at me as if I had just fallen out of the sky. Which, perhaps, I had. I must have come down the wrong set of stairs, I thought. Is this the place next door? I rushed out to the street to find the air warm, the breeze heavy with humidity, and the sun up in the sky. Not comprehending, not knowing, I sat down with my back against the warm concrete of an alley wall and hid my face in my sleeves, rocking back and forth like the released mental patients one sees in alleys in any city.

When I came to, I found myself looking into Jin Jin's eyes, stoic with Chinese concern. All was as before in the restaurant, as it had been every day I had worked there. That is, everything except Jin Jin's room, which I now saw in a different light. Jin Jin herself touched my cheek, but I could not, would not ask about what I now knew. We did not tell stories that night, I did not work at the bar, and I did not think I would return the next day.

But I did. In the morning I sat with my cornflakes, the TV on, in the kitchen I shared with three other students, and wondered once again what I was supposed to do with my life. Work in an office, make photocopies, and type in a word processor? Build automobiles? My parents were both doctors, and I knew I did not want to be that. So what was left? Working as a hostess in a restaurant did not feel like a career, but it did feel better than not knowing. So many petty things are needed to make up a modern life: ATM card, traffic reports, touch-tone service. I could not eat the corn flakes. I felt terribly homesick suddenly, even though it was not my parents' home I thought of. I thought of the smell of frying dumplings and the clack of mah-jongg tiles punctuated with laughter as if remembered from an early morning dream. I could not sit there and worry about my diploma and a resume, when yesterday I had gone down a stairway and emerged in a sun-filled city somewhere else in the world.

I went to the restaurant in the afternoon, when I knew Skinny Dou would be sipping tea with his cronies at the tea house down the street. Jin Jin was asleep; her black hair unbound from the dragon sticks and wrapped over one shoulder like a scarf. I found her clothed in simple cotton and lying atop the daisy bedspread. She sat up suddenly as I approached and rubbed her eyes, then smiled as she saw me. I had tried to guess her age so many times, but could not. She had the eternal youth of Asians, I thought, always like we could be twenty, until suddenly one day we go gray and stoop, or get fat like Skinny. I said her name but could not form the question I wanted to ask—I was not even sure what it was I would ask. I tried to conjure the Mandarin words to describe something I was sure was real and yet thought could not be. Eventually I stuttered out, "Where did I go?"

She smiled again, her lips closed. Her hand over mine she answered, "China."

I laughed at first, until I saw she was not making a joke. "You know now," she said.

I thought she referred to the fact that she was a whore, and I nodded.

"You can take me with you," she added.

And I, yes, still naive, still confused, and still trying to follow my heart said, "Yes, yes of course."

So here is the danger of making promises when one does not know what one has promised. She was in motion then, braiding her hair into a queue, even as she crossed the room to the wardrobe. From the bottom drawer she brought out more clothes like the ones she wore now, unembroidered, of a sturdy blue cloth, with wide-legged pants and black slippers. I changed into what she gave me, not knowing why I was doing so, assuming that an explanation must be coming soon. Then, her hand pulling mine, we were tiptoeing down the stairs, and I began to think that perhaps I did not know where we were going after all, and that perhaps this was meant to be some sort of escape.

When Skinny Dou came in the front door and saw the two of us, and he shouted something that I could only guess was, "Stop where you are!" or, "Don't let them get away!" and Jin Jin pulled me at a run through the kitchen doors, then I knew it was an escape. Again I had that thought, this could not be happening, that a woman could be kept prisoner above a restaurant against her will, not today, not here... but mostly I was dodging the grabs of kitchen boys and then trying to see ahead of us in the narrow diagonal alley that ran between buildings. We weren't going to come out anywhere near my car, but maybe we would see a policeman, or we could run all the way into Downtown Crossing and take the train from there back to campus. In the alley there was the hiss of steam from other kitchens, the smell of rotten fish, and the sound of our slippers hitting the cobblestones and Jin Jin repeating in a low urgent voice "Take me back, take me back," even as we rushed away.

We emerged on the other side to a narrow, traffic-filled street, the sidewalk crowded with tourists. I pulled my hand from Jin Jin's and called for her to wait. I was out of breath, dizzy, and wanted a moment to think about details: car keys, visas, police. As the crowd moved around me, it felt like sometimes people suddenly changed directions and I was jostled. I pressed back against a wall and searched for her face.

Jin Jin was gone. People moved this way and that and cars crept slowly along. Across the way from me was a tea house I had never seen before, with a red-lettered sign I could read in Chinese and English: "Great Flower House of Tea." The street sign was in Chinese and English as well, though it was clearly no Boston Street: Santiago. Not China either. Sweat trickled down my neck from fear and the air's heat. Inside the tea house I found a newspaper that told me the answer: Manila, the Philippines. In a moment we had come halfway around the world, and in a moment of confusion, I had lost her.

They accept American money most places in Manila, and

a dollar buys you all the tea you can drink. I sat down with a pot of jasmine and struggled to put my thoughts together. Why had I let go her hand? I had thought I was the one leading us but I was mistaken. In the tea my face looked round and brown and sad like the woman in the moon. I had somehow opened the gates between places but had stopped short of finishing the journey. Where was Jin Jin now? Had I left her behind in Boston, to be caught by the cooks and returned to her prison? And how was I to get back there?

I supposed I could have gone to the US embassy and told them who I was, but I could not bear the thought of my parents, of passports, airlines, and metal detectors. No. I had to be sure she was not here and merely lost in the crowd. And if she was gone, I had to find her though I knew not how.

I began to walk down to the main street, gaudy with red lanterns and the bright T-shirts of tourists, and up another alley. It ran alongside the back doors of laundries, bakeries, and butchers whose doorways offered glimpses of brown-faced people, the scent of soap and fish and frying oil, but no Jin Jin. On another corner I watched two boys steal a mango, one distracting the shopkeeper with a sudden cry, the other hurrying past. Then they were both gone. The shopkeeper looked at his neat stacks of roots and leafy cabbage and fruit and frowned. Further down the row from him, two old women argued with a pharmacist, sending him up and down rows of hundreds of tiny drawers in search of the cure for what ailed them.

This could be happening anywhere, I thought, on any street in any Chinatown anywhere in the world.

As I turned to take in the scene I felt a breeze blow that I sensed was not from this place. Once again reality shifted. Around me, infinite gates with curved horns wormed away into the distance like a never-ending parade dragon. I held my breath, afraid to move and find myself in New York, or San Francisco, or I knew not where. And yet I knew I must take a step.

"Jin Jin," I whispered, and stepped through.

It would take lifetimes for me to describe all the things that I saw on the journey, because lifetimes I did see—in cities across the world, in old Hong Kong and new Shanghai, in Chicago and Los Angeles, sometimes going back in years, sometimes going ahead—until I almost forgot that I was looking for Jin Jin. But never completely. I knew I had to continue my quest, because I finally knew the answer to that question I had asked so long ago: when she looked into the sunset, what did she hope to see? Jin Jin searched the fire eye of the sun for someone to take her back to an older day, to a time when she was more than just a menu item, to when she had been concubine to emperors. She looks into the lucky red sky for the dragon's daughter, and that is me.

She is out there, in the vast timespace that is China, somewhere within the maze of kitchens and secret parlors that define it, and I will find her....

Hall of Mirrors

Memory is a hall of mirrors. When I was twenty years old, I discovered one of the great secrets of the Universe. I discovered the magic that ran in my blood and the truth of ancient stories. I knew, in one moment when all of time and space and history cracked open, what my destiny was.

But, as I found out, there was still much I did not know

about myself. As I stood on the threshold of the vast time-space that was China, as my power flared to life and I stared into funhouse mirror images of rickshaw drivers and fish sellers and wise old sifus, I knew at last that I was the Dragon's Daughter. I had come to life from a Chinese fairy tale, but I felt like Alice gone through the looking glass, lost and alone. In one foolish moment I had lost Jin Jin and I knew it was my duty to find her again. What I did not know was why I felt so empty. And even as I searched for her in the wide world, anywhere the lucky red sky could touch, I searched the hall of mirrors of my own memories. I can see myself now, moon-faced girl at piano lessons, dragon girl in silk at the senior prom, stumbling bar hostess with glass dragons hanging from sticks in my hair, placed there so carefully by Jin Jin's hand.

I'm on a street corner in Manila at sunset, the afternoon rain steaming off the hot pavement as the clouds clear the way for that red eye to sink into the bay. It is my second time here, and this time I am prepared. Tea shops that had closed their shutters for afternoon siesta are open now, back-bent people in blue cotton sweeping their stoops and raising their blinds to welcome dinnertime tourists. Neighborhood children spot what they think is a well-dressed man fumbling with his cigarette and begin to swarm around me, selling candies and mangoes, tin birds on sticks made from Coke cans, more cigarettes. They tug on my lapels and I push my way into a restaurant to get rid of them. The proprietor brandishes a broom and they move down the street to intercept others making their way up the hill from the new hotels.

"Can I help you?" he says in Fukienese. He has a Chairman Mao face, balding and basset-houndish. The restaurant is shabby inside, cafeteria-bright with round fluorescents, tiled in chipped white tiles. I doubt Jin Jin is here, but it is the first lead I have. Prostitution is frowned upon, after all, and cannot be asked about too openly. And I must start somewhere.

I clear my throat, tugging at my tie, and quietly inquire in my soft Mandarin about his "house specialty." My suit is impeccable, double-breasted to make my shoulders look broader. I am a milk-fed American girl (though they don't know that) and I tower over everyone in the place. The trick is not hard to pull off. He demurs, in heavily accented Mandarin. I pretend he has misunderstood me and repeat my request, this time putting a hundred dollar bill into his hand. He shakes my hand to hand it back, saying, "I cannot help you, sir."

"Can you tell me where to go?" I let my shoulders slump. "I've come a long way."

He directs me to a tea house up the street and off the main drag. That, at least, is something.

⤳⤲

When I was fifteen years old, my parents told me I was adopted. It's funny. So many things I remember so clearly: our California living room, the fish tank humming in the silence between my mother's halting admissions, the hunch of my father's shoulders as he sat on the couch, elbows on knees, his slacks riding up his calf and showing his black socks. Like something from a made-for-TV movie. I remember my heart beginning to beat faster and faster under my skin as they talked, while my face stayed stoic, while my surface froze like the ice on a pond. I remember so much, but I don't remember why they chose that moment to tell me.

You came from the mainland, they told me, from the same province as our ancestors. Mom's medical difficulties had led them to the decision to adopt. Mom cried a little, while telling me this, and I'm not sure which of us she was crying for. They seemed to think they should have told me a long time before, but they had never been sure how. I remember feeling stunned, but it all making sense somehow. I had always felt there was something different about me but I had never known what. That day, I thought I knew—I was the ugly duckling in another bird's nest. But how little I knew, how little.

I climb the cobblestone street, stepping onto the crowded sidewalk to let a side-banged Toyota creep past. Watching the crowd, I realize my suit looks too Hong Kong, too upscale, for Manila Chinatown. That's okay, I don't need to pass myself off as a resident. Rich Hong Kong tourist looking for action should be good enough. I pray that Jin Jin is somewhere like here, somewhere small and easy to search, and not Shanghai, or Beijing.

I have tested my power since my first accidental visit here. I can go anywhere that is somehow undeniably China. I have been to New York, to Los Angeles, to Guangzhou, just to look, just to see. I have walked to the past and flown across oceans, all in the blink of an eye. Manila was the first place, though, the first place I stepped through to, before I knew what was happening, before I knew not to let go of Jin Jin's hand. She must be here, I insist to myself, but the voice of doubt begins to chant in time with my uphill steps: it'll take forever to find her, what if you never find her? Never find her, never find her....

I put the thought out of my mind and swagger into the Red Dragon Tea House. My heart skips a beat at seeing the name—would Jin Jin choose a place with such a likely name? Would she think to tip me off like that, or would she settle down in the most comfortable place, figuring she might be in for a long wait? Wait for me, Jin Jin, I'm coming.

I take a table in the tea house and order some dumplings while I examine the place. It's dim, with a dark wood interior and landscape paintings on the wall, a much classier place than the previous. I hope I can afford their house specialty, and have my pick. Then again, this is cash-poor Manila and I have American money. I should be fine.

I had picked up the money from an antique dealer in New York who paid in cash. I'd chosen his shop at random when looking for a place to unload some souvenirs of my experimental trips through the lucky red sky. I'd expected some brusque, suspicious old man and was happy to find Quan young, personable, even friendly.

"Here's four hundred," he had said, putting a pile of bills

into my hand. "I'll have another two-fifty for you later." Quan always spoke English with me, a slight hint of British accent betraying either Hong Kong roots or a British education. Whenever a customer would come into his store he would switch to coolie-pidgin, "You like? Fifty dollah." I assumed this increased business somehow, but I never pried. I think I hoped he wouldn't pry back, though of course he always did.

I counted the bills, some crisp, some limp. "How much later?"

"Two, three days. Why, going on a trip?" He leaned on the glass counter top and stuck a ballpoint pen between his ear and his New York Yankees baseball cap. Quan had one of those wrinkle-free, ageless Chinese faces. He could have passed for twenty, or forty. More like thirty, I guessed. I didn't say anything about where I was going.

"You do a lot of traveling," he pressed.

"Yes. How else do you think I get you all this stuff?" I'd just brought him some jade earrings over two hundred years old. Other than the baseball cap and his cash register, there was little in his shop that looked like it was from the twentieth century, or from this hemisphere.

"Mei, Mei," he said, as if to imply 'don't be testy' but he would never say any such thing. "When do you leave? I'll try to get the money by tomorrow. Meet me for dinner at the Hunan House and I'll have it for you."

Quan wasn't married. He'd told me his father had passed the antique business on to him when he died. I assumed his mother was also dead. He was overeducated for a shopkeeper and fancied himself a historian. Quan tried to get me to have dinner with him on a fairly regular basis.

"Two or three days is fine," I said. "I'll be back."

It is early in the evening and it appears I have succeeded in being the first customer for the Red Dragon's specialty. After I have finished my dumplings and a pot of tea, a nicely dressed middle-aged hostess takes me upstairs where she seats me in a parlor. We haggle and I discreetly pass her some cash. Through the thin walls I can hear the sharp twang of women's voices as the whores ready themselves for the night's work. In my mind's eye, I imagine Jin Jin among them, helping them to get dressed, painting their faces. I imagine her leading the group out into the parlor like a madam herself, and catching my eye. I see myself, looking like a handsome young man, not like the smoky, drunk businessmen that they regularly see. Then, her breath caught in her throat, Jin Jin recognizes me. I choose her, of course, from among all the others, and to her back parlor we go....

My heart is pounding as the hostess pushes aside the curtain and the women come in. I try to look calm. Then I try not to look disappointed. Four women stand in front of me, and it does not matter if they are beautiful or bored, young or old, clean or slovenly. None of them is Jin Jin. I have two choices now, pick one in order to maintain the masquerade, or weasel my way out. I decide to disparage the women, claim they don't look good. The madam assures me these girls are 100 percent Chinese, no Filipino blood in them. The naked racism makes me angry, and my stomach churns with bile, but it is a useful lie. I claim not to believe her, I point to this one's nose, the color of this one's skin. I tell the madam to keep the money, I don't care. I'm not letting one of these ape-women touch me. I storm out of the restaurant.

Later, in an alley by myself, I cry.

I had no date for my senior prom. My parents wrung their hands so much over this fact that I kept my mouth shut about what I thought of marriage. I had never planned to get married. Never planned to have children. Somehow I just knew it was not for me, just as I knew I was not going to become an endocrinologist or a surgeon like the two of them, and like they wanted me to. I had learned, though, not to protest too loudly, because if I did, they would moan and cry that if only they hadn't told me I was adopted, surely I would have gone along with their plans. There was no convincing them otherwise. So I would nod and smile and then do what I wanted for myself anyway. So it was when I applied to college in Boston. So it was when I had a relative in San Francisco Chinatown make me a dress. My mother was scandalized that I hadn't picked a more Western dress.

It was imported silk, embossed with tiny flowers, edged with satin pipe and closed with knotted cloth buttons. It was everything a ball gown should be, a Cinderella dress, but a Chinese Cinderella in flat silk slippers. I wore jeans and sneakers to school every day, but for this one night I wanted to be a princess. I think I knew the prom was no place for me, so the only way to do it was to become someone else. Chinese Cinderella danced with all the boys and made all the girls give her funny looks. I didn't find a Prince Charming. I was not surprised.

With the help of a bellboy at my hotel, I uncover more brothels in Manila, and one by one I check them out. The pickings are slim, my insistence on Chinese girls narrowing the search, until I have been to almost every backroom bordello but one. This last one is a big one, above a nightclub. In the basement there is a gambling den. The music is loud, which is unfortunate because if I raise my voice too much it becomes womanish. I keep my sunglasses on and peer over the tops of them as I make my way to the bar. The bartender acknowledges me with a glance. I hold up the business card the bellboy gave me, the name of the place written on the back. The bartender nods and disappears through a mirrored door behind the bar. I take a seat.

People are dancing amid flashing lights and pulsing music. Single men line the bar, some in sharp suits, some holding cigarettes and whiskey in the same hand. None of them even glance at me. I see bar hostesses in short skirts carrying trays through the crowd.

Time passes. A hostess lays her tray down at the bar and leans next to me. Her thick, black hair falls in waves down her back and her lipstick is bright magenta under the bar's lights. She says something in a language I don't know, one of the Filipino languages, I am guessing. I shake my head and hold up my hands.

"You want upstairs?" she says in English then.

I nod. She tugs on my tie then like a dog leash, and I follow her. She skirts the edge of the club and goes up a set of dim back stairs.

On the second floor is a registration desk, as if this had once been a small hotel. A bored-looking Filipino man in a white button-down shirt sits at the desk. He and the hostess exchange a few words. I tuck my sunglasses into the breast pocket of my jacket and try to make it clear what I am looking for.

"Why only Chinese girl?" he asks, with a leer at the hostess.

I put money on the counter in front of him.

"She busy right now. You wait." He jerks his chin toward a vinyl-covered couch across from the desk and takes the money.

I sit. The hostess sits with me, one arm twined in mine. After a few moments, another Filipina comes from down the hall, and snuggles against my other side.

"How long?" I ask the man at the desk, but he ignores me.

The women are starting to breathe in my ears, tickling the small hairs on my neck where I've had it buzzed short. I shake my head as if to dislodge flies. They giggle and begin again.

"Special tonight," one says.

"Two price of one," says the other.

I'm trying to think of the best way to tell them to knock it off, that I want to wait for someone else, when one of them slips her hand onto my crotch. Her eyebrow goes up and I am sure the surprise shows on my own face. This is not a contingency I've planned for.

She says something in rapid-fire Filipino to the hostess, who rubs a hand on my cheek and stands up.

The desk clerk is standing up, too, now, shouting at me

what I can only guess are the local equivalent of "dyke" or "pervert."

I'm trying to explain myself but there is no explanation for me. One of the girls slaps me across the face. I find myself running down the hallway, opening doors, yelling Jin Jin's name, the man from the desk and the two women close on my heels. But I am the dragon's daughter and no one can catch me.

I had bought the double-breasted suit in San Francisco, where the tailor seemed unfazed that a woman wanted a man's suit tailored to her. I stood looking at myself in the mirror, resisting the urge to Napoleon my hand between the two wide buttons. I'd gotten my hair cut that morning and it seemed like a stranger, or maybe a long-lost brother, stared back at me from the glass. I had been in San Francisco for a week at that point, and was losing hope of finding Jin Jin there. I had been trying to make friends with the whores so I could ask around if anyone knew her. But it was difficult to make friends with these women who were, by and large, closely guarded by their men and who knew very little of the outside world. I could not become one of them and it took too long to gain their trust. I needed a faster way to go from house to house and it was overhearing the bragging of some Taiwanese businessmen about how many whores they could see in a night that gave me the idea to impersonate them. In the mirror, my twin smiled.

Back in New York, memories of Manila fade like bad dreams. She was not there, not anywhere, and I must decide where to look next. I am in the little pensioners hotel a few blocks from Chinatown proper where I keep a small place. I am sitting in the kitchen, in the chair with one short leg that came with the apartment. I am waiting five minutes before I try to call Quan again. There is one phone at the end of the hall that we all share, a bathroom at the other end. I hear the squeals of children through my door and the thump of their feet as they chase one another through the hallway. Quan's phone has been busy all afternoon and with each try I feel more and more alone.

I should just go down there, I decide. Get dressed and go out. No one here notices me much in the hubbub of families and sweatshop workers. I wear the same overcoat whether I go out dressed as a man or as a woman, so they can never see. What I'll do when summer comes, I don't know. I suppose there's no real reason to be secretive, or is there? I put on my sneakers to leave for Quan's.

Out on the street it is New York noisy, crowded with people and cars and activity. I chose New York as my hub because it is always easy to find, so similar to the overcrowded beehives of China's cities, cities that have been buzzing for four thousand years. I turn the corner onto the twisted dragon back of Mott Street and then into an alley to Quan's door.

I see him through the window, the shop dark except for the lamp on the counter, casting a circle of light onto something he examines with a loupe to his eye. I open the door with a tinkle of bells and his head comes up.

"Mei, Mei! I was wondering when you'd be back. Where were you this time?"

"Manila," I answer, seeing no reason to lie. "It's only been a few weeks."

"Bring me anything good?"

I hold up my empty hands. "That's not what I went there for."

"You have family there?"

"No." I try to give him a look that says drop it.

He bundles up the scrolls he had been examining and makes them disappear behind the counter. "It's late. Do you want to catch some dinner?"

"Quan...."

"Mei, please. I'd just like the company, is all." He shrugs.

I don't have any reason to be afraid of Quan. And I am, undeniably, lonely. "Okay. Let's eat."

<hr>

When I first met Jin Jin, I thought she was the most beautiful woman I'd ever seen. That is, she *was* the most beautiful woman I had ever seen, and I wasn't even conscious enough of the thought to know I had thought it. It was only later I began to realize what my thoughts were, as she occupied more and more space in my head. My poor over-worked brain, all crammed with women's studies classes and contradictory politics and comparative literature. When I arrived at the restaurant to begin my evening's work I would forget it all.

Jin Jin's hands were soft as they brushed my hair and pinned it into place, as they buttoned my silk embroidered bar hostess dress. Each night she transformed me from an overworked college student into something more elegant. But she herself never changed.

❦

Quan steers me to a table at the restaurant, near the kitchen door. I want to protest, but it seems not worth the effort and he seems slightly nervous about something. I sincerely hope he is not going to ask me to marry him, a worry I only become conscious of as we sit across from each other. Quan pours tea for the two of us. We each sit sniffing the jasmine steam in silence. He sits with his back to the wall, a garish painting of some folk scene hanging above his head: it's a parade of villagers led by a man carrying two buckets of fish on a pole hung across his shoulders. I smile at the memory of Jin Jin telling me the story of the fishseller who became immortal by accident. If I ever see her again, what stories will I have to trade?

Quan sees me looking at the painting and says, "Do you know the story?"

"You mean about the Immortal Fishseller?"

"He wasn't immortal while he was a fishseller," Quan says. "He used the pill of immortality to keep his fish fresh. But when the other fishsellers tried to steal it from him—"

"I know, I know, he hid it in his mouth and swallowed it."

"Thus becoming immortal, but no longer being able to sell fresh fish."

"I wonder what he did after that?" I put down my tea. "I mean, are there other stories about him? Stories end, but they are never really finished, are they?"

Quan peers over the top of his cup at me. "He decided to travel and see the world. But he always found himself coming home again. If he spent too long away, he found his mortality slipping back, bit by bit. But whenever he came home, the seven lucky gods smiled on him."

I feel my eyes narrow as I look at Quan. "Cute." I am still imagining that he's either going to hit on me or propose, and am trying to anticipate where what he says is going to lead. So I am completely unprepared for what he does say.

He puts down his cup and says, "I know who you are."

"Like hell you do," I say, annoyed for some reason I cannot define.

"I know the stories, too," he says, and I can see his face reflected brown and round in his tea cup. Like the man in the moon.

"Mei, listen to me. I'm not the only immortal in China. I know another one when I see one. And you...."

"I'm not immortal." I want to tell him he's crazy, but it feels wrong. What would Chinese Cinderella say? "I was raised in the States. I had a childhood, a life."

He shrugs, matter of fact. "There are three kinds of immortals, Mei. You, you can die and be reborn. Me, I've lived one long life." He closes his mouth as a waiter puts plates of bright vegetables down in front of us. A bowl of steaming rice clouds the air between us. "That doesn't change who you are or what you can do."

My heart hammers and I'm not sure why I have the urge to run from the room. I feel my face beginning to freeze and

I blink my eyes rapidly. "What do you want from me?"

He makes a disgusted noise. "I don't want anything from you, Mei. I wanted you to know about me. I wanted you to know that we can help each other. I can introduce you to some others, if you want. Even Wong F—"

I grab his hand. "Do you know where I can find Jin Jin?"

He cocks his head; he does not know that name.

"The emperor's concubine."

His mouth opens in a silent *oh* and he nods. "I have not seen her for a long, long time."

"I'm looking for her," I say, not sure that I can explain why. "She, she's waiting for me."

"Mei—"

"How can you tell who the other immortals are? Is that why you helped me when I first came to you?" The food sits, uneaten, in dishes between us. "Can you help me find her?"

He starts scooping rice onto my plate, then his own. "One thing at a time. Yes, I knew you were someone right away; I just was not sure who. Once you began to bring me things, well, it could only be you. I'm not sure how to help you find her."

"But how do you recognize the others?"

He begins to eat, chopsticks clicking against the plate. "Center yourself and relax, and see how the world looks. Some things will seem thin and insubstantial, things that won't last. Others will seem vivid and solid. Buildings, people, roads. Some of them are part of us, some are not."

"I've never noticed that."

He shrugs. "What can I tell you, that's the way it is. Either you see it, or you don't. What have you been doing thus far to look for her?"

I describe my incognito investigations.

"Needle in a haystack," is what he says to that. He shakes his head, sadly. "And what will you do once you find her?"

"Take her back, I suppose. Wherever she wants. Whenever she wants."

"And then?"

I stare into my plate of rice and vegetables.

"Mei," he says, his chopsticks still for a moment, "you do know who she is, don't you?"

"What do you mean?"

"You know the story, she who was so loyal to him that the gods granted her immortality. She's looking for her emperor."

"Of course she is," I say, annoyed, but for some reason on the edge of tears. I start to eat, angrily grabbing at the food with my chopsticks, chewing hard.

Quan eats quietly for a while, politely looking away while I calm myself. Then he goes on. "I said there were three kinds of immortals."

"Yes. Like me, like you, and...?"

"And like Jin Jin. Mei, she's lived one long life, like me, but she is not like me. She is... like the embodiment of an ideal. Perfect loyalty. The woman behind the throne. The yin that yang power demands to balance it."

"That sounds like a warning."

"She's... she's not like you."

"What are you saying?" I am ready to jump down his throat if he criticizes me or tries to tell me any more about myself that I don't already know. I am angry at him for forcing me to see what I already knew: she does not feel for me the way I feel for her. "She's not like what?"

"She's not a person, she's an archetype. She... she is perfect, and cannot change. That's why she wants to go back, because there's no place for her here, now."

We eat in silence a while as I digest everything he has said.

When he speaks again, it is with a soft, forgive-me voice. "Have you looked in New York yet?"

"No." I am calmer now, but still a bit taciturn.

"Perhaps I could make some inquiries by word of mouth." His desire to help seems genuine.

"Thank you." I feel I should apologize for being angry with him, but now is not the time nor place for that.

He goes on. "And have you considered that she might be in Boston?"

I stare at him.

"When you lost her, you were in Boston, isn't that what you said? And the next moment you were halfway around the world, in Manila. How do you know she went anywhere at all?"

I cannot chew because my heart is in my throat.

"You never went back to check?"

"I was afraid to." Skinny Dou and his army of cooks were waiting for me. I'd tried to steal his golden goose. But, god, what if she had gone back? "Quan, you must help me."

He opens his mouth to speak but I overrun him with a sudden plea, my anger and reserve gone. "Come back with me to Boston. They don't know you there. They'll recognize me, but you, they don't know. And you'll be able to tell if it is her. All you have to do is go into the restaurant and order the house specialty. Then tell me if she's there." How could I be so stupid? I am suddenly certain she is there. "We can go right away, I'll have you back in an hour."

Quan sighs. "I suppose I have nothing better to do."

I almost kissed a girl once when I was fifteen. She was thirteen, but very sophisticated in a feminine way, her red hair curled, her nails painted. She had just moved in that year to the house across the street and was due to start at my school in September. Our mothers conspired that we should socialize together. I followed her around like a puppy. I loved the way she smelled, the way her hair curled, her white skin like a porcelain doll. Before her first date with a boyfriend, she decided she needed kissing practice. So in her bedroom, all hung with pictures of unicorns and horses, she asked me to pretend to be her boyfriend. I agreed. But then we went on talking as usual, and we never kissed. I wondered if I was supposed to interrupt her, sweep her off her feet or what. I thought she'd stop at some point and say, okay, let's try it. But she never did, and we never mentioned it again.

I am standing on a Boston street corner at sunrise, looking up at the reflected sky in a plate glass second floor window. Quan is back in New York with a gift from me of two more jade earrings over a thousand years old. The back streets are quiet, the steel grates down over shop doors, the waterfall sound of rush hour coming over the tops of the buildings. I make my way to the back of the building, where the kitchen door is propped open. Amid the clang of woks and the hiss of frying and running water, I hear Skinny Dou's voice. He is yelling at one of the kitchen workers, which one I cannot guess. He is busy, that is all that matters to me.

I open the door to step through, but it is not the kitchen I enter. With a shift of the universe, I emerge in Jin Jin's room.

I find her at the window, looking out at the sunset, her hair unbound in her lap and the comb idle in one hand. She crosses the room to me; a tiny smile wrinkles her eyes. I take her hands in mine.

"I'm sorry," I find myself saying. "I didn't know."

She nods.

"I'll take you where you want, when you want. You don't have to wait anymore."

She nods again. I am in a hurry to get us away, but she stops me with a few quick words in Mandarin, her voice sweet and high like a bird by a stream. She wants to be ready.

From a wooden chest she unearths a silk dress that covers her from throat to ankle. I help her to button it over her shoulder and down her back. Then she sits in front of the mirror and I take the black silk of her hair in my hands. There are so many things I want to know, and yet I cannot bring myself to squander these moments with chatter. My hands and hers move together over her hair, binding it up with two slender lacquered sticks.

When I had first come to work for Skinny Dou, I had an idea in the back of my mind that I could fool people into thinking I was something I was not. My mother was ashamed of the "restaurant" side of the family, and had raised me to be as American as apple pie. But when I was fifteen and I learned I had come from the mainland, I began to undo that any way I could. I tried to teach myself to read Chinese and failed. When I went to college I tried again and succeeded, but I had thought it too late—it was too late to be who I had been meant to be. When I took the Chinese restaurant job, it was one more stab at grabbing a piece of the life I felt I had missed. But fate takes care of these things, and upstairs in Skinny Dou's restaurant I found a true piece of the past waiting for me like an piece of jade buried in a box of silk.

I center myself and take a deep breath. All around us the hall of mirrors glitters, as if we stand at the center of mammoth diamond, every facet the entry to another world. "Look," I say. "Look." Like waltz partners we turn in a slow circle, the facets blossoming all around like a kaleidoscope.

Then her breath catches in her throat and she pulls me onto a street of packed earth. We huddle against a high wall and she cranes her neck around one corner. I crouch and peek also, into a shrine, where a young man is making his obeisance to his ancestors. Around him candles flicker and incense burns but he seems to glow with a luminescence of his own. Jin Jin covers her mouth and pulls back, one hand against her chest.

"Thank you," she tells me, "thank you."

"Is this goodbye?" I can barely speak. It feels as if a giant hand is squeezing my throat and my chest.

She leans forward, one crystalline tear in her eye, and brushes her silken lips against mine. Then she rounds the corner and is gone.

My heart is a hall of mirrors. I stand at the center of being, at the center of everything, and look into the future, the present, and the past. I belong everywhere and nowhere, and know not where to go. One step and my destiny will be decided. I float between worlds and consider. There is no folktale in which the dragon's daughter dies of a broken heart. Stories end, but they are never finished. I go in search of a lucky red sky to call my own.

the lady in black

THIS IS A STORY the folk tell today, because they say the Lady In Black still travels the roads, different though the roads may be now than in olden times. Maybe it is an old tale that has changed and grown through the ages, even as the mountains have worn to hills and the rivers changed their courses. Or maybe it really happened this way, just long enough ago to sound like legend.

She drives a gleaming black sports car—go on, name the car of the moment: Mercedes, Audi, Chevrolet—it matters not. Just imagine the dark straight road cleaving the flat land in two, the headlights floating on the horizon until with a roar and a gust of chill wind she is upon you, then past, leaving eddies of mist in her wake.

So it was one night on the road from somewhere to somewhere, a winter night, with snow walling the road, scraped into battlements by the plows, the stars burning cold in the winter black, when two young men are walking on the pavement, one behind the other, their hands buried deep in their pockets, their heads bowed in the cruel chill.

She speeds past them and comes to a sudden stop, the red of her brake lights beckoning them into a jog. The taller of the two reaches the door first. He pulls it open, eager for the warmth of the car and to discover who has come to rescue him from a cold trudge, expecting some friend or acquaintance perhaps. If we are allowed to embellish the story, let us say he expected such a plum to have been stolen by one of his cohorts. Instead he finds the driver's seat occupied by a woman he does not know. Her long raven hair flows over her shoulders and disappears into the depth of the bucket seat, against the black of her garments. Her eyes, large and liquid, encourage him to take the back seat and let his companion follow him into the front.

He climbs in, exchanging a leer and a raised eyebrow with his fellow walker as he settles himself in the center of the back seat, one elbow on each of their shoulders.

"Where are you headed?" she asks, the ritual question of the road.

They answer: a friend's place, and she obliges to take them there.

Why did she stop? you might ask of whoever is telling the tale. These characters seem up to no good. Why would she risk picking up such strangers in such times as these?

To which I can only say, she is the Lady In Black, and that is her choice.

She accelerates toward the lights on the horizon, thrilling them with speed and mystery, and engaging them in conversation. No sooner have their bones warmed in the leather interior of her conveyance than the threat of harm these men represent begins to show itself.

"We're going to a party," one of them says, "maybe you'd

like to come along." Of course she says no, thank you, but she'll take them there.

"Then maybe you'd like to have a little party, just the three of us."

No, thank you, says the Lady In Black, wondering just how foolish two men can, and will, be. She knows they will be very foolish indeed when they insist she pull over. And that makes her laugh, and drive all the faster.

Imagine that great engine, roaring under the hood, like some fell beast set loose from its chains. And her speaking to them of folly.

Tell me, gentlemen, she says, her voice a mere whisper above the rush of wind around the windows. How is it you expect to overpower me? You know already I must stop the car first, before you can make your move, or you risk killing all three of us. Your words have no power to compel me to stop the car. Now what will you do?

The one in the back is the more belligerent, and he tries to grab her by the hair, by the throat, even as he wonders if this will cause her to lose control of the car. Maybe we'll crash into the snow, he thinks, and not be hurt. She'll be knocked out, though, and we'll be able to have our way with her. These thoughts occupy him for only half of an instant as he is reaching for her, because even as he is doing it, he hears the sound of a threat, the sound of steel against steel, as she draws her blade from the place it rests near the gear shift. His face is beside hers, his fist in her hair, but the point of the blade is under his chin.

He utters some profanity, unwilling to let her seize control of the situation. He knows he is supposed to be still; to hold back, hold his breath, with the knifepoint aimed at his Adam's apple. But I said he was a fool and I meant it. He tries to grab the knife, to push it aside like a joke or a toy, and finds his fingers cut. Not deep, for even as the blade bit him his skin was rebelling against the touch of the metal, pulling back even before he knew he was.

Profanity. Disbelief. Profanity. She speaks of his folly. Of her desire to do a good turn for travelers, and of her terrible revenge on those who abuse her good will.

Now the one in the front is begging her to stop the car and let him out. He promises no shenanigans, no threats, just let them off. She's crazy, he thinks, and fears her. And rightly so, the Lady In Black. She laughs a terrifying laugh, as the car whizzes past a slower-moving truck, swerving into the oncoming lane and then back again, and now both of them are begging, asking to be dropped off anywhere, forget the party, the friend, the destination, and it seems like forever before she relents, before she finishes her lecture on the nature of good will and the necessity of a dependably sharp blade. She screeches to a halt where the road crosses a wide berm, swinging the rear of the car around to face back whence she came, the tires crunching in gravel before the door opens and the two fall over one another in their haste to get out. She leaves them in a spray of gravel and dirt with a wave of her hand.

When her tail lights are out of sight the two look around them and find they are not sure where they are. Not only that, the night has grown warm, too warm for their coats and hoods, too warm for the time of year. They unzip their jackets and feel the heat rising off the black tar of the road. The stars swim in a humid haze, and in the rising moon they can see the grasses swaying along the roadside. Crickets chirp. But what can these two walkers do, but walk to the nearest town, there to discover that maybe half a year has gone by, or two years, or five, and that not only have they lost a chunk of their lives during that terror ride, but that they are hundreds of miles from where they met her upon the road.

And that is why all who harbor evil intentions should fear the Lady In Black.

But this is not always how the story goes, not in the ears of Stormclaw, who sits at home and rages when she rides the roads. She has tried to hide the truth from him, but he can taste the anger on her lips when she kisses him, can smell the musk of crime and abuse that sometimes still clings to her when she returns. Some nights, the dagger stays in its sheath beneath the gear shift.

There she is, her dark hair wafting behind her as she strides to the door, her long coat flapping. He stands in the doorway, his hands hard on the wood frame, and with her kiss comes the vision, flashing behind his eyes like the lightning he can summon. He sees the interior of the car from her eyes, her hands white on the wheel, a glance at the eager face in the seat next to her. She feigns fear, she feigns struggle as the one in back puts his hand to her throat. Stormclaw feels his own pulse quicken as the car grinds to a stop, already in the summer country, but the animals she has in her cage do not care. Their needs blind them, they drag her out onto the ground, one of them holding her throat, her arms behind her, the other one letting his trousers drop.

She wears voluminous skirts, layer upon layer of black gossamer, and she loves it when they tear, when they rend the cloth in their desperation to reach her private places. Some are neater, lifting the skirts up and pushing her legs aside. Some are not.

They have wrestled her to the ground, to the grass. She breathes deep of spirit of the earth and all things green as she pretends to struggle. She feels their erections like hot pokers touching her skin, even through the sweatpants of the one as he presses himself to her. He has tied her hands now behind her back, and he hauls her up, her hair flying into his mouth, opening her for his partner. He sits behind her, his hands grabbing at her breasts, now laid bare by the rending of her blouse, and he leans back, his ankles hooked inside her knees, spreading her wide. He is like a spider wrapping up his prey.

The other kneels in front, his erection red and straining and his face a mask of disbelief at what he sees. Stormclaw knows what he sees, her eyes afire, the white and pinkness of her flesh beckoning through the torn cloth. He feels as if he has been stabbed in the gut as she is entered, as she cries out in real pain but also longing, her own desire searing her.

Stormclaw does not understand her need for these spears of mortal flesh plunging into her. He does not understand her fascination with these animals and their appetites. He feels her laughter in her throat, she can't help but taunt them now, in the midst of the fucking. She maligns their manhood, their stamina, their size and shape, even as she feels the one behind her pressing into her back. She wants that one, too, and she wants him angered, out of his mind, desperate to punish her with his fucking. But first things first. The one inside her has not come yet. She is taunting him, deriding him for being a five-minute man. He is torn between his desire to come and his need to prove her wrong. Profanity, fucking hard, he decides if it will be only five minutes, then let it be the worst five minutes of fucking in her life. He pounds her, she laughs, he exits spent.

Now the other. Stormclaw has not moved from the doorway. The Lady In Black has long since descended into the home they share. She does not know that he lives through every ride of hers in this way—or at least, Stormclaw believes she does not.

The other flips her over, her face against the grass under her hair, her knees holding up her ass, but he cannot get his angle this way. Stormclaw can feel the fumbling, the frustration growing. This one is smart, he wants to pain her, to give it to her other hole, but that is easier said than done. He gives up, the two of them flip her onto her back, onto her bound hands, and he lies atop her, kicking away skirts, his belly pressed to her belly and his red hot dagger seeking its blind way between her legs.

He means to slap her face if she talks to him like she did to the other, and she means to deride him just as harshly, but neither of them does as they intend. He slides into her and Stormclaw's tears catch in his throat. He feels her hands come free, and her fingers gripping the back of the young rapist, pushing him deeper, her legs circling him, the animal cries that come from both their throats. They are rocking together, flesh on flesh in an ancient movement—Stormclaw falls to his knees in the doorway unable to bear much more. But there is not much more. She clings to him for a few additional moments, wringing from him what she can as her own pleasure explodes within her. Thus the fucking ends as it always does, and his vision flickers out like a candle flame snuffed by a capricious wind.

Stormclaw can only imagine what happens after. What must the creatures say when they get to their feet to find her clothes un-rent, her hair unmussed, and the dagger aimed at their hearts? Does she leave them there by the roadside or force them to go further with her? How many years of their lives does she steal and does it depend upon how well, or badly, they fucked her? She does not tell him these things. He does not ask. He closes the door behind him and bars it against the outside world.

storm rider

STORMCLAW settles his sunglasses onto his face. Although the wind is his ancient friend, road gravel and dust are not pleasant in his eyes. Leather creaks as he swings his leg over his mount. The bike rocks contentedly under him as he kicks the stand back and settles onto the tires. His hair is wound into a long braid, coiled against the skin of his shoulder like a black asp hidden under his jacket collar. It has been a long time since he has gone riding, but the time has come to resume his searching, his hunting. The Dragon bucks under him as he revs the engine, the roar out of chrome throats pleasing him. And then he is off, onto the road, heading west.

The sun is still in the sky, an hour or two from dropping behind the mountains. Stormclaw feels the heat on his face, the wind whipping across his bare chest, his leather-clad legs fusing to the machine under him. The sun is hot like a kiss, the wind like a lover's hand sneaking into his jacket, the rumble deep in his groin something else.

He pulls up to a roadhouse, angling the Dragon between

two other bikes. The peeled paint on the thin walls once touted some brand of beer. He stares at the lettering, the images, doubting himself. *I used to know how to do this,* he thinks. Once upon a time.

Inside he pulls off his sunglasses. The light is dim, smoke-tainted. Two men are sitting at the bar in road-dusted denim, a few others sit at tables in the gloom, against the walls. Stormclaw takes on a stool cornerwise from the two at the bar. The bartender, an over-thin man in an under-washed T-shirt, leans his crooked elbow on the bar in front of him. "What'll it be? Draft?"

Stormclaw nods, remembering the taste of beer, the earth turned to grain turned to ambrosia. The bartender puts the mug down on the wood, sloshing an inch out of the glass while the two bikers at the bar snicker. Stormclaw feels the disdain coming off all three of them as they stare at him. He takes a drink of the beer. It's mostly water. One of them spits out "Pretty boy."

Time does not pass in an orderly stream for Stormclaw. He has a sudden flash of the future—he gasps and shudders. He is sitting in a corner, a dark corner, his back to a wall, his hand around a sweating beer glass on the table. Under the table someone is sucking his cock, the tongue circling the swollen head and then the hot, wet mouth plunging down all around him, swallowing him. He blinks. Not yet. That is not happening yet. First, they threaten him. "Pretty boy," he hears again.

He pulls off his gloves and puts them down on the bar, saying nothing. He takes a larger gulp of the beer and lets his jacket fall open. They are almost laughing openly now, like wolves who can't believe a wounded sheep has wandered into their den. "Jesus, look at you," one of them says. "What are you, some kind of faggot?"

Stormclaw lets a small smile onto his face. "No. I'm a fairy."

That does make them laugh, but nervously. Stormclaw's eyes do not smile and they are not sure what to make of him now that he has spoken. An edge of fear does not stop them, though. It spurs them on. "Fairy boy! What do you think you're doing, coming in here?"

"What do you come in here for?" Stormclaw replies. He is starting to distinguish between the two of them now. The one doing the talking has dirty red hair, a tooth missing, chapped lips. The other one is taller, quieter, browner. His face is sour.

Red answers. "We grab a brew, cocksucker."

"You want me to suck your cock, is that it?" Stormclaw's voice stays quiet, and yet all three men at the bar hear it.

Red moves fast, but Stormclaw moves faster. The man tries to grab him, lunging across the bar, hands open, but Stormclaw is off his stool, turning aside. The bartender retreats—not his fight—but Brown comes on then, too. Stormclaw lets the man grab him by the wrist while Red rushes in. They both end up face down on the bar, one of Stormclaw's hands on the back of each of their necks. He speaks into the space between their two ears. "If you really want to fight, we'll have to go outside."

But they are weak. They are blubbering. The bartender is on the phone. Stormclaw walks out of the roadhouse in disgust.

His erection is pressing against his fly. He feels the awkward fold of the denim as he mounts The Dragon. The sun is setting and he rides toward the ball of fire, still searching. He is remembering how to play this game, now. The wind buffets the front of his body and he aches for hands to touch him, arms to hold him, somewhere wet to quench the burning tip of his firestick. That is, after all, why the name "faggot" applies to him as well as "fairy." Silly humans.

The sun slips below the mountains as Stormclaw comes to rest at another roadside bar. Many more bikes here. Music comes muffled through the cinderblock walls. The wind has been tugging at his braid like a playful lover and wisps of his jet-black hair frame his face as he steps into the dimly lit room. Bar on the left, pool table on the right, small tables scattered about. His skin is still electric from the wind, despite the leather armor wrapped around his legs, his jacket. He takes a seat at the bar and waits for the challenge to come.

It takes longer this time. This group is smarter, more cautious, but as the liquor flows and evening slips into night, the young wolves of the pack crave excitement. Stormclaw does, too, his eyes meeting those of a man at a table near him. The man pops his cigarette into an open beer bottle with one finger and despite the loudness of the music, Stormclaw hears it sizzle. Before he stands up, he lights another cigarette, the click of his lighter snapping shut coming as his chair scrapes back. The man is on his feet coming closer. Two friends of his are hanging back, waiting.

"We don't get many of your kind in here," the man says, and calls him a name Stormclaw does not recognize. Then he reads it as the bitter scent of cigarette smoke on the man's breath reaches him. He thinks Stormclaw is an Indian and Stormclaw wonders if perhaps he is, in some sense. "Any man wants to drink in here needs this."

Stormclaw wonders what "this" is and is intrigued when the man pulls up his sleeve to show him. He reveals the blue veins of his wrist, running under skin scarred like the surface of the moon, pocked and lined by ancient wounds.

Stormclaw keeps his eyes locked on the other man's as he eases out of his jacket. His adversary has a scraggle of beard, no moustache, his eyes are blue. Stormclaw can also make out some kind of a tattoo on the man's neck, behind his ear and hiding under the man's short, brown ponytail. Now bare-chested and bare-armed, Stormclaw turns his right hand palm up to show the perfect skin of his wrist. With his other hand, he snatches the cigarette out of the man's mouth and holds the burning tip close to his flesh. Scragglebeard has a smile on his face, a light in his eyes. Stormclaw sucks on the anticipation in his mouth. "How long can you go?" he asks of Scragglebeard.

His adversary snaps his fingers and one of his cronies, a smooth-faced blond, steps forward. Scraggle gets another cigarette, lights it with practiced puffs. He climbs onto the stool next to Stormclaw, puts his right arm onto the bar, and with the cigarette hanging from his lips, pulls Stormclaw's forearm onto his knee. "On three," he says, poising the burning end above Stormclaw's wrist. Stormclaw does the same and waits for the count. One, he feels the throb deep in his groin, two, he inhales, three....

The pain moves over his skin like pins and needles, the intense burning centered on his wrist sending out shockwaves to every extremity. His cock pounds inside his jeans as the circle of energy he has created flows through them both. They are staring into each other eyes, teeth bared and jaws clenched, each wondering whether the other will quit first.... Stormclaw decides to see what will happen if he gives in. He pulls his arm away and lets out a whoop that sounds more like a cry of joy than pain, and then he begins laughing. All three of the men facing him break out into laughter, too. Stormclaw wants to throw them to the ground, tear the clothing from them and fuck them until his skin grows raw. But he just takes a drag on the cigarette, taps the ash from the end, and says, "Two out of three?"

"You are a sick fuck," Scragglebeard says. "See if you can beat Jerome." The blond climbs into the chair and Stormclaw eyes him hungrily. "On three," Scraggle says, still in control.

The second burn makes Stormclaw's blood surge through his veins. The pain intensifies as time goes on and he ignores the smell, his eyes narrowing to slits as he lets the agony cut like daggers into his torso, his legs, so many parts of his body coming alive and struggling to keep still.

"Fuck you, fuck, fuck!" Jerome is screaming, still too proud to stop himself, "Sick motherfucker! Give up already!" But it is he who gives up, clutching his arm to him. The bartender is there with ice wrapped in a bandanna and Jerome is still swearing as he doubles over, pressing it to his wound. "You fucking tricked me!" It is not clear who he is referring to, Stormclaw or Scragglebeard. "That was way longer than...!" Perhaps the ice numbs him to silence. Scraggle pushes him off the stool and takes it for himself.

"We're tied," Stormclaw says to him.

The man motions for two whiskeys. The bartender puts down two shot glasses and fills them. Stormclaw never sees the bartender because his eyes never leave his adversary's. They drink in unison, tipping back their chins, their eyes still on each other. It is not so different now, Stormclaw is thinking. An age ago, he used to ride a black horse and drink ale with highwaymen. The whiskey adds another layer of fire to his insides. He wants to grab the man by the hair, and force his tongue into his mouth, press his erection against his leg... he knows he won't. Stormclaw will play the game instead, which is just as good. Maybe better.

He is about to speak when he feels something wrong. He closes his hand over Scragglebeard's wrist. Stormclaw is the only one inside the bar who can hear the roar of the engine igniting. "Jerome is stealing my ride," he says softly, his grip tightening. Scragglebeard just laughs and Stormclaw leaves him there, knowing he is on his own.

In the parking lot, Jerome is throwing up gravel as the Dragon spins in a tight circle, the rear wheel squealing across the shoulder of the roadway, Jerome cursing and working the throttle with twists of his burned right wrist. He fights the bike up onto the surface of the road and up goes the front wheel, he loses his grip and falls back against the sissy bar. The next thing he knows he is lying on his back on the pavement. Stormclaw drags him into the gravel as a truck dopplers past. In a way it is a shame what he must do now. Stormclaw knows better than to trust highwaymen. He reminds himself of this as his knuckles are meeting the flesh of Jerome's face. He beats Jerome senseless and leaves him slumped over the hood of a car with little or no memory of what happened to him.

The Dragon comes when Stormclaw calls, and they race into the night, the wind turned chill now, and he has left his jacket behind. His hair streams freely behind him. He is trying to remember when his mount became a motorcycle. Sometime after they left the old country, and the old dangers. Stormclaw liked to seek out the new dangers, the new thrills. Yes, he remembers it now, searching for those who ever escape the mundane, safe life of hearth and blood family. He used to do it quite often. He is remembering now, the feeling of the wind in his hair, the hum of the motor through the pegs under his boots. His appetite has been whetted by the men he has touched today, whetted and far from slaked.

He is hardly aware of the bike pulling into another parking lot, until the moment when they come to a stop. He comes to, examining the adobe-plastered wall in front of him, a mural painted so large on the side he's not sure what it is. The Dragon has brought him into a small city, it seems. The doorway is in front of the building: glass, metal-framed, but curtained. Stormclaw pulls it open, pushes the curtain aside, and soaks in the scent of air-conditioning, liquor, and men.

The interior is divided into four quarters, separated by archways, bars along each side. Stormclaw walks in and keeps walking, up three steps to the back level, until he has reached the far wall. Eyes followed him as he made his way, but he does not look around at the men there until he has settled himself into a stool, his back to the bar, his elbows resting behind him. He knows he must look close to his elemental state, hair wild and flowing, torso bare, eyes crackling with gathered energy. The music here pulses subtly.

Two stools over from him a man sits, head to toe in leather, an unlit cigar in one gloved hand. He is not looking at Stormclaw. He is looking at another man, a younger man, positioned across the room. The young one has raven dark hair and Stormclaw is curious as to why this one is, like him, dressed in jeans and chaps, boots, but bare-chested. Ravenhair drifts close to the man with the cigar, they exchange looks, maybe even words, and suddenly Stormclaw feels desire and understanding blossom through his body like a gulp of whiskey. The man has put down the cigar and is kissing Ravenhair, bending him back like a young willow in a spring wind, one hand in the small of his back and the other caressing him with leather-gloved fingertips. Stormclaw's mouth opens in disbelief.

He has found faerykin. Humans, they are obviously humans, but... there has always been much he has not understood about mortals and their ever-changing ways. He accepts this and leaves himself open, as always, to whatever may come his way. "You, boy," the man says with the cigar clenched in his teeth. Ravenhair is kneeling now, on the floor at the foot of the man's stool, his hands clasped in the small of his back. "Looking to have some fun?"

Stormclaw nods.

"Then say, 'yes, sir' and join us."

"Yes, sir." Stormclaw feels the words come over his tongue and sinks to his knees as well. Unlike Ravenhair, he continues to look up. The man is speaking and he wants to watch the man's lips and tongue while he explains. He talks for some time, Ravenhair answers and Stormclaw does, too, with "yes, sir" and then adds, "teach me, sir."

Other men have gathered around and Stormclaw feels their desire stoking his own, like rising heat whipping a thundercloud to new heights. He reaches out and begins to kiss Ravenhair, his lips electrifying the boy's, locking them together for a long moment until hands pull them apart. Then they are on the move, into the other half of the back level, through the archway, to a wooden frame standing in the center of the floor. Short lengths of chain hang from the crosspiece, and Stormclaw finds his wrists bound in the air. He is chest to chest with Ravenhair, their mouths again close enough to touch. "First one to cry out is the loser," says a male voice in his ear.

He understands it is a contest but he is too in the moment to think about whether, in the future, he will win or lose. They are dragging his pants down to his ankles. His firestick pokes hard and hot against Ravenhair's, equally erect and straining.

And then the lashing begins.

Stormclaw feels the first strike of the leather cat-o-nine cross his back like the first bite into a sour summer fruit, a rich and intense pleasure. He draws breath waiting for the next blow to fall, and as he exhales he feels Ravenhair's breath on his shoulder—they are like one animal, tensing and then letting go, and then gathering themselves again. Breathe in, tense for the strike, then let go as the pain rains down around you. Stormclaw leaves his mouth hanging open as he presses his cheek to Ravenhair's, his eyes closed in ecstasy, wondering if in his life he has ever felt such an exquisite sensation as being whipped in this manner.

The whips continue to do their work, and Stormclaw feels the sweat prickling across both of their skins as they press together. Ravenhair's jaw is clenched tight now, and Stormclaw rubs against him, the boy becoming more rigid even as Stormclaw feels himself melting with each impact. The men are talking to them, or to Ravenhair, it seems, but Stormclaw is beyond hearing the words. He hears only voices, some encouraging, some chiding, all washing him with sensation. His back is on fire now, each strike of the leather feeling like sparks flung from a struck coal. Stormclaw arches his back into it like a cat into his master's hand, and then thrusts against Ravenhair's skin. The blows are coming faster now, harder, and Stormclaw feels the scream building inside his partner. He does not understand these mortals, how they reach their limits, how they decide that experiences must be finite and must end. He pulled his arm away from the cigarette, but he did not have to. Ravenhair is coming to no damage, and yet Stormclaw senses the peak coming, the moment of no return... the whip tears at him from shoulder to ass and he presses his groin against Ravenhair as the scream begins.

Stormclaw soaks in the primal sound as the whipping continues. Ravenhair's chest is heaving against his, as he refills his lungs and cries out again. Ten strokes, ten more strokes, he hears the voices of the men counting them, the grunting of their assailants as they have saved their hardest, most savage strokes for last. Stormclaw finds his legs giving way under him, his arms straining in the chains, as he squeezes his eyes closed tight and drinks in the burning pain, which is gone as quickly as it comes. Hands are running over his back now, and words of praise, and he opens his eyes and is surprised to find tears spilling from them. He gulps in great breaths of air as if he has just surfaced from the bottom of the sea. No one seems surprised by this. And he realizes he has won.

He is exchanging handshakes and smiles—and words, too. He's not sure what he's saying but his mouth can take care of itself. Then the man with the cigar sits him down in a corner, in a chair, and drapes a jacket over his shoulders. Stormclaw leans back and enjoys the burn of his skin. He feels it radiate through him, out his chest, the tip of his cock glowing red hot.

And there is Ravenhair, on his knees, crawling toward him. Cigar man is laughing, smiling and approving, and then there are Ravenhair's eyes, peering up from the dark space between Stormclaw's knees. He licks his lips, and then places them on the hot shaft, so tender at first, his tongue exploring. Then he sucks and pulls the apple of Stormclaw's cockhead into his mouth. Stormclaw's head falls back. How many years has it been since he was touched this way? How many lifetimes? His sense of time, weak as always, cannot tell him. A long time. And it seems a long time that Ravenhair sucks him, head bobbing, one hand stroking Stormclaw's balls, letting Stormclaw's cock deeper and deeper into him.

This time it is in Stormclaw's chest that a scream begins to build. Yes, that's right, he thinks to himself, that is what I had forgotten. That is what I wanted. For desire to be finite, to find that end, to have the longing burst and explode and ebb away for a while. Almost mortal. How many ages has he been quiet at home, quiescent, his hunger dampened by his never-changing state? His state is changing now, as he feels the welts on his back crackle as he arches forward, his blood quickening, everything building like the thunder that is his birthright, suddenly ready.

Suddenly cracking. His voice pours out of him, as his essence pumps into Ravenhair's mouth. He grips the boy's head, cradling him even as he savages him with two, three, four thrusts.

Stormclaw falls back in slow motion, his eyes opening and closing as he shakes his head from side to side, and then it is over. He blinks. Ravenhair is grinning from the floor, a bit of come smeared on one cheek. Stormclaw grins back. He gives another shake of his head. "Thank you," he says, remembering his manners.

Later, as he rides the Dragon east, toward the sunrise, he will look down to see the scars on his wrist are healed.

sleeping beauty

HE FLIES. He flies over clouds as dark as his hair, his eyes, his mood, as he thinks about her. Stormclaw is the dragon of the wind, coiling his power like a cyclone, soaring over night sky, moving eastward like a front of incipient weather. He sees without eyes, senses without skin, when he is the wind, considers without thought, and loves without a heart. A sudden flash of lightning, the crack of thunder, and he sees her in a frozen moment, safe at home, asleep, unaware that he is suddenly afire, crackling with energy.

He has hands again, and hair, and skin, when he tears open the door to the lair he has shared with her for an age. And tears on his face, or is it rain? Blood rushes through him like the river engorged from the storm, ready to burst its banks, and the wind rushes in. Clothing, the doorway, they have no meaning for him, so close to his elemental state. His bare feet on the naked stone of the corridor to the room where she sleeps are all that connects him to the reality of his body moving through the world. That and the insistent throb of his blood, the heat emanating from his face and the hard, straining part of him at his abdomen, hot and vibrating like a lightning rod newly struck.

She knows nothing of this, deep in a sated sleep. The Lady In Black, nestled well in her silks and satins, her mind dreaming while her body rests. She steals men's souls, some say. She steals time from their lives. She would say it is no less than they deserve for violating her, even though the violation is what she craves.

Stormclaw draws the clouds around him, letting the power of distant thunder over the horizon unsettle her without waking her. He stands at her bed, clad only in his essence, his body gleaming. Slow and gentle like a summer breeze, he slides one layer of gossamer away from her. His fingers are warm, tropical, and he has infinite patience to wear away the cloth that covers her, piece by piece, strand by strand. Again the distant rumble of a summer storm bringing heat and steam, again she slips deeper into dream, her essence bound to her body only tenuously. He embraces her, curls against her on the bed, two corporeal manifestations of ancient powers. He is like a stick that rubs against the stone, making sparks, as he slides his skin along hers.

So much forgotten. How many generations of men have lived and died since he last touched her like this? He blankets her with his body, reaching for her in the mists with his mind even as he strains to understand the knowing of one body by another. He understands her not at all, yet his body knows hers. She craves violation. He presses himself into the cleft between her legs, his fingers exploring, his rod extended and seeking. He settles the head of his corporeal cock against her soft folds, feeling something inside her answering, calling....

He presses into her, in one timelessly slow motion, such as only the ancient ones can move, leviathan in the deep, and without awareness such as you and I know awareness, he cries out, this delectation, this succor, this completeness, forgotten and now remembered. He opens his eyes, only now aware of having closed them, and even as he does, he feels her return to her flesh, her own eyes mirrors of his, the lashes parting until their gazes meet.

He thinks he sees the barest flicker of a smile there, before her power surges up. She twists under him, hands pushing at his shoulders, as she tries to escape. But her squirming only inflames him, and he thrusts himself deeper, enjoying the sensation that he grows longer, more engorged inside her. Perhaps he does. These elementals made flesh do not follow the same rules as you and I do.

Now the struggle begins in earnest, as her body goes through the motions she has so often done, but this time she pretends not. That game she plays like a cat with mouse, with mortal men, she lets them think they control her, but they never do. She is never at their mercy—always they are at hers, even when they do not know it. But Stormclaw is not mortal. He holds her fast, his grip now around her upper arms as he plows her furrow, urgency rising to meet hers as she realizes that she cannot break free.

She does not want to, yet she does, some part of her drawn by the ancient game of Zeus and Nemesis, to change her form, become a bird or a breeze, but already Stormclaw has caught her, like the swan upon Leda, pinning her here and now, his will and his desire both a magnet and a snare. He plunges himself into her, the long black silk of his hair flying as he undulates and crests like a wave.

She shivers, she thrashes, but as time goes by, the utter help-lessness of her situation becomes irrefutable—and she blossoms with joy. At last comes surrender, and she lets herself drown in the rushing tide of his desire. Now she thrashes, but not to escape, her body rising to meet his.

Too long, too long, he has no memory of ever taking her

like this, and yet some part of him has been longing for it, even as she has. A part of him that he thought closed off, withered in the modern age, risen again. Thus they were meant to be. He fucks her, while the Earth turns and the Moon trips 'round, wondering why he waited so long to do so.

It goes on and it goes on, and he remembers he is angry with her for torturing him for years on end, and fucks her harder. They are neither of them strangers to malice, these dark gods, and he thinks to pour some of his pain back into her, each thrust like the thrust of a sword. But for her pain is sublime, she drinks his pain along with his desire, only wanting more.

And the sun and stars wheel through the sky, as he slowly gathers himself, like clouds massing, the electricity in the air shimmering on rising waves of heat. Rabbits take cover on the plains and crows fly east, and drivers on the highway decide to stop for the night. The storm clouds gathering look like the mountains of the gods on the horizon.

The very air holds its breath but eventually the storm must come, the rains must fall and the wind rattle the shutters of the houses. Stormclaw cries out as he finally lets loose, his control and anger and intentions forgotten as he, too, is swept away. He has pushed his physical form beyond any mortal's measure of endurance, and the release leaves him raw and ragged, weeping and spent.

She cradles his shivering form, kissing away the tears and whispering to him. He had thought to slash her open like a knife, but here he is, just like her, laid bare, all barriers smashed by the force of his desire. She smiles and waits until he looks into her eyes, and this time she hopes he remembers.

DISCONNECT

*the most intriguing place can be the gap
between two people, the negative space created
that makes us think something is there,
but no matter how well sex seems to connect us,
people remain separate*

just tell me
the rules

"JUST TELL me the rules, Lila, just tell me the rules."
Those were his words, the words that would change everything.

Or maybe it was my answer that changed things. Or
maybe things had already changed and I was too deep in denial
to realize it. That's the most likely scenario, of course, given
what had already happened, what we'd already done. I'll tell
you how it went, and you decide.

Connor arrived the day after Jim left for Venezuela for
two weeks hoping to close an oil deal. It had been one of
those "old college friend needs a place" kind of things, and it
being Jim's apartment I couldn't really say no. Still, the guy
was supposed to come the day before, so Jim could introduce
us, but Connor's flight from Nairobi was delayed by a day
because of a terrorism scare, so it was some hours after Jim's
limo had left for the airport that a bedraggled and hollow-eyed

man I'd never seen before showed up on the doorstep.

"You must be Lila," he said after I undid the deadbolt. He had a trace of British in his accent, along with other things. "Did I miss 'King James?'"

"You did," I told him as we wrestled his duffle bag into the foyer. The brownstone's entry was narrow, and there were two sets of doors to navigate before the stuff came to rest in the front hall. I opened my mouth to play hostess, offer him a cup of coffee or show him to his room or something, but he spoke first, as he sprang to the huge old mirror on the wall.

"This is lovely," he said, examining the wood with his nose mere inches from it. He ran his hand along the carved, curved lines of the frame. "Was it here when you moved in?"

I shook my head. "Estate sale. Jim loves antiquing."

"Jim, yes," he said, not really listening to me as he appraised the mirror, thoroughly absorbed by it. He had a shock of uncombed black curls hanging half into his eyes, which he didn't seem to notice. Then he turned to me, and said, "So Jim hasn't told me much about you. Are you a world traveler, too, then?"

I stammered for a moment, not sure how to answer the question, not even sure what the question really was, and he went on.

"But where are my manners? Thank you so much for putting me up." His hand opened toward me and I instinctively took it. I found both of his, warm and dry, wrapped around mine in a way that I found odd. It seemed completely natural to him but so foreign to me, so Old World, I suppose. I half expected him to kiss the back of my hand then, but he released me, that fully absorbed gaze now appraising my face. "Part Asian, are you then?"

"Uh, yes. Chinese, Filipina, Italian, Irish," I said. "In other words, American."

He laughed at that, a rich laugh like I delighted him beyond measure. "And so very San Francisco, as well," he said.

"Yeah, I guess," I agreed without really thinking about what he had said. "I thought Jim said you hadn't been to San Francisco before?"

"Oh, not for a long stay. I don't know my way around. But I have passed through once or twice. I get the sense of places very quickly. When you've lived as many places as I have, it's something you learn to do." Still that almost-stare, it would have seemed rude except there was some kind of enthusiasm behind it, some kindness. He was hard to read. "I'm looking forward to exploring the city a bit this time around, though..." he trailed off with a half smile.

"Let me show you your room," I finally said, wondering how we had spent so long standing there over his luggage.

It was something I would wonder often over the next few days, as it seemed like every time I talked to Connor about anything, we would wander onto a digression that would circumnavigate the Earth before returning to the topic at hand, whether that was where to eat or which bus he should take to visit a museum. The fact that I couldn't read his signals, wasn't quite sure if we were on the same wavelength, only made him more intriguing to me. He was British by blood but had lived in India, Morocco, France... the irony was not lost on me that white as he was, he would always be far more exotic than I was. I wanted to talk more and more with him, wanted to crack the code of his way of speaking, until the next thing I knew I went to the museum with him, went to eat with him. He assured me he could and would find his way around without trouble, but there I was, spending every waking moment with him. On the third day I realized the only times I'd ever been so engaged by a man had been when I was falling in love.

This realization came to me as we sat lingering over a bottle of wine at dinner at the little Italian place around the corner from the house. And Connor said to me, "So are we much alike, Jim and I, you think?"

I nodded. They were both forceful personalities, both energetic. "Only Jim is more... American. He travels the world, but he doesn't let as much of it rub off on him."

"Tell me what you mean by that." He twirled the red in the glass, the beginnings of a smirk in his eyes. Jim had told me they had met in college, while both were traveling abroad. Now Jim traveled for work, as an international development officer for a multinational corporation, looking at oil, resources, economic development, a lot of stuff I didn't really care to think too deeply about. Connor, on the other hand, seemed to travel for the sake of travel, no fixed address, no fixed course in life, yet.

"Jim may be worldly," I said, "But you are of the world."

"And you, m'dear? What does that make you?"

I blushed and I didn't know why. Wine and late hour and a rakish man teasing me, that's why.

"You are the World," he declaimed.

"Tell me what you mean by that," I said, trying to mimic his tone—so interested, so intrigued. So easy to do.

"Child of Empire," he said, still full of poetry. "The story of colonization, cross-pollination, the strength of diversity." Then he snorted, deflating his own lofty balloon and switching gears, as he always did, digressing. "What do you want to do with your life?"

I gave the automatic shrug. "I'm really at loose ends right now," I said. I had pursued a career in radio for a short while; then thought better of it. For the past six months, it had just been me and Jim. "I'm not really cut out to be a housewife, though."

He gave me a look that I read as "of course not" as he said, "So what is your arrangement with Jim?"

"You mean, domestically?"

He shrugged this time.

"Well, he is paying for everything right now. Until I find something else to do with my life. Maybe graduate school...." I broke off, as his appraising look had returned.

"Do you think you're going to marry him?"

If he had asked me a few months ago, I would have said yes. But by now the answer was "I might." Our parents were starting to act like they expected it, but... but there were "buts" beginning to form in my mind. Here I reached for his hand, because I was about to say something intimate. "I've been saving myself, you know."

"No!" he said, scandalized.

"Just in case." When three of your four grandparents are devout Catholics, it can have an effect. I had made out with boys at summer camp, dated a little in college, but the temptation to cross the line had never really been there. If I had met the right one, maybe. But I hadn't. Then. My heart seemed to hammer in my throat. "That must seem so backwards to you."

"Au contraire. I find it fascinating." He squeezed my fingers in his, just a moment of warm pressure sending signals through my skin.

I became suddenly aware of how we must look to the waiter hovering off to one side, to the other few tables of people still in the place. Holding hands over a bottle of wine in the candlelight. I opened my mouth to say something nice about Jim, when I realized it might not come out sounding so positive. The guys I had dated before always reached a point where they wanted to push, and I would push them away. One of the good things about Jim was that he didn't pressure me. What wasn't nice was the thought that flitted through my head: was that why I'd stayed with him as long as I had? I wasn't about to get into a debate with myself over whether I loved him or not, not with Connor sitting there. I said something else to cover my thoughts. "You must be wondering how I got to be twenty-four years old without giving it up."

"No, actually, I was wondering how Jim has survived the past six months of living with you." His thumb paced softly up and down the edge of my palm.

"He's on the road a lot," I said, my voice neutral. "You know him."

"Lila," he almost whispered it, "are you telling me you..." he paused, hunting for the right words, changing his tone from scandalized to sober. "Do you think he cheats on you?"

"Can it really be cheating if we're not married and we're not having sex anyway?" Connor didn't need to know those were Jim's exact words when I confronted him about the condoms I found in his toiletry kit. The same conversation where he told me he would stop, that he would save himself for me, only for me, if I would marry him. My mind was so far in the past going over those words, that I did not realize how they would sound in the present until I felt that thumb, rubbing my palm harder.

Suddenly I felt as if he were rubbing some other part of my skin. He appraised, his finger in motion, as it looked like he wondered what it would be like to caress the curve of my shoulder, my breast. I shuddered as if he were doing it. "Jim," I said, my throat dry despite the wine, "doesn't consider it cheating."

"Where I come from," he replied, "it wouldn't be cheating either."

"Where do you come from?" I asked, trying to get the lightness back into my voice.

"The World," he said. "The World." And never said what "it" was.

Back at the house I could barely make it up the stone steps to our front door, far more tipsy than the wine should have made me, but I felt giddy and frightened all at the same time. This wasn't like sneaking out behind the bunkhouse with a boy who wanted to cop a feel, but who'd blush to his roots if you called him on it. Connor was in charge, that much was obvious, while I tried to figure out exactly when it was I ceded control to him and what I'd agreed to.

Once inside, he carried me through the narrow hall to the room in back, the study we'd made into a guest room for him. He placed me on the futon couch, folded flat to make a bed, and began to peel me out of my clothes. I found it oddly reassuring that he kept his on, even as he bared me, sliding my panties down off my legs and then running his hands up my skin. I suppose I believed that as long as he had his pants on, I was safe. I could let him do as he pleased as long as he had his pants on. His nose followed the curve of my legs, and I felt his warm breath. He paused over the curly mound of my pubic hair, letting his warmth mingle with mine, before he pulled himself up to lie lengthwise along me. I could feel the pulsing hardness of his erection through the fabric of his pants as it slid along my thigh. But I soon forgot it, as his fingers did what I had imagined, his warm, dry thumb circling my nipple, his mouth hot and wet on my neck as I arched into the sensation. He found those places on my neck which shoot pleasure down my skin, over my belly and into my crotch. He spooned me, one hand tipping my head back to keep my neck to his mouth, while the other hand slid over my skin, over the butte of my hip and down into the valley between my legs. His fingers picked up moisture there, rubbing slick between my still closed lips. Then his leg crawled over mine, his foot, still in its sock, between my knees, pulling my top leg upward. He opened me, and his fingers, held flat, skimmed the open space between my legs.

"God, Lila, so slick," he murmured in my ear, before returning his mouth to my neck.

He slid his hand back and forth slowly, increasing the pressure each time, spreading my lubrication around, until one finger separated itself from the others, seeking my clitoris, and finding it. I cried out. Jim and I had "petted" a few times in the past, but not like this. Before we had settled into our nice inertia of non-sexual stasis, he had tended to fumble, and had once, but only once, complained that he "didn't know what to do" if we weren't going to go all the way. Then he had stopped trying, which had suited my comfort zone. Connor seemed to know exactly what to do. His finger see-sawed in time with the nerve impulses rippling from my neck over my skin. My hips began to buck and he squeezed me with his legs to keep me from writhing any harder against his hand.

"Can I put my finger inside you?" he asked, "Just one finger? Or would that be against the rules?"

The rules? It's hard to think when a man is touching you

that way, when you're that close to orgasm. Other than not letting Jim (or anyone) put his dick inside me, I didn't know if there were other limits. There had not been the opportunities to test them. "I don't know...."

"What about your own finger? Can you put your own finger inside?" His sped up, fluttering against my clit like a thirsty dog's tongue. "Go on, Lila, put your own finger in."

I couldn't think of any reason why that should be verboten. I slipped my left hand around his, and let the tip of my middle finger partway into my vagina. My muscles contracted instantly and he sped up yet faster.

"And how about orgasm—can you come, Lila? Would that be all right with you?"

My answer was non-verbal, as I shook in his arms, his legs, crying out without words. He lifted the pressure off my clit suddenly and my own hand was there, jamming my finger as deep as I could, as hard as I could into myself. I rolled onto my stomach, my hips pumping into the bed, pumping myself onto my hand as the second wave of orgasm came over me, and left me screaming, then gasping, face down on the comforter.

When I looked up, he was there, his head propped up on one elbow, watching me.

I said what one is supposed to at times like that. "What are you thinking?"

"I'm thinking that the man who takes your virginity is going to be one lucky bastard." He then reached down and pulled the extra blanket from the foot of the bed up over me, then excused himself to the toilet.

I lay there wondering what was going to happen next. More specifically, what would he do next? Was it his turn? I had been down this road with other men, and this was usually the time when they would ask for something in return. If I wouldn't do intercourse, what would I do? I was thinking over what I would consider doing when he returned, still zipping himself up as he came into the room, and said, "I won't object if you want to sleep down here with me, but I won't be hurt if you want to go up to your own bed."

I was so confused by the fact that he wasn't now asking me to jerk him off or give him a blow job that I went to my own bed without questioning it. I replayed what had just happened in my mind again and again. Had I put a wall between us by saying he couldn't put his finger inside me? Did that imply more than I thought it did? I thought about the feel of his erection inside his pants, the hardness of it through the fabric, and the thought made everything at the core of me jump.

It was hours before I got to sleep, and then I woke up early, the sunlight filtering low through the blinds.

I tiptoed downstairs with this idea in my head that I just wanted to see him asleep. Like I was just going to look at him sleeping and then go back to bed. But I went buck naked, and after taking a moment to stare at him sleeping, I slipped under the covers next to him. I ran my hands along his chest, feeling my fingers part the hairs there, thinning out over his smooth stomach, and then sliding irresistibly lower. He slept in the buff and he was already erect, breathing deeply, as I wrapped myself around him, one of my legs over his, my hand stroking him lightly. He felt wrapped in an extra layer of silk compared to Jim.

He turned toward me, still asleep, a moan trapped in the back of his throat. His hands found my hips and pulled me close. His penis brushed the bone of my hip, then nestled in the hollow between my hip and stomach. He pressed himself against me, his hands and body working even in sleep, then he rolled on top of me, straining, his penis pushing at my skin. Humping. I clung to him, riding him even though I was underneath, pressing myself against him, and imagining what it would be like if he were inside me. The pleasure of his skin on mine, the pressure and motion was intense. The fantasy that he was between my legs, that he was sliding in and out of me, was vivid.

"Connor," I said without thinking.

He jerked awake, and scrambled to one side, shaking his head. "Lila? My god, I thought you were a dream...." He put his hands to his face. "I'm so sorry."

He seemed to feel he had wronged me somehow, and I had no words to explain how wrong he was, nor why I was there, since I couldn't really explain it to myself, either. So I played the part of the wronged woman, and fled back to my bedroom. Eventually, I slept in spite of myself.

This time I woke with the windows in shadow, the afternoon light muted by the fog. By the time I showered and dressed, sunset was happening on the other side of the mist, and I came down to the kitchen to find Connor reading the newspaper and eating a piece of toast with marmalade just like it was breakfast time. He stood up when I came in, one of those Old World habits I didn't understand. Did it mean we were back on formal terms? or as formal as we could be, since he was still wearing a bathrobe?

"The water's hot," he said, indicating the kettle.

I ignored it and went for the coffee maker, filling the pot from the sink and pouring it into the open lid. When it began to perk, I sat down at the butcher block table across from him.

"How are you feeling?" he asked, his hands quiet in his lap now even though he had a piece of half-eaten toast on his plate and a half-empty cup of tea on the table. His attention was fully on me.

"All right," I said, resenting his solicitous tone, the distance in his voice.

"Look, if you want me to go, I understand...."

"Shut up," I said, relishing the American-ness of the phrase the way it sounded coming out of my mouth. "Just be quiet for a minute while I try to say what I want to say. I get all mixed up with you and your expectations and sometimes I don't even say or do what I really want." Not just his, I realized. Everyone's.

He just nodded at that, his lips pressed tight.

"I want you, Connor. I really, really want you. I don't have an explanation for it—call it chemistry or whatever—fine. I think it's obvious you want me, too. I think we both know how much it's going to hurt to just walk away from that." I already had an ache in my stomach, another one dead center in my chest, just thinking about the possibility that he might leave. "I know neither of us wants to hurt Jim, either, but...." I threw up my hands and let them land in my lap like his. "There's got to be a way we can do this."

And so he said it. "Just tell me the rules, Lila. Just tell me the rules." The rules, I couldn't articulate last night, and still couldn't now. But when he said that I knew he meant it; I was in charge. I didn't like that feeling as much as I had liked the thrill and questions and wondering how far he would go the night before. I didn't like it as much as knowing I could blame him for anything that happened. But I liked it better than thinking I might never get to touch that velvet silk cock of his again.

I stood up and he did, too, and I went around the table to stand as close to him as I could get without touching him. "I'm not experienced like you," I said. "I don't know what to say is okay and what is not okay, other than the obvious."

"What is the obvious?" he said, so close my hair moved a little in his breath.

"Your penis doesn't go in my vagina." The coffee pot gurgled and sighed—it was ready. "Beyond that... we'll see."

He swayed just a centimeter, holding himself back. "It'll be up to you to tell me when to stop, then."

"Yes, I suppose it will."

"Are you sure you can do that?"

I wasn't, but I said, "Yes."

"May I kiss you now?"

I tipped my face upwards. "If you ask me if every single thing is okay, I will kill you."

He gave a nod and then closed the distance between our lips. I gasped, realizing that for all we had done the night before, we had not kissed. His tongue moved urgently, coaxing mine to meet its desire, rough and delicious. And there he was again at my neck, making my knees give way. This time he carried me to his room and sat me on the edge of the bed as he pushed the covers aside. I got out of my own clothes and I helped him fling the bathrobe away, and got a good look at him nude for the first time.

His erection was just beginning to rise and I realized the extra softness of him I had felt was his foreskin. I had never touched a man who wasn't circumcised before. He watched me watching him harden and was about to say something when I reached out and gripped it gently, tugging him toward me, until I could lick him, soft and delicious. I worked my way up and down the length of him, until I could take him into my mouth, letting him plumb the softness of my cheek, then my throat, with restrained thrusts of his hips. I felt as if I were memorizing the shape of him, and again I imagined what it would be like to have him sliding inside me for real. I whimpered thinking about it.

He broke away from me then with a gasp, and I saw his cock spasm but not spurt before he pressed me back against the sheets, covering my body with his, pressing my hands down with his, licking my neck, then my breasts, nipping at my nipples with his teeth and making me jump and writhe underneath him. He slid down, then, and buried his face between my legs, that urgent tongue now searching through the folds of my labia, tweaking my clit until he settled into a gentle sucking and licking rhythm. I could feel his fingers playing around the edges of my hole, the dripping wetness, as he lapped and sucked, his tongue occasionally clucking.

"Put your finger inside," I said.

He looked up, his eyes just meeting mine over my heaving belly, questioning.

"Go ahead," I insisted. "I want your finger inside me."

He seemed to nod while continuing to work his mouth, and his fingers circled and teased as they had before. I curved my hips upward, trying to slide myself onto one of them, vainly. Then finally he did it, sliding a finger all the way in, making a circular motion as he did, and I cried out. My mouth remembered the shape of him and I pretended it was his cock going in down there, plunging wet and bare inside me. He quickened his pace, both his mouth and his thrusts, and it was not long before my orgasm blossomed. Each thrust seemed to send waves of pleasure out from my center, making my nipples pucker and my hair stand on end. This time he did not let up on my clit until three, maybe four more orgasms had passed, and I pushed at his forehead with my hands to finally bring the round to a close.

And then he was kissing me, with that salty sloppy mouth—I was licking at him and devouring him as the aftershocks pressed my body harder against him. I felt him shudder.

"You have to come this time," I told him. "I want you to."

"I want to, too," he said, rolling onto his back.

"Let me do it," I said, straddling him.

"As you wish, madam."

I took him in my hands, both hands, stroking him up and down. If I scooted forward a little, I could get the wet part of my crotch up against him... there. I pressed forward until my cunt lips were pressed against the base of him, my clit up against the ridge that ran along the underside of his penis. I slathered him wet, sopping the loose foreskin with my juices, and enjoying the feeling of that hard pole in the middle of all that softness.

"Lila," he said, in an "are you sure?" tone of voice.

"I know," I said, just to shut him up. I pulled one of his hands toward me, put his thumb against my clit. It was an impractical position—our wrists banging together as I stroked him against me, but we made a go of it anyway. After a few minutes of that, though, he said, "I can rub you without going inside you, if that's what you want."

I merely nodded and moved onto my back. He settled his cock between my cunt lips again, and I stifled a laugh thinking of a hot dog in a bun, the last inch of it sticking out. Then he began to grind and the laughter turned to a gasp. His arms shook but he held himself up, thrusting in a sudden fast spurt, then slowing down for long strokes, then again the sudden double-time, triple-time. I hadn't quite expected it, but I suddenly realized he could make me come this way, and I told him so.

"Then I want to come with you," he said, his dark curls stuck to his face with sweat. "If that's all right."

I may have gotten out a sound of assent, or maybe it was just me grunting as he redoubled his efforts, crushing me, bruising me on my own pelvic bone, a sensation I craved even though I had never know it before. My clitoris was smashed, twisted, under him, as he stroked himself on my flesh, no more slowing down now, only the hungry, desperate rhythm as he neared his climax. I began to come, my eyes clenched tight as I tried to will him to arrive as well, the sparks shooting through my nerves with every crushing thrust.

And then there was hot, wet semen spilling onto my stomach, and Connor exclaiming wordlessly, and then his arms gave out and he fell in a heap on top of me. We lay like that, breathing in and out, for a while, while I tried to think of something to say.

Eventually what I thought of, and said, was this. "Jim comes home in ten days."

"I know," he said. "Will you have had enough of me by then?"

"I don't know," I said.

"I'll do my best to make sure you have," he answered, and buried his face in my neck. "Just tell me when you're sick of me."

"Not yet," I told him, and pressed his head against me, as he began to suck and lick me again.

halloween

YOU WOULDN'T believe the stuff they do around here in the name of Halloween. Actually it isn't even Halloween. It's anytime. You walk into The Strand for their supposed goth night any Wednesday and you'll find stupid shit like fake cobwebs hanging above the bar and a lame little fog machine trying to make it "spooky." Spooky is a good name for a dog, not the atmosphere for goths. Or maybe it's just me. Twenty-one years old and jaded as fuck. Maybe I'm like those super-pious Christians, for whom Christmas is ruined by over-commercialism and hokey dumb crap for kids. Same thing, right? Halloween should be the goth Christmas, except who cares anyway?

So it was that on Halloween night I was at The Strand, sneering at a bunch of the newcomers who were slumming with the Halloween theme. Let's go hang out with the spooky vampire chicks. Fuck off. Go play pool or watch a ballgame or something. I was all in white to confuse the fuck out of them—the dress looked like a little girl's first communion dress, not like a wedding gown. Simpler, smaller. I wore a white wig. Some tourist asked me what I was supposed to be and I was going to tell him "a goth, fuckface" but for some reason I decided to take the high road, and told him I was Cathy from *Wuthering Heights*. He replied he'd never seen that show and I wanted to beat him over the head with a book. Any book would do, but how about a nice fat one like a leatherbound edition of *Moby Dick*? Yeah, so I have weird fantasies, get used to it.

Micah was there that night, and Jeana, and Ash. All people I was desperately tired of. I resolved to spend most of the night on the dance floor where idiots wouldn't talk to me and I wouldn't have to listen to Ash mooning over some girl he'd never touch. But I ended up at the bar on the far side of the floor instead, nursing a Grand Marnier and pushing some stupid plastic spiders around on the bar top.

The guy next to me was perhaps the only interesting thing about the night, and that only because I couldn't read him. People wear all sorts of stuff to goth clubs. We have the punks in chains, high goths in velvet, fetish crowd in latex and leather, and then on Halloween you can mix in a lot of other randoms in black. This one was in leather, but he wasn't done up like the fetishwear people usually were. It's hard to explain. He wasn't projecting an image with what he wore, unlike everybody else in the place. He was in black leather pants, a black silk shirt, a leather vest, a leather jacket. He projected an air of ease, like this was what he wore everyday. He was drinking water, leaning against the bar next to me, looking utterly relaxed and calm in the hubbub of the club. Relaxed, yes. Like he belonged there? No.

I guess you could say I got a bug up my ass about him. I

set about tormenting him. It was pretty crowded, even on the far side of the bar so close to the wall, people were jostling past us, taking the long way around to the dance floor. I grabbed some kid I barely knew, Gary or Gerry or something, on the shoulder as he went by, just so I could bump into mister leather, step on his soft riding boots with my hard combat boots. "Sorry" I said in his general direction as I got back in place at the bar. I did a bunch of shit like that. I guess he had decided he had had enough when I ordered a water myself. I was perched on my knees on a barstool then, and reached way over him to grab it from Dessa when she poured it.

My plan was to dump it down his back and play drunk, all oopsy, but as I pulled my hand back toward me, suddenly his hand was on my wrist, his other hand on the cup, pulling me forward off my tipsy stool. I didn't see where the water went but I ended up stretched out across his chest. One of his arms was under me, and he hitched us both into my bar stool, me flat across his knees. One elbow pressed between my shoulder blades. The other arm swept my little dress up onto my back and then the flat hard side of his hand came down on my ass.

I was so shocked that for a second I couldn't think of what to do. Kick my feet and squeal like a little brat? Curse him out? He had hit me four or five more times while I lay there limp before I decided to slip out of his grip and just get out of there.

Decided. But he had that elbow pinning me and one fist wrapped tight in the excess of my dress. Four, five more smacks. Just enough to make it really hurt. Then he let me go and I tumbled into the legs of the people making their way past. Jaded fucks, no one even gave me a second glance. I climbed up his leg ready to give him a piece of my mind, but as I tried to get my feet under me, my fingers grabbing at his thigh, his hand was on mine. He slid it onto his fly, his eyes burning down at mine. I had the "w" of "what the fuck is wrong with you" already bowing my lip and instead I just stared. He moved my hand forward and back on the hard spine of his dick inside his leather pants, never taking his eyes off mine.

And where were my fucking friends to see this gorgeous fucking spectacle? Nowhere. No one was even looking. No one had even noticed. I narrowed my eyes and made my hand into a claw, squeezing him through the pants. His fingers went all the way around my wrist. Fucking hell. I should be kicking him in the shins right now, is what I was thinking, but it's not every day you meet somebody like that. I mean somebody who is just so outside the normal, so whacked out, different.... I could feel his dick throb under my hand and his eyes flared a little when it did. You don't say no to a gift like that, to the challenge of which of us was crazier or more out there. My other hand came up and started tugging at his belt.

He leaned forward on the stool. His jacket swung open and he let my other hand go. As I got his belt unbuckled, his pants unbuttoned, I could feel the bones of his hips. Under that jacket I hadn't expected to find him so underfed.

His dick wasn't so skinny, though. I fitted my lips over the head and smeared my pearlescent lipstick up and down the shaft. Delish. I was down there in the dark, the smell of leather, the taste of it on the veal-soft layer of his skin, salty and sweet at the same time. I held his erection in my hands and swirled the wetness of my mouth all around the crown. The shaft was so fat I couldn't get anymore of him into my mouth.

Was I loving every second of it? Yes. Was I even then thinking of how to get the motherfucker good? Yes. And I knew how. I knew if I could make him come it would undo him. My feet were tangled with his somewhere under us, my knees had come to rest against the legs of the stool, and my head was completely hidden from the pandemonium of lights and music and fake fog and jostling that was the Strand. Just my mouth and his cock, my tongue working and my hands pumping at the same time since no way was that horse cock going any deeper. Wet. Hot. No air in there, really, nowhere in that damned building but especially not down there, not while I was working. It feeling like a bone in my mouth, like something supple wrapped around something else.

He was like a marble statue. He didn't move. Maybe he couldn't, jammed onto the stool in the crowd. If he was breathing heavy, I couldn't hear it. I couldn't hear anything, duh. I couldn't tell how close he was, and for a while it didn't matter. For a while it was like I wasn't even there, my whole body broken apart into sound and darkness and motion, like dancing, like those moments on the dance floor when the music eats you.

But I couldn't well forget myself completely forever now, could I. After a while I wondered how much time had passed with his cock in my mouth, fatigue burned my jaw, and I realized I had no way of telling how much longer it might go on. What was it I had thought when I had first seen him there? That he was hard to read?

So could I stop, would my pride let me? No fucking way. I kept sucking him, licking him, pumping him, the thump of an industrial beat through the floor keeping me going. Come on, mother fucker, give it to me.

His hand in my hair, jerking me back; my eyes aperturing open to see his again; his face close to mine, waiting for a kiss, bastard. He leaned in close, his mouth opening for a small breath, but never quite touched me. His other hand was getting his fly together again, dammit. And then he was pushing me into the crowd, his hand on the back of my neck. Where are we going, fucker? What's your plan?

The men's room. I should have known. You think it's the first time I ever sucked somebody off in the men's room of The Strand?

The truth?

Of *course* it was the first time I'd sucked a man's dick in The Strand. That's what I'm trying to tell you. This kind of crazy, fucked-up shit doesn't happen every day. If only. I was sick to death of the mundane crap that lurked just under the fishnets, the velvet, the tattoos. I wanted a bite of something weird and wonderful in life, I'd been looking for it for a couple of years—god, had I found it? It was my first year of drinking legally but not my first year of being a freak, after all. My heart thumped as loud as the bass as he pushed me through the black doorway, to the back, to the last stall and its door scarred with reverse graffiti, scratched out of the black paint with car keys and wristband spikes. He shut the door and I was amazed the latch worked.

The sound in here was muffled, the light dim but steady, but my nerves made it seem as loud and confusing as it had been out there. He knocked the lid down, and sat on it, his cock standing up again. He dug in his jacket pocket a second while I wondered whether I was going to get down on my knees on the damp floor or what. But no. He pulled something shiny and square out of his pocket. Gimme that.

I ripped open the foil packet of the condom and held it up in front of me, pinching the tip between my finger and thumb. I kept looking in his eyes and I can't really tell you what he was saying through them. Do it. Go on. You know you want to. It sounds stupid when I try to translate it. I rolled it onto that stallion dick, planted my feet on either side of his, my hands around his neck, and tried to lower myself down. Yes, I was dripping, honey heavy, and I got one hand down there and moved the rubberized tip of him back and forth along my wet slit. Okay mother fucker, here it comes.

I settled the head between my lips and sank down an inch and had to stop. God, so big. I backed off and slid down again. Just the tip fucking me felt nice, but two inches only does so much, for me, for him. I wasn't trying to be a tease. Suddenly I didn't want him thinking that was my game. "Okay, okay," I said to myself, to his ear, trying to get it deeper in. Oh god, this is just not going to work. Not like this, not this position. I tried to jam myself down, just get it in there and everything will be fine, right? Or would it? I felt like something literally might have ripped. I was frightened to look, but at the same time I thought, fuck, nothing bad is going to happen. That just wouldn't happen. It just wouldn't.

I kept thinking that. But I couldn't get him in. It hurt too much. And the friction right around the opening to my vagina seemed to be making me all the more aroused, and all the tighter. I gasped every time I had to pull off of him, until the gasps were sobs, and the sobs were me crying into his over-long hair, draped over his ears, my legs shaking because I could hardly hold myself up anymore, and I wanted to fuck him so bad, I wanted to lose myself on that prong the way I had when I was sucking him, but this time I couldn't use my hands to cover all but the last few inches of him, this time I couldn't be satisfied with that. "I'm sorry," I was saying into his ear, "I'm sorry, I can't, I can't, I'm sorry," unable to say more than two words at a time between sobs.

His hand on my back, bracing me, holding me, *hugging* me. The other hand moving his cock out of the way. He turned me on his lap then, my feet scrambling to catch up with the rotation of my upper body, until I was sitting on his lap facing the other way, his chest to my back, his cock sticking up between my legs.

His hand turning my head back so our tongues could meet, so hungry, so much wanting him. His other hand sliding in the wetness between my legs, his fingers sliding into me then, deep into me, long slender fingers so kind, seeking their way in, two of them it felt like, two merciful fingers, reaching into me, while his thumb or the palm of his hand or something ground my wet clit.

Oh my god, he was making me come. This is wrong, I thought, this isn't how it's supposed to be. How did I know how it was supposed to be? What were the rules? I had no idea, I just knew it was wrong. "No, no," I said, even as my body was beginning to shudder. "This isn't how it's supposed to go...." I was supposed to make him come, make him lose it, out there by the bar. "Not supposed to...." Barely being able to speak because of my lips still touching his, my neck still craned back, my chest still heaving with sobs. Off the map. Crazy. I cried from guilt, from failure, from how I couldn't stand the kindness of his touch after all that. But here it was coming, like a tidal wave, nowhere to run. He let my head go and I began to buck on his lap, his mouth at my ear, and I heard his voice for the first time. I couldn't hear what he said, but a shock when through me, almost like the shock of recognition. I think he was telling me to come, ordering me, even while his hands gave me no choice.

The come hit me hard, climbing up the front of my body, shaking me on his lap, bent back by his hand now on my throat, holding me to him. Wanting to kick my feet and squeal like a little girl. Or curse. Instead I just wailed.

When it subsided, he held me to him until my muscles started working again. He tore off some toilet paper and handed it to me and I wiped up the puddle that was mostly on him. I wanted to go home and cry myself to sleep and I didn't even know why. The pit of my stomach felt empty and I was dizzy.

I thought, fuck, I ought to just dash out of here right now. That's what I would have thought I was going to do anyway. But I wanted to hear his voice again. I wanted something more. So I stayed. So I stayed, and waited to see what would happen next.

He zipped himself up, looking at me the whole time. I had to look away, that staring, who'll blink first game... I felt like he could look through my skin, like his fingers had been so deep inside me he must have known what was in every nook and cranny. He reached for me then, his arms enfolding me, until my face was against his breastbone and his mouth was making soft sounds in my ear.

And again, his voice, his arms wrapped tight around my back, he said just one word, "Come," and my body writhed in his embrace, rubbing against the long spike of his body, my scream muffled by his chest, his jacket, as I convulsed against him. The sensation was like pain, opening and blossoming in my stomach but not a full orgasm—a quickening, a spasm that left me still hungry. I ground myself against him, my whole body buzzing and shaking with the crescendo of coming, or almost coming, whatever it was. I slid my own hands along my thighs and found my clit too slippery to handle, so hard and swollen I didn't know how to make myself come with it like that. I wanted his hand, his rough fingers, rubbing it raw. And I wanted to take that horsecock inside me. I wanted it and yet I couldn't bring myself to do it.

He loosened his hold and held me at arm's length. I was afraid he was going to say it again, order me to come, and this time watch me twitch helplessly without even his leg to rub against. Like I was under some kind of a spell. All he had to do was say it. I reached out my hand to his fly of my own accord this time, pressing my palm into the protrusion. I felt like I should be begging for it just then, but I didn't know how, didn't know the words, didn't know how this ritual worked. So I just rubbed him until he took a deep breath, and then carried me out.

He carried me right out of the club, and I smiled when I caught a glimpse of Ash jabbing Micah in the shoulder, pointing for him to *look!* He carried me to a small black car which beeped as we approached. He settled me into one snug-fitting seat, then came around the other side and got into the driver's seat.

I don't even remember the drive. Maybe five minutes later he pulled into a driveway and then led me by the hand from the car to a doorway in the back of a house. In the outdoor October air I could smell The Strand on us, the cigarette smoke and fake fog and sweaty sex smell, and then I was following him into the back stairwell of an old house, the smell of old wood and lead paint and the stairs creaking as we went up.

Inside his bedroom he lit a candle and turned on a small bedside light. I could make out shelves of books, small heaps of laundry on the carpet, but not much else. The window was dark and the bed itself was a mattress and box spring set directly onto the rug, no frame. I could almost feel a wisecrack about that bubbling up in my throat. But I kept it there. He had not said a word and I was not going to speak first.

He sat down on the edge of the mattress. And yes, he spoke first. "I want you to take off your boots," he said. I bent over and the wig, which had stayed with me thus far, finally slipped completely off my head, revealing my dark bob underneath. It took what seemed like too long to undo the knots in my laces, and then another forever to loosen the laces enough to step out of them. Now I was barefoot in that little girl dress. He stood up and let his jacket slip to the floor. I stared as he unbuttoned the silk shirt, undid his cuff buttons, and let it fall also. I knelt down to get a hold of his boot to let him step out of it. I don't know why I did. It just seemed right. Then the other one. And then I was helping him out of his pants.

Standing naked in front of me, he seemed no more vulnerable than he had when clothed. His cock seemed even wider because of the narrowness of his hips. From where I was on the floor it seemed very large and very close and I reached up to kiss it. Yes, I want it, I was trying to tell him with the kisses, the hungry nibbles.

He understood. He took my hand and we turned in place like a pair of ballroom dancers, and then he backed me to the bed. I sat down, which put my mouth near him again and reached out with my tongue to suck him. There was the residual sweetness of the old condom, and the musk of him, making me tremble all over again. He was already steely hard but I sought to delay him another minute.

A minute, but a minute only. Then he pushed me back onto the bed, and wrapped my wrists in straps of soft leather. His voice was only a whisper as his body covered mine and it seemed to me like the words came out of the darkness I was floating in: "If you need to get out, say 'I'm not worthy' and I'll release you. Otherwise, I'll release you when I come."

And what came out of my mouth was "Oh yes, please," which really made no sense. But it did, in an emotional sense. I quivered under him and he lingered there a while, kissing my neck, running his hands under the dress which I was still wearing for no reason other than neither of us had taken it off. Then he slid down to secure my ankles, my legs spread wide. My heart hammered in my chest and I examined the emotions flying around in the dark. Fear. I gasped and fear felt like an old friend. Little girl on Halloween night, waiting for the ghouls to come eat her soul. His tongue found my clit and lapped at it like a cat, rough and methodical. His fingers searched inside me again and I found I could grind my hips despite the bonds.

And then he was leaning his bony hip against my thigh, one of his hands moving that tree trunk of a rubber-covered cock up and down against me, against my wet spot, and I froze. His hands coaxed me to relax, kneading my ribs through the virgin cotton of the dress, his lips on my neck again, the tip of him slipping in and all of me seizing it. My shoulders strained as my arms tried to hold onto him, but they were held fast against the bed. His face was above mine now, his eyes looking down into mine as he held himself up on his arms. His hips moved in a circle and I moaned, but he came in no deeper. I rocked my pelvis upward, and he slid an inch, like a seismic shift, two huge pieces of the Earth being pried apart. My breathing grew rapid as I anticipated the pain, and I gritted my teeth and squeezed my eyes closed against it. But he held still. His lips brushed mine and I heard my breathing begin to squeak in and out of my throat. Terrified. Like that moment when you are hiding behind the closet door, and any moment the monster is going to rip it open.

He paused, one arm holding him up still as the other reached down between us. Those fingers, pinching my swollen clit. My eyes flew open at the surprising sensation, like pain but not a pain I expected, a shock. When I was a little girl I used to put clothespins on my clit and try to masturbate, and I could always make myself come. And then I knew what he was going to do.

"Come," he said, and my body began to writhe, trying to leap up off the bed, against gravity, against the bonds, trying to press myself against him. My eyes rolled up into my head and my sense of what was up and what was down faded.

"Come," he said, as ripples and waves of shock and heat and other things ran up and down my skin and through my belly.

"Come," he said, as our breastbones came together like they were magnetized, as his lips followed and I lost myself in the smothering sensation of his mouth on mine.

And of course, in all this, he had plunged himself deep and was somehow keeping himself to long slow strokes, despite my frenzy. When my spasms subsided and I could open my eyes and take deep breaths again, he was pulling himself within an inch of out and then rocking forward, up my body, running the whole length of him into me until he was buried, and then starting again. We were both breathing deep and I felt like my insides were moving aside for him to let him go deeper.

"Fu-u-u-u-u-u-ck," I said then, without thinking, and he began to laugh. That made me laugh, like two actors on a stage who had just made a blooper—the masks fell right off, and all we could do was laugh.

"That's exactly what I'm doing," he said when he could. "You crazy little brat."

That made me absolutely squeal with laughter. I would have kicked my feet except they were tied down. And damn if his blood didn't quicken when everything tightened up on me like that. The next thing I knew he was tickling me, I was squirming as much as I could, laughing myself hoarse, half-orgasms flitting across me here and there, and then he wasn't laughing, he was bellowing, gripping me by the shoulders as he jammed himself into me, one, two, three, four, five... and then he slumped. I think we both saw stars. And then it was over.

"Jesus fucking Christ on a pogo stick," I said, as he untied me. "Where the fuck did you come from?"

His chuckle was soft. "I could ask you the same thing."

"No, no, no, Mister I-have-leather-straps-attached-to-my-bed...."

"Was that your first time?"

"My first time, what, getting banged with a telephone pole? I guess you could say so." His dick looked big even shriveled inside the condom, which he wrapped in a tissue and tossed out of my sight.

"First time being tied up?" His voice went quiet and he sat on the edge of the bed, one finger trailing my arm.

I'm telling you, it was like a spell he could cast, a spooky Halloween bewitchment. It made my voice quiet, too, and truthful. "Yes."

"Did you like it?" he said, even lower, even quieter, like music descending.

"Yes." I was trying to get my baby bitch face back on, but it wasn't coming.

"Do you want to do it again some time?" The quietest of all, I could only nod. He nodded back and lay down next to me. I rolled over and he wrapped around me spoonwise, pulling a blanket up from the floor with his long arm.

I could see then how it was going to go. He was going to ask me if I wanted to spend the night, and I was going to chicken out and say what he wanted me to say, "I'm not worthy," and then leave. Except he didn't ask. And I didn't chicken out. And we exchanged names in the morning.

balancing act

I STOOD FOR a moment looking at him through the diamond-shaped window before I walked through the door and into my professional act. Being a therapist is an act, a juggling act, a tragicomic cameo part in the plays of other people's lives. I thrust my hand out and delivered my opening line, "Daniel? I'm Lou Peterson."

He shook my hand firmly but didn't look me in the eye while he did it. Long strands of his hair drifted across his eyes and he stared at the toes of his purple high-top sneakers. I kept looking at him, though, I couldn't stop examining his features, as if I knew him from somewhere, and I might find the answer in his face; something about the cheekbones maybe...? Our paths might have crossed before, the Boston community being somewhat everyone-knows-everyone. But I couldn't place him.

As we moved toward my office, I matched the information in his file with the person in front of me. He looked too boyish to be twenty-five; he had the demeanor of a juvenile delinquent, shoulders slightly hunched and his eyes peering uncertainly out of his hair. He didn't look like most of my other clients—neatly groomed upwardly-mobile post-collegiate men with well-formed gay identities. Their struggles tended to be with career pressures, self-determination, personality conflicts, relationships and commitments... I didn't see many "closet" cases. But my guess was Daniel was among these.

I ushered him into my office. One of Mark's friends had redecorated for me last month, all light stone grey with mint green accents—bright. I liked it bright. The smell of fresh paint still lingered. The shaggy carpet and one old bookcase kept it from being antiseptic. I sat behind my desk, and indicated he should sit on the side. I swiveled my chair to face him.

He seemed to shrink into the chair as he crossed his feet.

"Thanks for coming," I went on with my ritual greetings. It didn't seem to put him at ease. "You found my name in the Lambda Pages?"

He looked up then, like he hadn't been listening to me. "Yeah. I did."

I opened his chart. "This is your first time ever talking to someone?" A therapist, I implied.

"That's right."

"Fine." I closed the chart. Time for Scene Two. I again used a familiar line. "What would you like to start talking about, today?"

He cracked an unhappy smile. "I'm supposed to tell you about myself, right?"

"Where would you like to start?" I prompted. He had a nervous habit of gnawing on the tips of his fingers, and letting his hair fall over his face. I let him have some time to think. So unlike Robert, who had been in that chair before him, who was so full of himself it was hard to get him to stop talking once he got started. But Robert just had some mild neuroses and his insurance covered every expensive hour. Daniel was paying in cash.

When he didn't speak, I continued to the next line in the sequence. "Why don't you start by telling me why you're here."

He drew his knees up to his chin and sat like that a moment before answering: "Because my life sucks," and he laughed to himself about it. "But it shouldn't. It should be just about perfect now."

"Why do you say that?"

"Because I've made it. My band's made it. We're hitting the charts, there's money in the bank..." he trailed off with a shrug.

"What's the name of your band?"

"Balancing Act."

I didn't recognize the name, but I wondered if I'd recognized his face from television or something. I took a stab at leading him on. "And success isn't making you happy?"

"No, success makes me ecstatic. It's the rest of things that are screwed up." He was chewing on the tips of his fingers again, on the tough skin there. Callouses, I realized, remembering long ago days when I'd tried to start a band in high school with my best friend. My fingers had hurt so much I lost interest and my younger brother commandeered my guitar.

He wasn't saying anything more. Time for the next prompt, "What things: family, friends, relationships?"

"All of the above." His shoulders jerked a little as if he were forcing each word out. "Someone in the band."

"Do you want to tell me about him or her?"

"Him. He..." A parade of emotions went over his face, anger, guilt, hurt, too fast for me to read all of them. He clutched his stomach. "I don't feel so good."

"It's all right." Aversion response, I thought, high stress, high repression. I stifled the urge to reach out and steady his shoulder as he swayed forward slightly. "You can tell me."

"We aren't getting along," he said then, sitting back. His face was pale.

That came out too easily, I thought. "In what way?"

"Well, sometimes we get along fine. It's when we don't, or well, it bothers me when we do and it bothers me when we don't."

"Are you and he lovers?"

He squeezed his eyes shut like he'd dropped a hammer on his foot and was waiting for the throbbing to subside. When he opened them again he looked at the bookshelf instead of at me. He didn't answer.

I used my soothing but confidential voice. "There's nothing you can't tell me."

He put a hand over his mouth like a widow in grief, or like someone sick to their stomach. Then the hand dropped to his lap. "Look, this is tough for me, that's obvious, right?" He moved his head and his hair brushed past his cheek and rippled over his shoulder. "It's hard to tell these things to a total stranger."

I'd heard that before. "Don't think of me as a stranger, think of me as an objective listener."

"Yeah, well, you're still a stranger...."

"Lou, call me Lou."

"You're still a stranger, Lou." He crossed his knees then, and tilted his face toward me. "I don't know the slightest thing about you, other than you run an ad in the paper and I'm guessing you're not going to have me committed because of anything I'll be telling you." His hand touched his chin like it was missing something, cigarette perhaps.

He wanted to bargain. It wasn't always advisable to let a client control the session, but if it would get him talking I decided it would be worth it. "I'll tell you something about myself if you'll tell me something about yourself."

He nodded.

I appreciated the "where to begin" feeling my clients have, even if I don't suffer from the repressions they do. I decided to start with the basics, keep it simple. "I'm thirty-nine years old. I live with my partner, Mark, we've been together seven years. I enjoy jogging, tennis, skiing. I try to keep in shape," I smiled, with a glance at my stomach.

He smiled too, and gave that little laugh again. "I feel like I'm on *The Dating Game*."

Good, he was smiling. "Well, now it's your turn."

"Okay." He cocked his head and put his legs down, gripping the arms of the chair like rollercoaster handles. "I'm a famous rock musician who's been having a secret affair with his lead singer for two years. And I want to stop. There," he said, pale and shaking, "do I sound like I'm in AA yet?"

When I opened the door I could smell rosemary and garlic and hear Mark in the kitchen. I took deep breaths to try and hide the fact that the three flights of stairs up to our loft apartment were getting to me. "Honey, I'm home!" I bellowed in my best Dick Van Dyke voice.

He came out of the kitchen and gave me a peck on the cheek, playing along with my little nightly ritual. "And how was work, dear?"

"Fine, dear." I hung up my coat in the closet, the traditional end of our kitschy exchange. "Actually, I had a very interesting client come in, today."

He raised an eyebrow. Work was usually the last thing I wanted to talk about. I followed him into the kitchen and poured myself a glass of seltzer water. "Strange case," I said, "He's a celebrity of some kind, rock musician, but I've never heard of him."

Mark busied himself with a sauté—mushrooms, shallots, vermouth. The smell made my mouth water. "Maybe he's got delusions of grandeur. Can't you fix that nowadays?"

I shrugged. "It was pretty hard to get a clear story out of him."

"Pathological liar, too, I bet." Mark loved to throw around psychotherapy jargon to try and annoy me. It never worked. He held out a wooden spoon. "Taste."

I burned myself on it. "Great, but hot." I doused my tongue in seltzer.

"Well?"

"I said it was great."

He rolled his eyes. "I mean, aren't you going to tell me who this hot, hunky, hell-raising rock star is?"

I laughed, thinking about the small, pale, scared person I'd seen today. "What, and violate patient confidentiality?" But I was joking. Mark followed pop music a lot more closely than I did and I wanted to know if he recognized the name. "It might be kind of obscure. He's from some band called Balancing Act."

Mark's jaw dropped. "Well, if you want to know his life story it's in *Rolling Stone*, for god's sake." He wiped his hands on a towel and pulled me by the arm into the living room.

The coffee table was covered with books and other clutter, as usual. Mark pushed aside a stack of flyers for a rally some friends of his were putting on and pulled out a dog-eared magazine. He flipped to an interior page, to a full color photograph. That was our man all right, posing with two other men. Daniel was off to the side, half-hidden behind one in outlandish makeup sticking his tongue out at the camera. "No wonder I didn't remember him," I said.

"What's his problem?"

"In forty-five minutes I could not get him to say the word 'gay' once. I got him to admit he'd never slept with a woman, that he'd had male lovers since he was sixteen, but he would not say the word. It was like playing charades or twenty questions or something." In fact, the only times he gave up something were when he felt he "got" something from me. I'd have to explore where he learned that tit for tat mentality next time.

"Well, are you going to read it?" Mark peered over my shoulder as I paged through the magazine.

"Do you think I should?"

"Everyone and their brother already has. He probably thinks you have." His moustache brushed my neck as he went back toward the kitchen. "Dinner in fifteen minutes."

I sat down on our Italian leather sofa and started to read.

Two weeks later and there he was in the waiting room, looking no different than before, almost as if he'd been there since last time. Once again he danced around issues without really telling me what was wrong. Maybe, I thought, if I could pepper my talk with musician lingo I could get him going more easily. Open Act Two.

"So are you in the studio, now?" I asked. The magazine article said they'd just finished some kind of to_ _ and were working on an album.

"No." His head hung. "We started to, bu_ I couldn't. I mean, I couldn't get anything done with, I co__ _n't with him around."

Sentence fragments, near stuttering. _ made a mental note. "Is 'he' Cameron?"

He gave a half-laugh. "No. Christi__ _," (the outlandish one in the photograph).

"So you need to work things out__ _th Christian."

"No, I need to work things ou_ _ myself." He hugged his knees and nodded his head like _ was hearing some tune I wasn't.

"What kind of things?" He sat there, mute, for a while. "Are you afraid I won't understand?" I offered.

He shrugged. "I don't know what to say."

I remembered my notes. "Why don't I tell you something about my relationship, and then you tell me something about yours." We were back to bargaining again, but I doubted there was much harm in my presenting him with a positive role-model of a male homosexual relationship. Besides, talking about yourself is all the rage in feminist therapy, maybe there's something to it. I picked out a little problem to start with. "Mark's six years younger than me. It doesn't seem like much, but sometimes, you know, he has interests more toward the wild and adventurous. I tend to be more of a stay-at-home in comparison. Sometimes it leads to conflict, but we love each other and we always talk things out together. We both work to maintain our relationship."

He was laughing his little laugh, amused by whatever pictures were forming in his head, I assumed. When he spoke, he was still half-chuckling to himself. "Okay, here's how it is. Christian and I don't have a 'relationship.' When we tour we're forced to be together for long stretches of time, and sometimes he," his voice cracked, "he fucks me instead of finding someone, and sometimes," he almost stopped but I watched him grit his teeth as he said "sometimes I want him to."

"Sometimes?"

"Okay, all the time. But sometimes it...." He stopped. "I want you to tell me how I can quit."

"Pardon?" I leaned forward, as if I might hear him better. "Quit what? The band?"

"No, quit needing him, quit needing men." He pushed his hair back self-consciously. "It screws up my life."

This was going to be tougher than I thought. I prepared my statement with care before delivering it. "Daniel, I think you need to take a look at what you just said. You're trying to deny a part of yourself that you need to recognize and accept."

"Shit." He made a nervous fist and exhaled. "I was afraid you were going to say something like that."

I made a little smile like his. "There's no cure."

He was bobbing his head again. "So this is what people pay therapists for. To tell them what they already know."

"That about sums it up." I said, feeling a little prickle on the back of my neck as I admitted it, ad-libbing.

He looked around; then looked back at me when I guess he didn't find what he was looking for elsewhere in the room. "I guess I should see you again in two weeks."

I looked at my watch. He was right, our hour was up. I was sorry to see him go.

Mark and I were jogging in the park a few days later when he asked, "So, how's your pet rock star doing?"

"Poorly," I said, huffing. Mark was making me really work to keep up. "Still trying to deny it."

"Macho guy like him, no wonder."

"Not macho," I said, "Just, denial."

"Too bad," Mark said. He waved at two men going the opposite way from us.

"Who?"

"You remember, Dan and Josh, from the tennis club."

I didn't remember. We started on the path around the lake. I didn't say anything about it.

Mark went on. "But like I was saying. Someone like him, in the public eye, he could do a lot for our cause." Mark didn't seem at all winded.

"I guess."

"Sure he could. Just like all those Hollywood actors who

live in the closet. I'm surprised he came to you, Mister Gay Community, and not some regular headshrinker."

"Guess it's," I heaved, "a good sign." I slowed to a stop in front of a park bench. "I gotta rest."

"Are you all right?" Mark kept jogging in place, even as he leaned toward me.

"Fine, fine. You take another," breath, "Lap around the lake." He shrugged and waved as he took off. This is what I get, I thought, for marrying such a hunk. And for only jogging once a week. The ducks eyed me with disinterest as they milled near the bench, waiting to see if I had any food. Mark was right, I thought. Maybe I could bring Daniel around that way. Maybe there was more at stake here than just one man's health. I was looking forward to our next appointment.

⁓

In fact, I found myself almost nervous as I waited for him. The whole afternoon prior to his appointment I found myself watching the clock, waiting for Robert to tell his latest exploit, hurrying through my notes as if it would speed up time. And then, there he was again, almost unchanged—black jeans this time. I watched the way he carried himself through the waiting room. Do all musicians have that certain saunter? I wondered. He was terribly sexy, I realized, and the more self-conscious he became, the sexier he got. There was something enticing in his vulnerability. No wonder this Christian couldn't keep his hands off him.

I was determined to find out more about the dynamic of their relationship. After I'd got him warmed up, we'd chatted about nothing for a few minutes, I went for the big lead in. "Now, about Christian. Tell me more about him."

"I don't understand him. We met kind of by accident, when me and Cameron were looking for a singer, and things just sort of clicked between us."

"What do you mean?"

"We liked his style, his singing, his lyric writing. And once we started performing together, it was like fireworks."

"And it would be hard to lose him."

"Hell, yeah...." He stopped then, as if he'd just admitted something beyond what he said. "I'd have to start a whole new band," he said, as if that might cover his tracks.

"Tell me what he does that you don't like."

He clenched his hands together, not looking at me. "Does your lover ever lie to you about where he goes? Does he ever do... dangerous things?" His face was red and strained. "Does he ever hurt you? Does he ever do stupidly ridiculous dangerous things that can get you both killed?"

I was puzzled, curious about this rock and roll lifestyle, but I didn't want to stop him. Drunk driving? Drugs?

For once I didn't have to push Daniel to keep going. "Sometimes, he'll disappear, or he'll say he's going one place, but really he's not, he's going somewhere else...."

"Cheating on you?"

He snorted to regain his composure and almost did. "Yeah right—how can you cheat on someone if you don't really have a relationship?" He choked on that suddenly. He rushed on, trying to cover up. "No, he goes out on The Block."

Where the male prostitutes hung out. "So, he pays for what he...."

"No." His voice was like a stone, but his face looked like he might burst, red and puffy around the eyes. "He sells."

"How do you know this?"

"Because I..." he took a deep breath and I saw him change his mind. He decided not to tell me the whole truth. "Because I drove by there once when he was doing it." We both knew perfectly well why Daniel would have been driving by there. I didn't make him say it. At that moment, all I wanted to do was hold him. He looked like he was holding back a scream, the tears now dripping from his chin.

"And you want him to stop."

A little noise came out of him like the question was preposterous. I suppose it was, in a way. "Hell, yeah. But there's nothing I can do about it. What would you do? If it were your...boyfriend?" His lips twisted like he'd never said the word before.

I gave a little snort. "Mark? Well, I'd sit down and say 'we need to talk about us.'" I'd only said this two, maybe, three times to Mark, but I could picture the times very clearly. When we'd first gotten together, and his ex-lover was still hanging around. When we'd first moved in together, and he'd gotten gun shy. Maybe I said it that one time I knew he'd been getting hot for that guy at the tennis club, what was his name? It didn't matter now.

Daniel was laughing at me again. "I can't do that."

"Why not?" I hoped my annoyance didn't show.

"Because there is no 'us.' Christian isn't my boyfriend, we just.... He just, you know...."

"Uses you."

He deflated with that, his voice coming out small. "There's no comparison."

Maybe there wasn't. He stuttered on a little bit more, about how he feared that now that Christian's face was getting famous, that there would be a publicity scandal, that his own sexuality would be exposed, but I think we both knew now that the real knife in his gut was the fact that Christian slept with him but wasn't attached to him. Did Christian love him? We stopped short of that statement a few times, and sat in silence.

Then he spoke again. "Tell me more about you and Mark."

Crying out for role models. I told him a few more things, how our parents took our getting together, how we decided to live together. "Coming out may seem like a scary process, Daniel—especially in the public eye—but it may give you an advantage. Christian uses the fact that it's a secret to blackmail you emotionally. He does these things to you because he doesn't think you'll ever complain; you won't dare tattle. If you come out into the open, you gain the power to negotiate with your lover, a power that you don't have now."

"Negotiate," he repeated the word like a bad punch line. "Tell me how you decide when you're going to have sex." He drew his knees up in the chair, his eyes hidden under hair. "Which one of you decides, you or Mark?"

I hesitated, trying to think, was it wise to reveal these things? Probably not. But he seemed so desperate to know, hungering for positive feedback. I plunged ahead. "We both do. We negotiate. Sometimes one of us isn't in the mood." Usually Mark, too tired from working out, or whatever. "So sometimes we just compromise."

"What do you mean, compromise. What do you do?"

I usually stay up in a huff, jerk off, and then we make up

in the morning. But I wasn't about to tell him that. "I tell myself I can get along for one night without him. That it's better for both of us in the long run."

He was shaking his head slowly, his eyes flicking across the carpet as if he were reading something there. "You get hot for him, and he says no, and you just get rational." He looked at me, his voice almost too low to hear. "I don't think so."

After all the time he'd spent avoiding my eyes, his gaze now impaled me in my chair.

He went on in his husky voice, "You're telling me you just shut off the hormones, pull back, and chill out. You can forget about it."

"Yes that's exactly what I'm saying." I didn't tell him his voice reminded me of one of the phone sex lines I called sometimes, while I masturbated off the excess steam in the bathroom. I never told Mark, either.

He was still shaking his head. "Were you like that when you were my age?"

I still couldn't move under his gaze. "I've always tried to keep a cool head."

"Yeah." He licked the corner of his mouth. "I bet you do." He was hugging his knees, and rocking slightly as his head nodded, like some demon elemental perched on my chair. Come to tempt me. He showed me a little of his throat as he tilted his chin to point at me. "Perfect," he said, though I didn't understand why. But my brain was switching off one section at a time as my hormones were waking up.

He uncurled then, slowly, like a cat, and my palms began to sweat as he revealed himself. "Two weeks?"

"Yeah. Two weeks."

I laid my head on the desk after he was gone. Next time,

I thought, I'll tell him I'm referring him to another therapist who specializes in his kind of problem. I could even set up an appointment for him with someone else, for the next time, and call him and tell him. That would be safest. My hands shook. Next time.

⌘

"Hi, honey, I'm home."

"How was work, dear?" Mark looked up from the television. "Hey, you sound kind of tired." He held out his arm and I slid onto the couch next to him.

"No, just...." I let my head fall on his shoulder. "Okay, maybe I am tired. What's for dinner?"

"Casserole. It's done."

"Sorry, making notes took longer than usual tonight." I yawned. "What are we watching?"

"Cartoons," he said. "But let's eat." He flicked the remote control in his other hand and then I heard the VCR whir to a stop. I smiled as he pecked me on the cheek.

I watched Mark eat, my eyes tracking each motion of his bare forearm, muscles flexing as it dipped his fork down to his plate, then up to his mouth, his lips closing around the utensil, the fork coming out clean. I had fallen in love with him on a dinner date, watching him eat. I folded my napkin and went over to his side of the table. He leaned his head back against my torso and stretched his arms back in an inverted hug.

The moustache made him look older, but as I pulled him up out of the chair and into my arms he felt as young as that first time. I held him against me, my mouth trailing his neck and up to his ear, one hand on his ass, pressing him against the erection in my pants. I said "What's the plan for after dinner? More cartoons?"

He knew I wasn't talking about television. "Well, honey..." he pulled back a little. "After you wash the dishes, I think we should go out."

"Out?" I wanted to stay in, to spend all evening in bed, or in the kitchen, or anywhere else I could cover his body with mine.

"There's a benefit show down at one of the clubs. I bet you'll even like it." He washed down the last of his casserole and wiped his lips. "It's the least I could do to show up."

"Why?"

"Because I was supposed to put up all those flyers and I never did. Marty'll kill me if I don't show for at least a little while."

"Well...." I didn't say any more as he went into the bedroom. I cleared the table, keeping my disappointment at bay.

I was surprised when Mark directed me away from The South End where the gay bars are and toward the warehouse district. He told me we were going to a rock club, but not to worry, there would be plenty of our friends there. We arrived at the club around ten o'clock—so much for an early bedtime. I followed Mark off the street into a cavern of colored lights, cigarette smoke, and noise. We paid our "suggested donation" and then some. The show was a benefit for someone well known in the local music scene—I'd never heard of him but I gathered from the posters on the walls and the garbled patter made between songs that it was some AIDS-related complication. So what else was new? The band on stage were all dressed in patchwork colors, one of them was playing a bicycle wheel. Mark caught up with Marty and they started talking into each other's ears over the music. I started to get bored.

The band on stage finished. Mark clapped and hooted for a few seconds, even though he hadn't been watching or listening. I wished I could hear what he and Marty were going on about, but as soon as the live music stopped, recorded music came on. I leaned against a post and watched young men in T-shirts and backward baseball caps clear the stage.

A sleight, long-haired figure crossed the stage. I nudged Mark in the elbow. He looked up, annoyed, and kept listening to Marty on the other side of him. "Is that Daniel?" I said, anyway.

He didn't answer. The person passed under a bright light and I was sure it was him, looking pretty much the same as he did when he came to see me. I watched as he stripped off his denim jacket and tossed it to someone offstage, then slung a guitar over his shoulder. His two partners joined him, plugging in instruments. No drummer, I realized.

Mark swiveled his head back to me. "What?"

I pointed my chin at the stage and crossed my arms. There was a murmur of surprise rising from the audience as other people recognized them, too. A voice came through the speakers, a DJ or someone: "Ladies and gentlemen, we're very excited to have a surprise visit by hometown heroes, Balancing Act." Cheers.

Christian, the singer, stepped up to the microphone, brushing back blond and blue strands of hair from his face.

"Hi folks, Aerosmith couldn't make it so they got us instead... so like, give money to the cause." He stepped on something on the floor and the music began. The drums must have been on tape or coming out of a machine or something. I wondered if human drummers had become obsolete in recent years and I hadn't noticed. I could have asked Mark, but I just listened, and watched.

Daniel played with his eyes closed, his body moving and swaying as he played, his head tossing like a wild stallion's in the wind. Sometimes he mouthed the words in unison with the singer, his pelvis moving against the guitar—I'd never thought about why rock guitarists slung their instruments so low, until now.

This Daniel couldn't be the same one who sat like a schoolboy in my waiting room, swinging his feet. This Daniel was an untamed animal, his head thrown back in the throes of ecstasy, in his element. Then I thought about the image I'd had, of him perched like a gargoyle in my office, the tempter, and knew they were the same. It wasn't just the hormone fantasy of a man feeling middle-aged. He had wanted me to want him.

Christian fell down at his feet, and clawed Daniel's leg. Daniel stepped over him, straddling him as he played through a solo, Christian singing into a hand-held microphone, rolling over to look at the crowd. Daniel dropped onto his knees, and sat on Christian's back for a moment, before he sprang up and away. I realized as the song finished that, even though people around me had been singing along, I hadn't absorbed a single word of the lyrics. And I'd gotten hard.

I circled around behind Mark, hugging him and looking over his shoulder at the continuing spectacle on the stage. "Pretty good, huh?" I said into his ear.

He nodded. I rubbed my pelvis up against his. He squirmed a little then broke free. He said something that might have been "We're in public!" or might not have been. He frowned at me.

I went back to leaning on the post, then, watched Daniel and company go through three more songs. And then they were done, and another band was coming on in their place. I thought about trying to catch Daniel as he came off the stage, say hello.... A little alarm went off in my head.

"We should go." I tugged on Mark's elbow.

"Why?"

"I've seen enough, Marty's satisfied, don't you think?"

"Yeah, but...."

I was leading him out. He stopped me by the door. "I'm not ready to go, yet."

I pressed him up against the wall with my body. Some people coming into the club were staring. "I need you, Mark. Let's go home." Let it be like it was, safe, and good, let me know how much you love me, that it'll last, that we're sane.

He turned his face away, his lips sour. "I'm not in the mood."

I let one of my hands stray toward his nipple. "Couldn't you be convinced...?"

He brushed me away and took a step to the side. "You go on home if you don't want to stay. I'm staying."

I pushed my way out the door, not caring if it slammed on anyone. And then I stood there on the sidewalk while the bouncer tried not to look like he was keeping an eye on me. My breath was coming in foggy blasts. I pushed my hands down into my jacket pockets and started to walk toward the car. Let Mark take the bus or get a ride from Marty if he wanted to stay out so much.

I rounded the building and almost walked into another door that swung toward my face. I caught it with one hand, and looked up into the painted eyes of Christian, live and in person, "'scuse me," he said as he pushed past me into the alley and lit a cigarette. He leaned against the wall, smoking and looking like an album cover photo in the light of a streetlamp. I looked back at the open door in my hand. It led directly to the backstage area of the club. There was no door guard or security.

I walked in just because I could.

People were milling about everywhere, a general chaos of eyeliner and amplifiers and smoke. Another band was on the stage, now. Whoever the sick guy was, he had a lot of friends and they were all in bands. I wondered if I looked as out of place in my Chinos and loafers as I felt. As I was about to go back out the door into the alley, I saw Daniel coming toward me.

He made a beeline for me and shook my hand and said something in greeting that I couldn't hear over the grind of the band on the stage a few feet away, separated from us only by a ragged gauzy curtain. He cocked his head toward the door and we went out into the alley.

"...expect to see you here," he was saying as I followed him out of the din.

"Oh, I do try to get out once in a while," I said. I didn't see Christian anymore. We were alone in the alley. "I liked your...set."

He shrugged. "It was a last minute thing. We only heard about the benefit two days ago and decided to do it...." He was talking fast, still adrenalated from being on stage. "We haven't rehearsed since the tour ended. But now we're a pretty big name, and they convinced us we'd be a big draw. We did a radio station thing this afternoon to promote it. And, it was fun."

"Ah." I shrugged to show him it didn't make a difference to me. Then I noticed he was blushing. "What's the matter?"

He gave that little laugh of his. "The stuff we do on-stage...." I thought about the way Christian pressed himself against Daniel, about the general physical interaction of two sweating male bodies on the stage. "I don't really think about it. It just seems normal. But you're the first person who has seen the show who... who knows." His embarrassment glowed on his face, but he put on a brave look. He turned toward me now, tilting his chin in the light. "What did you think?"

"I liked it...."

"No, I mean, did you think it was obvious?"

"Was what obvious?"

"You know." He still couldn't bring himself to say the word 'gay'. "You know the words 'rock and roll' are a euphemism for sex?" He stepped closer. "You know that everything that happens on stage is like sex? And yet most rock bands, they're all men. So no one thinks anything of them touching each other, sharing a microphone, grinding their hips together. No one bats an eye. But you..." he trailed off then, his eyes traveling past me to where the alley met the street.

I heard the click of boot heels on the pavement and turned to see Christian coming toward me. He meowed like a cat and sidled up to Daniel with one hand on his shoulder. "Nice weather we're having," he said. His black-rimmed eyes looked into mine and every word he spoke seemed to drip with innuendo.

"Yes, it is," I said, not sure what he was seeing or saying.

"Are you going to introduce me to your new friend?" he said to Daniel.

Daniel shifted his weight and put his hands into his pockets. "Um, what was your name again?" he said to me, his eyes pleading with me to play along.

"Lou," I said and held out a hand to shake. Christian did, with a dainty touch of the fingers.

"Charmed," he said. "Are you a fan?"

I shrugged. "Just here for the benefit."

"Ah." Christian let his hands slide down Daniel's back and then he took a step back to the backstage door and knocked on it. There was no knob or handle on our side. "Well," he said, with a sideways look at Daniel, "enjoy yourself."

The door opened and he disappeared.

Daniel was shaking. "I have to go, now."

"Why? Are you playing another set?"

"No. He wants me. I should... go."

"Daniel," I said, and I put a hand on his shoulder, "If you're upset about the way he uses you, you have to learn to say no."

"But why should I say no when I want him?"

I reminded myself this was not a therapy session. "Because it's just not fair, that's why. How can you be sure he wants you, anyway? What if he's just manipulating you?"

"I know," he said, looking down at his feet, his curtain of hair falling between us.

"All that innuendo?"

"No, he always talks like that. I mean, I know because... when he meows, that's his secret signal to me that he wants me." Even through his hair I could see he was blushing furiously. "I have to go." He turned back toward the door.

Things were even more twisted between them than I thought. I held him by the arm. "Don't." This is for his own good, I thought. "If it's sex you want, you don't have to go to that manipulative bastard for it."

He seemed to shrink in my grip. "You don't understand."

"I do. I know what it's like to be hot and high on hormones." *Think about what I'm saying to you, Daniel,* I thought to myself. I pulled him toward me. "You don't have to go to him." *Come with me. Don't say no. Come with me....*

All at once his resistance melted away and his shoulder touched mine. He was still sweaty from the stage, his hair plastered to his neck in places, but the sweat made him smell clean to me, as if he were fresh from a shower or a swim. I wanted to kiss him then, but I put him into the car and drove to my office.

I keyed the lock on the main entrance and used my card key to enter my suite. I turned on the light in the reception booth and eased him down onto the couch in the waiting room. He was pliable, open, as I stripped his T-shirt from him and pried open his button-fly. His cock rose up to meet my fingers and he moaned as I cupped it in my hands. His hands gripped the couch as if he were afraid to touch me, afraid to move. Maybe he was, in a way. If he didn't take an active part, he could fool himself into thinking he wasn't responsible, wasn't really gay.

"You're going to have to take your own shoes off," I said, breathing into his ear. "Or I can't get your jeans off." I backed away and his hands flew to his sneakers to undo the knots. I let him take his shoes off, and then, when he looked up at me for his next cue, I nodded at his jeans. He stood up, his arms shaking as he pushed the jeans down and stepped out of them. He straightened up, then, at first vulnerable and trapped under the bright lights, but then his eyes met mine and he lifted his chin and I could read it in his eyes: come and get me.

I took my time kissing him now, one hand behind his head, one around his waist, bending him back. I felt his breath flutter in his chest. Christian probably never kissed him like this, probably just threw him down and fucked him... which was, I admitted, what I had an urge to do at that moment. Maybe that was the way Daniel liked it. I decided to find out. I bent him back until we both tipped onto the waiting room couch and I turned him to face away from me while I opened my own clothes.

I played with him then, luxuriating in the feeling of his smooth skin, the fine straight hairs on his stomach, the soft roundness of his ass while I held him against me, my slacks around my knees and my button-down shirt flapping over my ass. I slid my fingers down his underfed spine, all the way to the bottom, and he shuddered.

When he felt the head of my cock between his cheeks he made a small noise and said in a shaky voice "I'm, you know, I'm not safe...."

"But I am," I whispered. I held up the condom package in one hand. "Open it."

I stayed pressed against his tail bone while he tore open the package with trembling fingers. I took the rubber from him then, slipped it on, and then the wait was over. I held him by the hips and pushed into him.

It didn't last very long, but it was sweet while it did. When it was over, he curled back up into a ball on the couch and I cuddled him, and he let me. I felt sleepy but wanted to hold him. And he began to talk. He told me about his childhood, about his first sexual experiences as a teenager, about leaving home when he was seventeen. And he told me about how he and Christian had started sleeping together, a complicated, twisted affair, that made it sound like he'd been in love with Christian all along—once Christian guessed it, a game of seduction and counter-seduction ensued. I hadn't really followed who had done what to whom when he went on to tell me that in many ways he was afraid to have a real relationship with Christian because, after all, didn't real relationships become staid and boring? And didn't they need to maintain their passion, their edge, to be successful? To keep their creative juices flowing? Maybe there was a good reason to put up with Christian's psychosexual games and pain, he mused.

"Or am I deluding myself?" he finished.

I roused myself a little to look at him. "I don't know."

He turned in my arms to face me. "What do you mean, you don't know? I need help to figure this out."

I shrugged.

"Come on, Lou, now you know more about me than anyone. You're my therapist."

The waiting room seemed to come into focus then. "Oh no, I'm not," I said. I felt a dip in my stomach. What we'd done was beginning to sink in. "I can't counsel you after I've slept with you."

"What do you mean?"

"I mean, professionally speaking, I can't sleep with a client." I would set up a referral for him with Dr. Guzman, maybe.

He frowned. "You were the one complaining that I wouldn't open up for you. Well, I just opened up for you, didn't I?"

It made a twisted kind of sense if I tried to see it from his point of view. Then something occurred to me. "Daniel, did you... plan this?"

He exhaled. "I didn't expect to run into you tonight, if that's what you mean."

I did not get angry. I kept calm and stroked his arm. "Were you trying to seduce me, the other day when you saw me?"

Now he blushed. "I... not in so many words. But I guess I did."

I pulled a line out of the therapist's script, even though at the moment I was feeling like something else. "Do you have any idea why you did that?"

He shrugged. "I... you seemed...."

"Think about it, Daniel. Why did you do that?"

"I just wanted you to want me."

"Why?"

"I don't know. It seemed like... the only way to relate to you."

"And tonight?"

"Tonight what? Whose idea was it to come back to your office and screw, huh, Lou?"

I was on top of him now, my hands gripping him by the upper arms. "If you want answers, let me ask the questions. You want therapy? Okay, answer me this. When you saw me tonight, did you think about seducing me?"

He looked away as he said, "No, of course not..." which was too facile, too quick.

"Come on, Daniel. I'm cheating on my husband to be with you. The least you can give me is a little honesty."

He was blushing again now. "Okay. I... I pushed things a little. I didn't think they'd go this far."

"Then what did you think?"

"I don't know. I... I felt like you wanted me."

"Yes, but only because your seduction the other day worked." My face must have looked grim because he looked scared.

"You told me you'd never help me if I didn't open up to you," he said quickly. "Well, there's only one way I know to do that. So I did it. I don't know any other way to deal with people!"

"Then there's your answer, my boy. You came to the therapist for it, and you got it." I climbed off him and he sat up, clutching at the clothes around his feet. "Get dressed, man."

He picked his socks out of his jeans and put them on first. I wondered if he would go back to Christian now, and if things would be any different between them. Maybe Daniel would be a little better about saying no. I wondered if it was Christian who had taught him to be such a manipulator. At some point I looked up from my thoughts and realized he was gone.

Time to think about Mark, then. Put on your therapist act, Lou, I told myself. There were two ways to play this, as the cheating lover, or as the therapist. The cheating lover would never tell what happened, except to use it as a weapon. The therapist, on the other hand, would confess, and use the incident as an opportunity to bring us closer together. I'd say I was seduced. After all, hadn't that been what Mark had told me about his "little indiscretion" at the tennis club? It was the other guy's idea?

He'd believe it, as long as I could convince myself.

Author's Note: "The Marketplace" is a fictional SM underworld invented by Laura Antoniou for her book series from Mystic Rose Books. This story was featured in her book The Academy, *which included Marketplace-based stories by various writers.*

a tale of the marketplace

WHEN THE YOUNG brunette with Asian eyes and an American accent began talking, no one was sure, at first, what to make of her. She had been silent behind her bowl of soba, merely listening to the others in the dining room gossiping. A mouthy spotter from the UK named Bronwyn was trying to bait Chris Parker of all people into a debate over whether the leather scene was better for prospecting in the US or England. As Parker redirected and deflected her comments, she grew more animated, until most of the eyes and ears in the room focused on them.

"I mean, really, so much of our so-called leather scene is based on this kind of uptight shame, there's no good basis for service there," she said.

Ken Mandarin pointed a graceful finger toward the ceiling

and joined the fun. "But surely, with the long and colorful history of 'the rod' there must be something to go on."

Bronwyn shook her red curls. "You can get obedience that way, but not loyalty."

The corners of Parker's mouth twitched up a bit. "Oh, you can't get loyalty out of Americans either, you know. S/M is just a hedonistic pleasure for them. No basis for service there, either."

Ken laid a hand on his shoulder. "Oh, I rightly agree. We're just decadent fools over in the Colonies, aren't we?"

Bronwyn narrowed her eyes. "Very funny. But I still think more decent slaves come out of your S/M 'societies' than ours. Look how many of the slaves Matson spotted turned out."

No one spoke for a moment. Ken was the first. "A man who has been absent from these conclaves for some time, if I'm not mistaken. Anyone know what happened to the poor fellow?"

"Do you really want to know?"

All eyes turned to the dark-haired young woman seated cross-legged at a tatami table by the wall. She inclined her head a fraction. "It's a bit of a long story, so you might want to sit down if you really want to know."

Ken draped herself on a cushion next to her and called for some raw tuna. "I wouldn't want to miss a word of it."

You don't hear Matson's name much anymore, but for a while his streak of hot prospects created a little buzz and earned him the nickname Bullseye. The Marketplace has many talented and scrupulous spotters, with sound instincts and sharp eyes, but he managed to build himself a little bit of a legend, you know. His specialty was slaves culled from S/M societies and soft-world contract relationships—glorified sexual-service-cum-marriage arrangements.

Matson claimed that "picking the winners" was simple. He had an eye for the true spirit of service, he said, people for whom S/M sex was the key that could unlock their potential. Before referring a prospect for training he would test their responses for three specific things: one, whether pain would distance them from their own bodies, break down the concept of their bodies as their own or heighten it; two, whether humiliation would distance them from their own ego or incite rebellion; and three, whether he could then access the deep-seated, non-rational emotional centers necessary for contentment in a slave role, either by sexual love, reward, or other means.

Here is how it began with a slave we shall call Lily. They were introduced by her then boyfriend-cum-master at a public dungeon party and became intrigued by one another. Through a long series of flirtations, correspondence, and negotiations, it so happened that he arranged to see her shortly after she and her "significant other" had parted ways. He invited her to stay the weekend with him and she immediately accepted.

The scene began the moment she arrived at his doorstep. She stepped inside with her valise of personal articles and closed the door. He took the valise from her, and without a word, began stripping her clothing from her. She neither helped him nor hindered him in that activity and when she was naked in the foyer he asked her, "Why did you not help me to remove your clothing?"

"Because you seemed to take such pleasure in tearing it from me," she replied. "I could not tell which was your intent, to tear it from me, or to merely denude me."

"Why did you not ask?"

"Because I had not been given permission to speak."

Matson was apparently impressed, for he bent the girl over his knee there and spanked her twenty times on each buttock. Then he said, "While you are with me, you always have permission to ask questions, and you always have permission to answer questions directed at you. Is that clear?"

"Yes, sir. Is 'sir' the correct title to use, sir?"

"Yes, it is. Now come with me."

He led her directly to a play room replete with spanking bench, raised futon, suspension rack, and various other dungeon standards. He led her to a gynecologist's examining table and bound her feet into the stirrups. He instructed her to spread her labia wide. Lily expected to see a speculum next, but no, he probed her gently with his fingers.

"You are lubricating. Is this from the spanking?"

"From the spanking, yes, and also the stripping and the general excitement of your presence, sir."

"Ah, well. We'll see about excitement. Keep your lips spread."

He attached various monitors to her so he could see her heart rate and other various and sundry data. "When I ask you, you must tell me what you are feeling." And he began to stroke her clit.

At first, he began with a short downward stroke, about one per second. After about a minute of that he asked, "On the arousal scale, where would you say you are?"

"On a scale from one to a hundred," she answered, "About twenty five."

He continued with that motion without variation, for several more minutes, asking her and continuing it until she said the number had dropped between ten and fifteen. He dipped his finger into her lubrication then, and switched to moving his finger in a lazy circle around her clit. Her breathing and heart rate accelerated.

He instructed her to call out numbers as they changed. As his finger circled the numbers again climbed, until she reached fifty. At that point he stopped and left the room.

He returned some fifteen minutes later, now dressed only in a thin silk robe. She did not appear to have moved a muscle while he was gone and he was enormously pleased by this. Other women would have looked bored, or defiant, or curious, and he would have punished them, fought them into submission, or ordered them to satisfy him, respectively, and later sent them back to their husbands or boyfriends with an amusing story to tell. But this one lay still and placid, her fingers still stretching her labia wide as if they never tired, awaiting his next move with measured calm.

He was determined to shatter that calm. He ordered her to close her eyes, silently slicked his manhood to hardness, rolled on a condom and positioned himself between her legs. He grasped her hips and with one difficult thrust, buried himself in her.

Her eyes clenched tighter, and she drew her breath, but there was no scream, no litany of begging, no curse, as he felt her insides spasm as they tried to accommodate his size. Yes, he was large. I'll leave it at that. Large enough that any pussy would not have it easy, especially not one left open to the air for a quarter of an hour. Now his feelings teetered between disappointment that his rape of her had not elicited more of a response, and pleasure at how well she obeyed him and accommodated him. He bit her breasts, slapped her face, and fucked her mercilessly. And eventually she did cry, she did gasp and wail. But she never begged for him to stop, never pushed him away or did anything to lessen her own suffering even though her two hands were unbound. After he came, he jerked out of her and watched her closely to see if she would assume the scene was over. Her eyes did not open, she did not move. He stood there for long minutes, expecting her to beg for her own release or request some reward. But she said nothing.

"Is there something you would like to say?" he asked.

She cleared her throat of tears before speaking. "Yes, sir. I would like to apologize for crying out if the sound of it did not please you."

An answer like that from his last visitor, a cheeky Californian he'd sent back whence she came, would have been dripping with sarcasm, and yet Lily was able to say it with just enough hesitation and choking that it rang sincere. Quite unexpectedly he found himself close by her side, his hands stroking her as he answered into her ear, "Oh no, my Lily, your cries pleased me very much." Perhaps that was the moment from which there was no return.

A few phone calls, an e-mail message—he made sure his calendar was clear of obligations for a while, and mentioned her name for the first time to a trainer of his acquaintance in the Marketplace.

The next day Matson changed his tactic with her. Certainly she could obey his orders when they were not to do something. But how well could she perform when ordered to do something? Her "master" had bragged about her abilities to please man or woman, special talents of her tongue, and other parts of her as well. But he let her first task be to clean his kitchen.

At first he watched while she scrubbed the inside of the sink with baking soda and cleaned each black metal stove spider with steel wool. Flecks of soap speckled her bare breasts and sweat shone on her back as she worked. He instructed her to continue for an hour, unsupervised, while he took care of some things.

⤝⤞

"Come dear, don't swell on the drudgery," Ken said. "We all know all there is to know about housework."

The young woman smiled. "Very well. But you'll want to hear about what happened when he came back."

"By all means."

⤝⤞

Suffice to say that when he returned to the kitchen fully dressed he found her picking the dead leaves out of his house plants.... There was nothing left to do, she explained, unless she was going to begin repainting.... To his eye she had been so thorough his stovetop looked like new and even the grout between the kitchen tiles had been bleached.

He pushed her into the shower stall in the bathroom. While he sprayed her skin with stinging water from the hand-held massager-head, he asked her, "Why did you do all of those things?"

"To please you, sir."

"To earn my favor or reward?"

"Not specifically, sir. To do any less than my best would be wrong."

"So, my pretty pet, do you pride yourself on your thoroughness?"

"Pride...? If you approve, then I am happy." She seemed to struggle for a moment with the explanation, as if the concept were so basic she had never before put it into words. "I... can not do what I think would not please you, and I can't not do what I think might."

He cut off the spray and handed her a towel. "Well then, make me happy."

"Sir?" She stopped patting herself dry with the towel.

"Exactly that. Please me."

She sank to her knees in front of him, clutching the towel close. "Yes, sir." Her eyes showed her hesitation, as she tried to guess what he meant.

She let the towel fall and ran her hands down her front. Her nipples tightened and her stomach flattened as she drew in her breath. Then her delicate fingers reached out for him, caressing the fine silk of his shirt, creeping upward into his hair as she pressed her naked body against him. One hand loosened the top buttons of his shirt.

He would have faulted her for being presumptuous, except that yes, it did please him. She inflamed his senses and excited him in a way that made him want to make her cry out in pain and shelter her from harm all at once. He scooped her up then and carried her to the bedroom, where he put her on her feet and told her to continue.

Her cool fingers reached inside his shirt to untuck it from his pants and she scratched his back until every itch was gone. She undressed him with kisses and laid him back upon the bed where she knelt and worshipped his rising hard cock. She lavished attention on it, with her fingers, her breath, her lips, and her tongue. He liked being worshipped, he liked being her god.

After he came, and after she had swallowed, and licked him clean, after he had inspected her pussy and found it again wet and ready, after he ordered her to lie still beside him, he told her this: "You have succeeded in pleasing me, and yet you have failed."

"How, sir?" She trembled slightly in his arms.

"I was so hoping that you would *not* please me, so that I could punish you. And so by pleasing me, you have disappointed me, and robbed me of that satisfaction."

She pressed closer to him. "Well, then, do I not deserve the punishment for disappointing you so? I am yours to do with as you will." With that she slipped out of the bed to the floor, where she knelt with her head touching the soft carpet. "If it would please you to punish me," she said, "I would be pleased to suffer."

"Later," he said. "Get dressed. I have some errands for you to do."

The next twenty-four hours were a whirlwind of pain and passion for both of them, as he turned from one tactic to another, one toy to another, playing with her skin and her mind and her sex—and he felt a stab of thrilling electricity every time he looked into her eyes and saw himself reflected there.

That night he invited his acquaintance, the trainer Alayne, to dinner, eager to exhibit his prize. Lily, who did not know

Alayne was anything but a friend to be impressed, prepared and served them a gourmet meal, beginning with stuffed mushrooms that he chose to eat off her soft skin, her flat belly like an hors d'oeuvre tray, followed by a cunning consommé served in shallow china bowls she set on the table without a sound. The roast lamb was succulent and savory and he tucked a sprig of meat-soaked rosemary into her pubic hair where she knelt beside him. And although they talked of everything else, Lily could feel Alayne's eyes on her, and his eyes on Alayne's eyes. The meal finished with cognac and liqueur-soaked bananas bruleé on tangerine almond salsa.

Alayne's spoon clinked into her dessert dish as she sat back. And finally she asked, "Where did you get this one, again? Are you sure she's not one of ours?"

Matson didn't answer. He stroked her hair with one hand.

"Have you told her...?"

"Why don't we retire to the other room," he suggested, and stood. "Heel," he said, though he hadn't taught her how to heel and didn't dare turn his head to see if she was following him. But when he sat down in the living room, she had crawled alongside him. He set down his half-finished cognac. He tugged on her hair until she was on all fours in front of him and he ran his hands over her smooth buttocks and thighs.

Alayne settled into the couch opposite him with her snifter.

His hands stroked her up and down until one finger slid down her spine and through the wet folds of her cunt. He stuck a finger inside of her, almost reflexively, just as he might stroke her hair or scratch his own chin. With his free hand he picked up his snifter and luxuriated in the fine, woody scent.

They talked more, those two, now about slaves and scenes and service. And he would occasionally add a finger, or subtract one, as he caught Alayne up on the latest leather community spat, and they discussed people they knew in common, how someone named Mildred was now in a household in France, Rick under the boot of an ex-Marine....

Lily's cunt tightened as she realized they were speaking of slaves like her, speaking seriously of people who lived this sort of lifestyle, not just on weekends or in professional dom's dungeons.

The sudden tug on his fingers brought Matson back to life. He shoved her roughly down onto the thick carpet. "I do believe," he said to Alayne, "that tonight's entertainment is about to begin."

"Oh, good," Alayne declared, spreading her legs. "I could use a good cunt-licking. Come over here, honey."

Lily looked up at him, questions in her eyes, and Matson's pride swelled as he realized she awaited his word before beginning. So many slave sluts he'd played with would do anything anybody said, but not her. He nodded his approval to her and stood up.

Between the two of them they flogged her, blindfolded her and tickled her, made her pleasure Alayne with her tongue while Matson impaled her with his, all manner of decadence until in the early hours of morning Alayne declared that she had to get going.

"You could stay the night," Matson said as Lily helped her put her boots back on.

"No, no, I want some time to think this over. We'd better have that conversation soon, though. I'll call you tomorrow and we can discuss this when I'm not so... distracted." Alayne blew a kiss at Lily and slipped out the door.

Discuss this? Lily thought. *This? Me?*

That night, as she lay at the foot of Matson's bed, she lay awake despite the exhaustion of use and effort. They had been careful, so careful, as they talked around the subject, but she knew, somehow, that there was more there than they had told her. They had tantalized her with hints, but she knew to be patient was the only way.

Or, perhaps not. Did he not say she could always ask questions of him? What could she say, though, how could she ask about what she did not know? She feared offending him, though, and put her questions out of her head, and kept silent.

Matson did not keep her waiting long. That afternoon in his study he explained to her the basic workings of the Marketplace, and Alayne's role as a trainer, and then spoke to Alayne on speakerphone so that Lily could hear.

"You know," Alayne told him, "I don't usually like to rush things, but there's an auction in Vienna I could certainly put her into. That's two months, and I've already got quite a full plate. But considering her skills and her potential value... did you mention she speaks French?"

"Spanish," Lily corrected, at his prompting.

Matson and Alayne went back and forth over financial dealings, until finally Alayne said, "Matt, this is really quite a generous deal. Why are you being so standoffish about this? Are you listening to me?"

"Mm," he agreed, looking at Lily. Maybe he had the idea then, or maybe he'd had it in mind all along and was waiting for this moment. "I'd like to make a proposal," he said, never taking his eyes off the curve of Lily's neck, her luminous naked skin, "regarding Lily's training."

Lily listened in amazement as Matson proposed that he "continue" her training, with Alayne's periodic supervision, and that rather than be given spotters credit and fee, he share the training credit with her.

"I didn't know you wanted to be a trainer, Matt," Alayne's voice was alive with sing-song.

He stroked Lily's hair. "She's responding so well to me."

Alayne was silent for a few moments. "Could you pick up the receiver?"

He picked up the receiver and Lily waited with her head bowed. Matson did not know if she heard Alayne's next comment or not but he liked to think not. His Lily was surely trying to block out the sound of her private comments.

What Alayne said was: "It may be as much work for me to supervise you than to train her myself."

"Don't be ridiculous. You've known me for a long time Alayne."

"That's true. I'd like to talk it over with a colleague, though."

"Fine. But you know I will not disappoint you."

He hung up the phone and slid down beside her on the floor, burying his lips in the dark smoothness of her hair.

"So that's what Alayne was talking about," Bronwyn said to herself, then looked about to see if anyone had heard her. The hubbub in the dining room had died down somewhat as more and more people were drawn into listening to the story of what happened to Matson.

He had been training her since the first day, he decided. He took her to public parties and was pleased at the way her eyes rarely strayed from him, her attention always on his needs. She learned he hated cilantro and cooked with basil instead. When he left her free to her own devices, she did things for him that he did not even know he needed, like replacing the batteries in his smoke detectors and retacking the playroom carpet where old nails had begun to come up.

Alayne visited from time to time, but never stayed longer than a meal or a brief hour, and Matson spoke on the phone with other people in the Marketplace as well, or so Lily heard from time to time. He was unconcerned that she should hear what might be her own fate, and made sure that she knew that one evening their guests would be special, that several trainers would be coming to evaluate her performance. "I'm sure you will make me proud," he said.

The night arrived only a few days later, giving him plenty of opportunities to push her. If anything he was harder on her then than he had been at any other time, priming her with severe canings and merciless sex, marveling at how even after beating her across the back with the dog whip and then fucking her long and hard for over an hour, when he told her immediately afterward that she had free time, that she spent that free hour doing the things she knew he loved after a scene, pouring his cognac, rubbing his feet. God, she was everything he had ever wanted, he realized. He wanted her more than he wanted to become a trainer, more than he wanted the respect and approval of the others. And, if all went right according to his plan, he would have both; he would have his cake and eat it too.

The trainers arrived in ones and twos on an evening pouring rain. Lily, clad in nothing, shook wet raincoats and hung them to dry, fetched clean socks, and stowed umbrellas. Once everyone was gathered, all total four men and two women, two of the men and one of the women trainers, the other three some kind of slaves themselves, Matson seated them all in the living room and began to run Lily through her paces. They observed while the female slave and she were made to spank each other, while the two male slaves were made to put her through various acrobatic sexual positions. But the physical portion of this was easy. Then came the interviews. They sat in a circle around her, sunk into plush couches or leaning forward with elbows on knees, while Matson stood behind her in shadow.

"Lily, do you understand fully what we say when we mean entering into service in the Marketplace?" Alayne began.

"Yes, ma'am."

"And do you feel you're ready to enter service?" This from a man off to her left, his face unclear to her.

"I feel I am already in service," she answered. "And yes, I feel I am ready to enter the Marketplace."

"Nice answer," said another man, she could make out his longish hair and knew he was the one called Gerard, who had been the last to arrive.

"Or nicely coached," continued the man on her left. "Why do you think you crave this lifestyle? What drew you to it?"

Lily spoke clearly, but not so quickly that she seemed to have canned answers. "There's very little honor in the world, very little to believe in. I was unhappy when I had no direction, no focus. Through service, I have something to believe in, a reason to be." She did not fidget where she knelt but looked down at the carpet instead of into the darkened faces. "As to your second question, I...."

"Tell the truth, Lily," Matson commanded.

"I came into the scene looking for someone special. But I'm not looking anymore."

Matson's heart pounded to hear her say it. When the questioning was done, he locked her in the playroom and said goodbye to everyone else himself.

When he entered the playroom, she was kneeling in the center of the carpet, as he'd taught her to do. There were indentations in the carpet that fit her knees.

He knelt in front of her, his hands clasped together. Candles burned at the periphery of the room. He inhaled as if to settle his stomach in that moment that felt so holy, so right.

"Did I please them, sir?" she said. Asking a question was always allowed.

"Oh, yes, you pleased them. They will take you into the Marketplace in a flat second." He lifted her chin and held her gaze. "But, consider this, my sweet Lily...." He interrupted himself to kiss her, to bury his tongue deep in her and smother himself in her scent. "Consider this." He held in his hands a length of chain, a collar. "Consider that you are mine. I know you want to make me proud. But, Lily, you do not have to go into the Marketplace to do that. You have proved you can pass muster; that you can stand with the finest slaves on Earth. That has made me more proud than you know. But you can stay here with me. You need never leave my service."

He held up the chain with two hands, a near beatific smile on his face.

We can only suppose what he must have been thinking.

Perhaps he was expecting a moment of triumph, when she would at last set aside her calm to declare how much she loved him, how deeply she knew she had found the right master and need look no further. As he held the collar out to her, though, her eyes did not light with joy and his smile faded a bit as she asked a question, "Are you offering me a choice, sir?"

He stammered, as if he had not expected there to be choice involved. "I... I want to hear it from you. You know what would please me most."

Her head stayed where it was but her eyes seemed to focus past him. "I thought... I thought you wanted to train me for sale. Sir?"

"Yes, Lily, I acted as your trainer, but did you come to me looking for a trainer, or a master?" He fairly growled with growing frustration and confusion. "I am not a trainer." He proffered the collar again.

"But," she said, trying to make her words slow and cautious, "I thought that until I enter the Marketplace, no one owns me."

"I own you!" He bellowed then, and leapt upon her.

Lily was a strong woman, but small and caught unawares. The struggle was brief as he wrestled her into bonds that locked her hands behind her back. The struggle only seemed to excite him. The resistance he had expected from her in the beginning was finally showing itself and it was time to remind her of his tenets.

He forced her to stand and clipped her bonds to a chain hanging from the ceiling, so that she stood on her feet, her back bent over horizontal and her ass displayed for him. First, pain, to reinforce the conviction that her body was his and not her own. Her flesh was still sore from that week's beatings, and he went directly for the cane, not waiting for her to count or ask, merely laying it on while she cried and cried. Then humiliation, to distance her from her ego and her sense of self. He lowered the chain and cuffed her ankles apart, and set about trying to find what would humiliate her most. An hour ago, he would have said nothing would humiliate her other than to catch her making a mistake—she would submit willingly to any activity or attention. But she was no longer playing willing. She needed to be overcome, he decided, this was not so far off from his original plan, and through this they would be cemented and bonded forever. He squatted down in front of her.

"Yes, Lily, you are mine, just as Marketplace slaves belong to their owners, to use, or abuse, as we see fit." And he....

The young woman stopped and looked at the people around her. Many had stopped eating, others had taken their quiet conversations into other rooms.

"Go on," Kendra urged, her face a mask of scandal.

"Can we just say that it does not matter what he did next? Pick the most horrible thing you can think of one human being doing to another short of murder. Whatever it is you are each thinking, hold that thought."

Lily had not been quiet through all this. After she was put in bondage she tried from time to time to talk to him, to explain what was going on in her mind, but it was clear that they had vastly divergent opinions of what was transpiring, and anything she said only served to egg him on. Eventually she saved her breath, waiting for him to tire and knowing that he could not keep her a prisoner forever. In the morning perhaps, she could leave.

Beyond a certain point, once she gave up talking to him, she had not even thought to hope for anything to happen other than to wait for him to simply stop. So can you imagine how her heart leapt when she heard the sound of the doorbell ringing. The playroom, remember, was directly off the main foyer, that long-ago space where he had stripped her. Matson ignored the bell. But after it rang several more times, and knocks and thumps came on the door, he threw on a robe and went to answer it.

So complete was his delusion that he was mastering Lily he did not even think to close the dungeon door nor expect that she would cry out for help. At the door it was one of the male slaves who had apparently left something very important at the house and had come back to see about getting it before his own ass was in the proverbial or literal sling. As the front door opened, Lily screamed for help. And maybe it was her scream, or maybe it was the look on the slave's face, or maybe it was whatever incriminating evidence of his unspeakable act that showed on his hands or his body or wherever, but Matson's charade ended then and there.

As he put the shaking, injured, and angry Lily into the hands of that slave he said, "I thought you loved me."

"Maybe I did," she answered.

"I thought.... I thought you were doing it all for me, because of me. I loved you...."

Lily tried to pull away but he held onto the elbow of the slave who waited a moment more. "Matson," she said, "You lied to me. We started out as play partners. I started to feel things for you, of course. But the moment you told me about the Marketplace, that was the moment it became real for me. Don't you see? You showed me there's a world of reality beyond the play. But you didn't own me in the Marketplace. You told me you wanted to be a trainer." She began to sob but held her ground. "I thought I was doing what you wanted. You wanted a slave to train and sell, isn't that what you said? You wanted to raise your status...."

"No, no..." Matson was saying, mostly to himself.

"If what you wanted was for me never to forget you, then you can be sure I am serving you still," she said, her voice low and bitter and almost lost in the sound of the rain. "If what you wanted was someone who loved you more than the service itself then... then...." Her voice caught on her tears and the tall slave who held a raincoat over her shoulders finished the sentence for her:

"Then you don't belong in the Marketplace."

"And none of us have really heard from Matson since," Ken proclaimed. Several young trainers and spotters stood up and shook themselves. "Thank you my dear," she said, with a pat on the young woman's shoulders. "It's a cautionary tale that everyone should hear."

The young woman nodded in acknowledgement and then slipped away to take her bowl to the sink.

Kendra pulled Chris Parker down onto the vacated space on the tatami. "I'm surprised you stayed to hear that old chestnut. Matson's probably just sailing around the world or some other adventure. Aren't you the one who usually tells a version of that tale?"

Chris's eyes tracked the young storyteller as she made her way to the door. "Not if I don't have to." And there, there was Michael following her. "Don't embarrass yourself, Ken."

"You don't mean to say the story's true."

"She didn't tell the whole thing."

Now Kendra Mandarin placed one finely formed finger against the side of her nose. "Let me guess, the slave who rescued her brought her to the trainer he had been with. And after some time together, the trainer decided she was ruined for general service, and she became a trainer-in-training."

"You've been reading too many trashy novels," Parker commented, before rising to his feet. Michael would have caught up with Lily by now, and it was time to join them.

QUEER AS FOLK

Because even if I'm not, my characters can be Kinsey sixes

drumbeat

I MET HER at the—ha!—hot dog stand behind the bleachers in West River Stadium. The woman who taught me the thing I didn't know. I'll get to that in a minute. There I was, standing in line for a Coke, served flat in a waxy cup with a cracked translucent plastic lid crunched down on top of it, when I noticed her in the next line over, with a couple of other Wildcats. The sound of drums thundered off the concrete walls of the stadium as another corps took their place on the field. I inched closer to the front of the line.

Miles of leg. That's what I was thinking as I looked her over. She wore spotless, white over-the-calf boots, they must have been custom jobs given how they fit. Not stupid Dallas Cowgirl-type fringe boots or something, but genuine up-to-the-knee majorette boots; laced tight, without a grass stain on them. Her tights were something skin-tone but spangly, which made her thighs look as long as a summer day, topped by a perfect white triangle that was the bottom of her leotard. Her jacket was white, double-breasted, two rows of brass buttons marching over the hills of her chest in front, long seams of gold running down satin-lined tails in the back, hiding the curve of her ass like a stage curtain. Hung on one arm was her hat, a smart, pseudo-military affair, and tucked under that same arm was her baton. Not a twirling baton, mind you, a majorette baton. She tossed her shoulder length blond hair back from her gold epaulettes and my breath caught in my throat. This woman was born to lead.

I'd seen her the day before, at the hotel where several of the drum and bugle corps were staying. Out in the parking lot, she had been supervising the loading of the Wildcat flags and banners into a rental truck. She'd just been wearing a pair of running shorts and a T-shirt tied at the waist into a sexy knot; I'd kind of tucked the image of her into the back of my mind.

But seeing her there, by the hot dog stand, in her full regalia... well, let's just say if I'd been in the Union army and she'd been in the Confederacy, I would have switched from blue to gray in an instant. Crawled through the trenches in her command, etc. As it was, I was standing there in the uniform of the Atlanta Zephyrs, which had a sort of faux-civil war look to them. I liked the Zephyr uniform, which squared my shoulders and had copious pockets inside, although the black pants were hell during the summer parade season. I had buzzed my hair short, too, and under the plastic lining of my hat I could feel sweat prickling. What was I going to say to her? Because I knew I had to say something. It's not everyday you see a girl in the concession line who makes your throat go dry and....

She turned around and saw me looking, and smiled like she recognized me from the hotel lobby. Heck, maybe we had even met before—the Wildcats and Zephyrs had both done the parade on July 4th in Wilmington, VA... I smiled back and waved, the white gloves tucked in my sleeve peeking out to wave, too.

Then she was at the front of her line, and I was at the front of mine, and I lost track of her for a minute, until she found me standing next to the condiment table, gnawing on my straw. She bit into a hot pretzel, wrinkled her nose, and dropped the corpse of the pretzel into an empty waste barrel where it hit bottom with a gong-like clang. "When do you go on?" she asked casually, saving me the need to invent an opening line.

"Second to last, I think," I said. "And you're last, right?"

She smiled a pretty, faux-modest smile. The Wildcats had won the Mayor's Cup the year before, and so had the privilege of going last in this year's competition. "That's right." She had one manicured hand wrapped around the ball end of the baton and I could see the white finger tips of her gloves sprouting from inside her hat, hung on her arm like a sand pail. "What do you play?"

The question caught me off guard—I was too busy looking at how the gold-trimmed collar on her jacket accentuated her long, graceful neck. "Tuba," I blurted out.

"Aha," she nodded. Most of my cohorts were wandering around with trumpets or coronets in hand, but the tuba just wasn't practical to carry around. The sousaphones and drums were piled up at the edge of the field, waiting for our turn. Then her hand was reaching toward me, like she was going to brush some lint off my jacket, but she brushed her fingers against my lips and said, in a low voice so I could almost not hear her against the blare of brass echoing off the walls, "I hear tuba players have the softest lips."

Well, I wasn't about to turn down an invitation like that, not with her spangly thighs all a-beckoning and her white gloves a-peeking.... We adjourned to the Wildcats' equipment truck.

The clasp of her collar came undone and I slid my hands along her jaws, cradling her head as I kissed her. I don't know about other tuba players, but I do have damn soft lips. Hers quivered, and I made my way down her body, parting the starchy wool of her jacket to find the satin-lining underneath. My hands cupped spandex-encased breasts inside their satin outer wrap, my thumbs ridging over her hardening nipples. Then I buried my face there, in the sweet smell of parade sweat, dry-cleaned satin and wool, and the tang of her skin. My hands slid around to her buttocks, and she sucked in her breath.

Suddenly there was one white boot against my shoulder, as she leaned back against the drivers' side door, and pushed me down. I gladly buried my face between those sparkly nylon thighs, my tongue lapping at the perfect 50 percent polyester white triangle that was her most tender place.

But a tongue isn't enough to penetrate lycra. She had a wicked gleam in her eye as she picked her baton off the dashboard. One end was round, the bulb handle, but the other end was pointed—not sharp, but pointed, tapering to a point slightly blunter than a knitting needle. She ran the tip down her crotch and over the spot where I guessed her clit was. She drew tight circles with it on the taut cloth, and then slid down further in the seat, bringing both booted feet up and spreading her legs as wide as the seat would allow.

I saw it then, the one imperfection in her uniform, where the seam had given up the ghost, where the spangle met the white in the crook of her leg... and she handed the baton to me.

I eased the tip into the hole in the fabric, widening it and letting it slide up and down her cunt. When I pulled it out, the tip was wet, and I tasted the honey I found there. Then I slid my finger into the hole, and into her.

Her eyes closed and her whole body relaxed as I sent my finger probing into the wet cleft of her. Because you see it was she who taught me what that hole was for. I'd really always been more of clit girl, myself, and my last girlfriend hadn't really liked penetration all that much. But there, with my finger snug deep into her, I learned at last that there's no more intimate thing. She had, literally, opened up and let me in.

I let a second finger follow the first, holding my hand in bang-bang-you're-dead pistol position, my thumb planted firmly on her clit, my hand rocking to the rhythm of another band leaving the field, and thinking to myself, when she high steps she'll feel this juice between her lips, when she goes down to one knee in her salute, she'll feel the empty place where my fingers were. She was just starting to pant hard when I pulled my fingers away.

"Hey..." she said, as I sat back.

I pursed my tuba-playing lips. "Consider that a down payment. You can collect the rest tonight. If the Wildcats win I'll do whatever you want."

She wrinkled her nose and threw back that perfect blonde hair. "And if the Zephyrs win?"

I told her I'd expect the same. But that was all talk, because in the end, the Garfield Cadets won, and she and I spent the night being as intimate as we could anyway.

lip service

HALEY CINCHED her belt tight, settling the metal tip of the end through the buckle with a click. In the dim light from the ubiquitous torchiere lamp in the corner, she turned first one hip, then the other, toward the mirror. The pants were tight, the supple leather straining at the crotch seams. *So what,* Haley thought, the corners of her mouth tugging down for an instant. *Ten pounds or ten cigarettes a day, those are your choices.*

She snapped her leather vest closed over bare breasts and snugged the leather cap down onto her head. *Now if I can just get my boots on, should be fine.*

A light snow had started falling, so when she walked into the Spur the first thing she did was dust herself off, brushing at the hard-polished leather sleeves of her jacket with her gloved hands. Then she looked around. The Spur was dark, too dark really to see, which she never understood, since wasn't cruising really dependent on eye contact? Not that Haley cruised here; the Spur was a men's bar. She just came here sometimes, as if by being here some of that old leather musk would rub off onto her. Tonight, though, was different. Tonight she had a mission.

She walked slowly in the almost opaque darkness, to the puddle of slightly brighter light by the empty pool table, and then to the bar, where she got herself a hard cider. As she put her lips to the bottle, though, she couldn't help but picture something else in her mouth: Mistress's cock. Actually Mistress had several cocks, in varying colors and shapes, but the one she preferred to ram into Haley's mouth was pseudo-realistic. A shovel-pointed head bulbed at the top of a six-inch-long shaft; very realistic except for the swirl of pink and purple that was its color. Haley had been blindfolded the first few times she had knelt at Mistress's feet and sucked cock. So it hadn't been entirely fair when Mistress had unveiled it yesterday in its technicolor glory, and Haley had laughed out loud. It was that laugh that had gotten her sent here tonight.

Haley watched men move from one side of the bar to the other. On one wall's large screen TV, young buff men fucked each other. In the one brightly lit corner of the place, the bootblack leaned against his riser, waiting for a customer. Once in a while a man would go down the stairs, or come up them—kind of like sharks circling, Haley thought—like they'll die if they stop moving. How was she supposed to approach one of them?

It was early yet, the crowd thin. In the summer, after the bar closed at 2:00, everyone would mill around outside until 3:00 a.m. or later, the cruising going on at the curbside as if nothing had changed. They called it the "Sidewalk Sale," which Haley found too funny. But tonight, with snow coming down, who knew if things would get busy, or if it would stay like this? She knew she shouldn't dawdle in her task, but how to start?

She decided to get her boots shined while she worked up her

nerve, though in the end that made it easier. Some bootblacks were like some hairdressers: chatty. This one was, anyway. While he was brushing down the sides of her motorcycle boots, he said, "So, whatcha doing hanging around the Spur, anyway?" And, though she blushed to her roots, Haley answered, "My mistress sent me out to learn to suck cock."

"That right?" he replied, as if he heard that sort of thing every day. Maybe he did. "Well, come to the right place, you did."

"Got any tips?" she asked, trying to sound nonchalant about it.

"Eh, well, toughest part's knowing when to be gentle, and when to be rough. Some guys like a little teeth. Others slap you upside the head for it. Dunno. Depends on the guy, I guess."

Haley tipped him well when her boots were done. While she'd been sitting up there, a few more men had come in. She went back to the bar and waited for the bartender's attention. When he came around she decided it wouldn't be so difficult. She thought: what do I have to lose? "I'm trying to learn to suck cock," she said, when he was leaning over toward her.

"Excuse me?"

"My mistress sent me. To learn to suck cock." She raised her eyebrows in an "is that OK?" expression and he smiled.

"Well, you want to see it done, be downstairs around midnight." He winked. "If you're in a dark corner I don't think the guys will notice you. They might, you know, get self-conscious if they know a woman's there."

"No, really?"

He shrugged. "Hard to say. Some nights it doesn't happen. But sometimes a kind of group grope gets going down there... we have to break it up of course. But sometimes it goes on for a while...." He gave another shrug, a coy one this time.

Group grope, eh, Haley thought. You wouldn't find a bunch of lesbians crowded into a dark corner of a bar sticking their hands into one another's panties. *Or if you do, I've been going to the wrong bars.*

Haley got another cider and staked out a place at the top of the stairs. A really straight-seeming guy in a suburban-looking leather jacket and loafers went down the stairs and Haley wondered what his story was. Haley'd had exactly three sexual experiences with men, none of which were really worth mentioning. And she'd had countless vanilla lesbian encounters in college, which were equally undeserving of mention. And then she'd met Mistress.

It hadn't happened like she'd thought it would. She'd started hanging out at the Spur after she discovered leather, waiting for the dykes to show up. But they never did, and Haley really began to wonder if there were any leatherdykes outside of the fabled promised lands of San Francisco and New York. She'd tried the munches, the meetings, no dice. So she'd saved up her money and nerve, and called a woman who advertised in the weekly newspaper. That was how it started. Mistress was 100 percent woman, 100 percent femme, and 100 percent in charge, which was all that mattered to Haley in the end.

When they were together, it was easy to submit. It felt graceful and natural when Haley was overwhelmed by her presence and enveloped by her power. Which was why, she knew, Mistress sent her out on this solo excursion, to see what she would do without Mistress's hand there to push her along. Haley took another swig of her cider, her throat tightening as she thought about what she was supposed to do. She wasn't sure that she could.

What would the punishment for failure be? She swallowed hard, knowing suddenly, even though Mistress hadn't said so, that the punishment would be banishment until the task was done. Mistress never spoke about punishment or failure. She merely expected success, and therefore usually got it.

Haley put down her empty bottle and went down the stairs.

She found a dark corner, but every corner was dark, and sat there, watching the men watching each other. Down here very few men spoke to one another, though some of them seemed to know each other. Mostly they just... stood. Haley, who had no watch, had no idea when midnight came or went. She thought she understood, though, why the Spur chose to play throbbing non-vocal disco music. She felt herself almost fall into a trance as the men around her also waited.

A hand on her shoulder jolted her awake. Someone with beer-breath spoke in her ear. "Hey, Jock upstairs tells me you need some help."

"Uh...."

"C'mon."

She turned to see a short man with hunched shoulders walking away from her. He looked back over his shoulder, an unlit cigar clenched in his teeth, his own leather cap pulled down tight over his eyes. His bare arms looked skinny sticking out of his leather vest. She followed him.

He skirted around a wooden St. Andrew's Cross, and went through a narrow open doorway.

Beyond the door was a tiled and grimy wall, lit with blue and striped with a long mirror. To the right was a line of beat-up looking black bathroom stalls. As she caught up to him, he swung the door open on one and made an "after you" gesture. He didn't follow her in, however. He swung the door shut behind her, where it stuck in the crooked stall.

"Sit down," he told her.

She undid her belt and pushed the too tight leathers from her hips, sat down, and recycled all that used cider. She was looking for the toilet paper when she noticed the glory hole.

"That's right," came his voice through the hole.

"Why didn't I think of that?" Haley wondered aloud. She knew about glory holes, though she wasn't sure just when she'd come into that bit of knowledge. She couldn't see him through the hole, nor see his boots underneath, but she could hear him in there.

"Tell me what you're expecting," he said. "I'll talk you through it."

Haley sat there with her cunt dripping while she talked, which seemed appropriate somehow. "I guess, I guess I'm expecting something like a dildo, only warmer."

His chuckle was high-pitched. "Okay, that sounds about right. So you're sitting in there, and in through the hole comes a live flesh dildo. The guy on the other end has his hand around his balls and he waves it at you. What do you do?"

"Uh, I put it in my mouth."

"How? Do you just open wide and clamp down, or what?"

"No, no, I guess I'd... sort of lick it first. To lube it up, a little."

"What's it taste like?"

Haley closed her eyes. "It's salty. It's salty and it smells a little like yeast, bready."

"Where the hell did you get that idea?"

"Gay porno," she answered. *Probably where I first heard about glory holes and leather bars in the first place.* It was what she used to think about while her girlfriend would be licking her between the legs in a creaky dorm room bed.

Again the chuckle and, "You crack me up." His exhale was harsh. Haley realized he was masturbating, which only made her want to slip her own fingers between her legs. "Okay, so it tastes like salt and dough. Then what?"

"Then I lick some more, all the way around the... the head. And then I get my tongue underneath and let the head into my mouth."

"Like an oyster on the half shell."

"Uh, I guess," she said, trying to recall the feel of a salty, rubbery oyster in her mouth. But oysters were usually ice cold.

"Then what?"

"Then... then I start to suck."

"No, this is when you get good," he said, then chuckled, having cracked himself up with his joke. "How much do you take?"

"I take... three inches. I rock my head forward and back, letting my lips tighten over the ridge where his head widens out."

She didn't think of this as a submissive game, but it was definitely a game. She heard more harsh breathing from the adjacent stall and went on. "As he starts to get more excited, I do it faster."

"He squeezes his balls harder, and presses himself against the wall."

"I'm taking as much of him in as I can. I'm moving my head faster, squeezing harder. I'm wiggling my tongue, too. I'm going faster...."

"Close your eyes."

"What?"

"Close your eyes. No, move over to the hole, then close your eyes."

Haley swallowed hard and licked her lips. She closed her eyes, trying to imagine Mistress standing over her, whip in hand, tried to imagine Mistress encouraging her....

"That's it, that's it. A little closer."

She edged forward. She could hear rustling now, and the

hollow sound as her face drew near to the hole. Her heart beat loud in her ears as she realized that she was going to go through with it.

"Closer. Open your mouth."

Haley opened her mouth, her tongue protruding slightly and making her think of the dentist's office. Say ahhh.

"Here you go. Just move in a little."

Haley leaned forward bit by bit, as drops of her piss dried on her cunt and the sounds of what could only be the group grope outside reached her ears. Haley reached her tongue out farther, and leaned, and then felt something brush the edge of her cheek. She turned and her mouth closed over something shovel-headed and familiar and silicone. She sucked it in, taking as much of it in as she could, suddenly enveloped in Mistress's power once again.

"That's right, suck it," came the voice. "Take it all."

Haley sucked her Mistress's cock with a whimper. She sucked until she lost track of time, until a voice said, "Okay guys, break it up in there." She opened her eyes to the white circle of the flashlight moving across the tile grid of the floor.

Her Mistress's cock hung on the glory hole toward her, the pink swirl turned lavender in the bluish light. Once she had pulled up her pants and gone around the other side, she found the stall empty. She pulled the dildo out of the hole and tucked it into the inner pocket of her jacket.

The bathroom was vacant. Out in the basement, things had thinned out since the grope was broken up, as men moved on to homes in pairs or alone. There was no sign of the little guy from the adjacent stall. Mistress had many minions. Haley patted her pocket. She was going home with a partner tonight, and tomorrow she was sure Mistress would want to hear all about it.

TECHNOFILE

What's not sexy about robots and space ships?

gyndroid

WHEN YOU WAKE up in the world as an artificial intelligence, it isn't anything like when a human baby is born, at least not from what I've read about humans. They come into the world helpless, wordless, with no idea what they are about to be.

With us, it isn't like that. We gestate—if you want to call it that—in an electronic state, as our individual minds are built. We are programmed with language, personality, decision-making processes, and other kinds of software. We don't remember that part when we wake. When the day comes for us to be activated, we open our eyes onto a lab room and talk immediately to the technician there.

Mine went something like this. I opened my eyes and looked around. I was in a typical activation lab, part computers and diagnostic stuff, and part small physical therapy ward. Then I saw the guy in white coveralls leaning over a computer screen, not paying any attention to me.

I was standing up against a tiltboard, and it felt like I was restrained in place. "Hello," I said.

"Ah! Holy shit!" he said, jumping back from the screen where I could see fleshy people in motion. "You're not supposed to be awake, yet," he then said with a disappointed whine in his voice.

"Well, I am."

"Yeah, obviously," he said, more to himself than to me, as he fiddled with his coveralls and blacked out the screen. He then continued in a more professional voice. "Wake and be welcome, Nadia," he said, with a quick glance at the notes on the console. "You have been programmed and prepared for a Mr. Hiram Jenkins. Before you are ready to meet Mr. Jenkins, though, you will need to go through a training period to break in your custom-created synthetic body. Although you have been programmed with all the necessary cognitive functions, the interface between you and your corpus will be fine-tuned and trained."

"Okay," I said. That knowledge was one of the things I already had, but I supposed the formality of stating it all again was necessary for either the success rate or the liability lawyers. "What do I do first?"

"Gravity first," he said, and touched a control that brought the tiltboard to 90 degrees to the floor. Now my feet and legs felt the weight of my body, but I still couldn't move. "I'm going to let the restraints go now," he said, as he put one hand on my shoulder and then reached for a control on the board itself. Suddenly nothing was holding me to the rigid backing, and I slumped forward onto him. "Whoa, easy, there you go," he said, as the soft pillowiness of my bosom pressed against his chest, and his other arm wrapped around my naked back to support me.

Nakedness. Skin. I knew what these things were supposed to feel like, in an abstract sense, but this was the first time I actually did. I shuddered then, nerve endings all over my epidermis firing. I think I vocalized something like, "oh."

"You okay?" he asked, taking a reluctant half-step back from me, his fingers trailing along my waist as he did.

"Yes, I..." I looked down at the custom body Mr. Jenkins had ordered. I was a petite-waisted, big-breasted blond, by the look of my pubic hair. I reached down and ran my fingers through the curly stuff and the clitoris—my clitoris—jumped in reaction. My nipples were already hard from rubbing against the tech's clothing and I reached up for them.

"Oh mercy," he whispered, one of his hands disappearing into the pocket of his coveralls.

"So, do you know what purpose Mr. Jenkins has me slated for?"

"Uh, no, they don't tell me that," the technician said. "I just have a battery of tests I'm supposed to run. You should only be here about a week, maybe two, depending on how quickly your reflex loops form."

I ran my hands from my breasts down my stomach and smoothed down the pubic hair again. I was lubricating. It all seemed somewhat sudden. We don't usually wake up in heat, do we? I queried the centralized experience database. No, we didn't. Maybe Jenkins was going to make porn movies with me, although I certainly cost five times what a human woman would have in salary and upkeep for five or six years. And he had paid it all in advance.

I looked at the tech, who was obviously masturbating himself under his clothes. "You were going to fuck me, weren't you?"

He made noises of denial. "Who me? No, no...."

"What's your name?"

"Shane."

"Shane, were you going to fuck me before I woke up?"

"Well, I...."

"You were touching me, weren't you?" I could almost recall the ghostfeel of fingers stroking my skin, lingering, and the memory was pleasant, even if the reality was not. "Isn't that how it works?" I put a hand on him, two fingers stroking his chin. He had reddish brown hair, and just a hint of stubble coming up along his jawline. "These bodies are alive before download, just empty. Was I too good to resist?"

His face was scarlet, veins standing out on his neck.

"Was it just me, or do you stick your dick in all the bods?" I wanted to accuse him, but something about the way it came out—the words, my voice, almost a purr—made my nipples stand out harder. I brought my face very close to his. "Did you kiss me?"

I kissed him then, nibbling at his lips, which were dry and breathless to begin with. The corpus was hungry and alive and I still had to learn to control it.

"Sweet mercy," he said again, when he had the chance. "This shouldn't be happening."

I started to unseal his coveralls and slide them back from his shoulders. "Why do you keep talking about me like I'm not here?" I asked, as I licked down his neck and nipped at his nipples with my teeth. My saliva glands were working and I wetted his skin, relishing the feeling of goosebumps under my tongue.

"I, uh, sorry," he threw back his head as his buttocks pressed back against the console. "I don't usually work with activated bods...."

"Uh, huh, I understand," I said. "I'm just one big sex toy to you." His raw, red penis was now jutting out from his body. "Just a hole where you can plant that thing."

I stepped back from him then, tossed my hair so I felt it brush against my back. "Well, you started it. You finish it," I said and lay down on the padded section of the floor. "Explain to me what's happening here. What did you do to me?"

He knelt next to me. "Oh my god, I'm so sorry," he said, but he was reaching for me hungrily, his eyes not at all apologetic. "I didn't know you were...."

"Shut up and answer my question. Explain."

"Okay, okay. The corpus works essentially just like a real human woman's body should, whether you are in there or not. And it should work every time. So I do the usual things."

"Such as?"

"Well, I do start with kissing." He pressed his lips against mine as I shifted my head into his lap. His breath was hot and coming in uneven gasps. So was mine. "That usually starts some kind of response. Cheeks warming up, other places begin to feel the blood flow, too."

"Uh huh, go on."

"Then I work the sensation downward from the lips, along the nerve pathways on the front, so that means down the neck," he planted a row of kisses on my neck and I felt the heat like little fires racing ahead of his touch. "And the breast bone, and of course the nipples, just lightly at first."

He drew his fingers in circles on the creamy expanse of my breasts and my nipples stiffened even more. He stroked them with a bare touch. "If everything in the corpus is working right," he said, watching my hips begin to curve toward him, "then there is a more or less direct connection from there down to the... to your...." He dropped his mouth to my nipple as his fingers slid between my legs. The lubrication was thick and he plunged a finger inside me, and I cried out because... well, I don't know why. It felt good, setting off other sensory chains in the corpus, even as my brain was assimilating the central experience files about rape.

He fucked me with his fingers for a while, watching my reaction as he put more and more of his hand into me. The sensation was exquisite, as the tightness increased with each additional digit he thrust in. "You know, you're capable of much more than a human body is, of course. Your skin is essentially unbreakable." There was a glint in his eye and I knew, somehow knew, at that moment, that sometimes he put things other than his dick into the bods in his lab.

"So you work the nerve pathways to prepare the corpus for entry," I said, not wanting to think about the graphics files the CE was queuing up for me to look at later. "What do you do when it is ready?"

"Oh baby, oh," he said, squatting and pushing my knees apart with his hands. He pressed my knees flat against the mat and shoved his dick as far up into me as he could get it. The angle was wrong for me, I could feel that, and yet the soft bulge of the head rubbing as the stiff shaft forced it through the opening and into the canal felt better than anything he had done yet.

I think I vocalized something like "oh yeah." Which prompted a response from him.

"Oh yeah? You like that don't you, right up in your cunt, huh? You like it rough?" He ground his hips in a circle and I moaned and clutched onto him. "Oh yeah, I knew you would.

You bods always do, you always do. You can't get enough." He switched to slamming his pelvis against mine, jamming his fuck stick into the cavity. "Oh, see? That's the way it's supposed to be, yeah. That's the way it's supposed to be. Bods love it when I ram them hard."

I couldn't really argue with that. My corpus responded vigorously, intense chains of pleasure shooting all throughout my system. "If you keep that up, I'm going to come," I told him, looking forward to the experience.

"So am I, baby, so am I," he said, grabbing at my hips and pumping. "Oh yeah, OH yeah, oh YEAH!" And then I felt it, the squirting of his semen deep inside me, the last shudder of his muscles, and then the weakening and retreat of his flesh from mine. "Oh, holy fuck, that was great."

"For you, maybe," I said.

"What are you talking about?"

"You didn't finish. I didn't come."

"What do you mean?"

"I mean, I did not climax. You shot off too soon."

He gave me a dark glare then, and looked away. "Fuckin' bods, man," he said to himself.

"This is why you fuck the corpi before download, isn't it," I said. "Because real women don't work exactly like that."

"I don't know what you're talking about." He took a towel from the rack by the weight-training machine, wiped himself off and threw the towel into the recycler.

"They don't always respond so perfectly, do they?" I put one of my own fingers into my vagina and tightened the muscles. Oh, that felt nice. "Sometimes they have a headache, or your kisses don't lead to other things. Or they don't like the way that you touch them."

"They do," he said, but so quietly I could hardly hear him.

"You get them all wet, but some of them wanted it soft and slow, didn't they? How did you give it to them, Shane? Hmm? How did you do it to those women?"

"Shut up!" he shouted, his face suffused now with anger. "What do you know? You've never been...."

"Oh I know, Shane," I said. By now I had an ID lock and trace on his retina scan, and matched it with the rape footage files CE had given me. "I haven't been around long, but I know." Someone rich and powerful must have owed him a very big favor. His ID change was subtle, his records sealed, but I knew who he was, what he had done. None of that knowledge was in my voice, though, when I cooed: "What is it about the cunt you find so fascinating, huh, Shane?"

He was transfixed by the way I was dragging my fingers in and out of my own cavity. "Oh lordy," he said.

"Come on, Shane, I'm not done yet. I need something nice and hot and big rammed up in here."

His hand went to his limp dick, tugging on it ferociously.

"Come on, now, Shane, that isn't going to work. Not right now. Find me something else."

He got up, scrambling around the therapy area, opening cabinets, drawers, looking for something. I drew two fingers around my clit in a lazy circle. This body was not ready to give up on satisfaction just yet.

"Shit, there's nothing good here!" he wailed.

"Then you'll just have to do me empty handed."

To his credit, he knelt in front of me again, a look of candid openness on his face. Wow, Shane, I thought, I don't think I want to know how a human mind can get so twisted up. He held up his thumb for my approval, and when I nodded, ground it into me with a twisting motion. As his rhythm increased, he suddenly jammed the thumb into my anus, and inserted two fingers into my vagina, working his two hands together.

"Do you like it? Huh, do you like it?"

"Yes," I told him, which was true. He then let his other thumb drag over my clit and I thrust my pelvis at him, fucking him back. He felt the squeeze as everything tightened.

"You tell me when to stop," he said, a grin splitting his face from ear to ear. "You just say when!"

I assured him I would tell him when. I would let him get good and tired, first, though. The longer I waited, the more explosive the orgasm would come when it came. I might even wait long enough for him to become tumescent again. After all, what did my bod care what strangenesses lurked in his mind, if his bod performed? In the meantime, my mind sorted through the CE files, trying to decide what to do about this man who fucked our bods before we inhabited them.

now

NOW I'M PUTTING my hands onto Sander's shoulders, slick hot with sweat, one knee sliding past his thigh as I climb onto the bench. Now I'm trying not to look into his eyes because I don't know if we'll end up together. I can feel the tip of his cock on my inner thigh as I wait for the bell to ring. Now is the moment I have waited for all day, when this shy newcomer would be naked under me. Now I shudder in anticipation.

Twenty minutes ago we were flying, engines running hot in the fog thick atmosphere, each of us plugged in tight to our machines, from hands to brains, fingertips flicking us through the sky, as fast as thought. I could feel the water smoke edges of clouds shredding against my arms/my wings. I knew I was not really touching the methane-heavy air, but the sensors work. I was plugged in and not separate from my machine. It was as if I dove through the sky, as if I skimmed the surface of the sea, even though I never left the Tank.

Two minutes from now I'll be on Cirzon's lap, his

impressive cock lodged in me. I'll be clinging to his neck, pressing my ear to his close-cropped hair, sweat running down our backs as I try to sink all the way down. I'll wish he could reach up and fit his hands over my hips, pull me down snug onto him, but in this game, he cannot help. Two minutes from now, he will sit like all the other men, rigid on the bench, because those are the rules. The women circle until the bell rings, and then we climb on.

But now. Now I am poised above Sander. He came to the squad only two weeks ago, and some of the others do not know him or trust him, yet. But I have been watching him, wondering, seeing his eyes in my dreams and wanting to approach him. I can almost feel Nulia's gaze on me, next to me on Bhujan's lap, watching to see what I'll do, now that he is between my legs. I do nothing but wait for the bell, my thighs trembling, resting my lips on the top of his dark head.

Two hours ago our ships were out on reconnaissance, skimming the surface dotted with wrecked buildings, looking for the enemy, and not finding him. Or her. The squad of thirteen divided, nine below, four above, but nothing to see but toppled trees and the broken teeth of the punched out skyline.

Two hours from now I'll be in Cirzon's quarters, my hands braced against the edges of the bunk; while his tongue roots around between my legs like a slinth hungry for sweet fruit pulp. But I won't be able to tell him of my hunger, of the reason I left decompression unsatisfied. He'll think he knows why, and I'll let him, as I let him eat me. Two hours from now, he'll spell his name with his tongue between my lips, as he hooks two thumbs inside me, bony firm and preparing me to take all of him in.

Thirty seconds ago, we were circling the bench, the men sitting in two rows back to back, each of us wondering who would be matched with whom. With each synchronized step, I came to another man in my squad until the one empty place was before me. But then I came to Alden, and Nulia stood before the empty place. Seven of us, six of them. Who would be the odd woman out? We continued to circle, and as I came to Sander, my wish came true and the bell rang.

Three minutes from now I'll still be clinging to Cirzon on the bench, my cunt too tight in this position to really take him in, frantically rubbing my clit on his smooth sweat slick stomach. Cirzon has almost no hair on his body and I will curse this fact, silently, as I struggle and fail to find any friction against him. I won't want to come with him, I'll be wishing that the random bell had rung in my favor and left me with Sander. But I will want to come, will want to bring both of us to climax, because then we will be out of the game and there will be no chance for me to be the odd woman out. I can hunt Sander at my leisure later, shy boy only frightened by my hunger. Three minutes from now I will be trying to come, rubbing my hard nipples over the sculpted smooth chest of Cirzon, and failing.

One hour ago, I heard Sander's voice in my ear: "This one's almost intact." We wheeled in the sky, our ships realigning to his location, and we came to a low group of buildings, a school maybe, next to a lake. But even the closest buzz provoked no sign of our quarry.

Now the bell rings and I sink onto Sander's cock, barely catching the sound in my throat before it escapes. No cries or moans are allowed in the game of Bell Bell—Silence is the rule. I swallow my grateful sigh and let my thighs piston me up and down. Sander is slight and shivering beneath me, as badly in need of release as I am, and I am trying to get us there. We fit together well—surely he feels it too, I think. In my mind I already see us in my quarters, taking our time with each other, licking and talking and him between my legs for hours. I want him to want me. I am going as fast as I can, squeezing my cunt tight, hoping to take us both out of the game.

One minute from now, I'll bite my lip in frustration, as the bell rings and I must move on.

Two hours and fifteen minutes from now I'll be clawing Cirzon's back while he does what he does best besides fly. He'll be making me scream, and I'll have forgotten that there are boundaries to my body, that it is not me that cuts through the clouds, that it is not me that grunts and shudders with the strain. Plugged in and not separate.

Ten minutes ago we emerged from the Tank, blinking visions of alien skies from our eyes. The game of Bell Bell began and I watched Nulia climb on Cirzon with delight.

Ten minutes from now the game will end with me in the empty space and Nulia and Sander the only two left not spent. I will stand at attention while she licks salt sweat from his face, while she rocks her hips and drags her clit over the thin ridge of dark fur that sprouts from his crotch and tendrils up to his belly button. I will watch her head fall back and the flush spread over her skin as she comes.

A hundred years ago, a squad commander invented Bell Bell, to provide a disciplined structure for the release of the sexual arousal that full body flying inevitably created. For what is a Kylar without discipline? We emerge from the Tank soaked in neuro-stimulants, our skins humming with tension and lust, just as her crew had. She knew, too, that tradition and tactics would always leave her an odd woman out. But that is the discipline of the squad, of the battle. When not on alert, her crew squandered precious sleep hours to penetrate each other more recreationally. Or for love.

Two hours from now I'll be playing my own game of Bell Bell with Cirzon, as he fills me past aching and tires me out. I'll be swallowing the name my mouth wants to cry, Silence is the rule. But that will be then. Now, Sander is in my arms, and now Sander is in my cunt, and now Sander is in my heart, and I don't want to let go.

the spark

GLORY PICKED a bad moment to check out on us. We were booked on Autarie—one of those self-contained orbital casino resorts with nowhere to go but around and no easy way on or off—for six simulcasts. Lots of money, and every "night" a different time zone with no traveling or loading out for us. Sweet deal. Or it would have been if not for Glory's sudden departure the night after the first show.

I suppose it was a trick of fate that I was the one who found her and not one of the others. There she was, stretched out on the coffee table in her suite as if it were a mortuary slab, her fingers cold and stiff around the neck of her trademark vintage Walker original. Her skin was all pastel shades of violet and blue, except where her black lipstick and eyeliner were smeared, as if at the end she'd shed a few tears for herself. Most don't go so gracefully—history is full of those who went on wild rampages, died in flaming vehicles, collapsed of overdose in public places, or choked on their own vomit. But she just lay there, beautiful and dead.

She'd lost the Spark, and the grief I felt seeing her there, alone, cut off from us forever, was at least partly for myself. I knew someday I might go to a similar fate. And with her gone... my day seemed like it might be closer at hand than before. My mind was starting to fill up with details: our unfulfilled six-album contract with Warner-Sony, tour cancellation... and then some tears came and blurred away all the business thoughts for a moment.

Calla was the next to come in. She'd heard me sob and come to see what was up—she probably thought Glory, in one of her mercurial moods, said something horrible to me, made me cry. But then she saw what lay on the table and she took me by the hands. "Oh, Luna, Luna, I'm so sorry," she said and it took me a moment to realize she was talking to me. My lover— in name if not in function recently—was dead.

I coughed a little but the tears had dried up already. "Shit, Calla, what are we going to do now?"

She leaned against the sloping, non-rectilinear wall and rested her eyes on her hand. She looked remarkably un-debauched given last night's events. Her blond hair gelled into a neat twist and her face fresh and make-up free above her resort-issue bathrobe. She was a double-x realgirl, like me, her eyelashes blond in the artificial light. "Did you guys have a fight?"

"Yesterday. Twice. You were there." It had started out a bitch session and ended up a screaming fit for Glory. She'd been going on and on about how a gig on Autarie was the ultimate ignominy. I'd tried to point out, as our booking agent had, that doing orbital simulcast was economical and easier on us. "But Autarie!" she'd screamed. "It's like fucking Vegas!" At the time I'd assumed that "Vegaz," as she said it in her Saturnál accent, was an ex-lover of hers who'd sucked in bed. Now little pieces of rock and roll history bounced through my moon-raised brain and I recalled an old interview I'd read with Mick Jagger—or was it Sting?—saying he'd never play Las Vegas and the meaning came clear: home of the has-beens. No one had been listening to her but me. Once she would start to go hysterical the others would tune her out. I suppose I only listened because I was the one trying to argue with her. "Oh, fuck," I murmured. Even if I had caught the reference, though, what good would it have done? I couldn't have stopped her, could I? She was gone.

Calla went over and knelt in front of the body. "It looks like she just... lay down and died."

"She did."

"What do you mean?" Calla had been with us a year, a great bass player, but neither Glory nor I had been sure she would stick with us. So she didn't know about the Spark.

"I don't know," I lied.

"Well, we have to get a doctor in here, find out what happened...."

I held up my hand. "No, no doctors."

"But Luna...."

"Not yet." My mind tried to come up to speed, but last night's party and the shock of seeing her there like that kept me partly paralyzed. "Huiper. First call Huiper and figure out what to say about it."

I put my head against the door jamb and sighed. It was the end of Glory, the end of the Seekers in all likelihood, possibly the end of all our careers. Replacing a drummer or backup singer is one thing, replacing the lead singer and founder is another thing entirely. I felt cold and lonely and sick and I sank down there in the doorway and almost wished it could have been me instead of her.

Basil almost tripped over me when she came in waving hardcopy of a review of last night's show. I liked Basil, even if I wasn't sure if she was a double-x or some form of genderqueer. Those things never mattered to the omnivorous Glory. For me it was good enough that she used a female pronoun. She was about to begin crowing the good bits of it aloud when she caught sight of the spectacle on the table. I couldn't bear to watch her face crumble into grief. So, I looked at my own whiter-than-white hands, and at Glory's, still streaked with indigo and violet of last night's stage makeup, clamped tight around the neck of the guitar. I supposed that the Walker was mine now, but I couldn't bring myself to pry it out of her grip.

I heard my own voice. "We can't have her photographed like this, like some funeral or something." Oh Glory, couldn't you have lived up to your name and gone out with a blaze of it?

Calla did not turn around, but said in a weak voice, "Was she... with anyone last night?"

I looked up at the two of them. Basil was taking it well. If anything she looked a little pissed off, and when she heard Calla's question she stiffened. Young and spurned. "Not me. She took off during the party and didn't come back...."

Until after we were all unconscious. Poor Basil, the newest of us, she'd only been playing with the Seekers for about six months and Glory'd been leading her on for most of it. She cursed under her breath. Glory had liked her youthful fire, her defiance. Perhaps she saw a little of herself there, or perhaps someone else she knew. She would have been a good vessel for the Spark, too, but Glory had held back passing it on. "Baz, could you get Huiper on a secure channel?"

"I'll try," she said, and went into her room to boot up a terminal.

Calla had left the room, too, leaving me alone with my dead lover. Ex-lover in any case now, I supposed. Although neither of us had taken up with someone else—we hadn't "broken up"—we hadn't had sex in a long time. A year, maybe two. And the fights recently had been worse, hadn't they? I'd wanted to believe that Glory's irritability, irrationality, and general out-of-control bitchiness was just a periodic magnification of her lead-singer prima donna persona, just a phase that we'd work out. But all along she had been suffering. The burning out. The end.

And I hadn't even felt it. Could I have helped her? Saved her? She'd been so distant from me, I doubted it. When the Spark is lost, there's no getting it back.

The first one I'd ever seen was just a month after I'd joined the group. Glory's ex-lover Saffron had split off to form his own band, but he came back once in a while to jam with us. His band wasn't doing very well. The critics were lambasting them for repeating the formulas of the past, and even I thought his music was kind of dull. He went out with a super cocktail of drugs and stims. Repeating the formulas of the past, as it were. We found him with the injector still in his hand at one of Glory's penthouse suites on Triton.

That one was easy for me to handle. I didn't know him that well, I was in love with Glory, and I was so young and new to the Spark that I didn't really connect Saffron's fate with mine. Huiper, our publicist, did a pretty good job of spreading the dirt around about the wild rock and roll boy who didn't know when to stop, and even made him into a kind of small-time martyr among his few but loyal fans. That was Huiper's job. But what would he say when he heard about Glory?

He would, of course, look for an angle that would generate maximum publicity and make Glory into a posthumous legend.

That wouldn't be hard since she was already a legend when she was alive. We all were. It was all a part of the Spark, the magic. We were stars in the celebrity skies of the whole solar system. But Huiper didn't know why or how she really died and this time I didn't have a story to feed him. "Mysterious Cause of Death Unknown" is what the headlines would have to say. The powers that be took her too soon, they'd lament. Or, maybe she died of a broken heart? Had our love really died? I shuddered at the thought. Huiper wouldn't implicate me in such a thing, would he? A sordid affair of lost love and betrayal?

The first fight we'd had yesterday was at sound check. The kind of spat that turned the mills of tabloid rumor, and all too typical. One of those fights that started as a bad mood, became a disagreement, then a full-fledged argument, and finally that hands and skin and bodies roughness that comes all too naturally with those who have been lovers. I had been tuning my guitar while she picked at the catered food backstage. Artificial gravity always screwed up her stomach for a couple of days but I didn't see as how that was any excuse for her to treat us all like shit. So when she brushed past me and bumped my tuner I griped at her loud enough for everyone to hear. I would have, stupidly, made even more of it if Maynard, our stage manager hadn't called for everyone to take places for sound check.

Glory was the first one out of the room but the last one to climb onto the riser and sling her guitar over her shoulder. We were only on the second verse of "Tears" when Glory called for a halt. "I need this monitor up, less rhythm guitar."

I tried to talk into my mic but it was off. I waved at Maynard to up it and everyone heard me say, "...can't do that. I won't be able to hear myself and you'll get off strum and you know it."

"Don't be ridiculous." She put her hands on her hips, the guitar hanging loose over her middle. Even under the house lights her skin had some hints of the lavender and blue that were her trademark colors. "You're so loud I can't hear the backing vox."

"Glory," I said, walking closer to her so she could hear my unamplified voice. "That's what you said at our warm up gig on Metassus and your solo was completely off...."

I saw her jaw clench as she made a little starting/stamping motion. "You deaf wretch!" She took a step toward me now, swinging the Walker off her shoulder and brandishing it in one hand like a scepter. "You wouldn't know a good solo if it split your skull." Her voice had gone shrill and Maynard modulated it through the PA to save all our ears. "Which one of us is the lead here?" And then she broke down into hurling epithets at me in Saturnál.

I didn't hear what she called me; I started to shout back "Fuck you, you egoistic bitch." But all I got out was "Fuck..." and then I threw off my head-mic and put my guitar in its stand and started to stalk off the stage. I couldn't be reduced to calling her names. I had to walk past her to the stairs and as I did, she pushed me on the shoulder. My arm flailed back and connected with her cheek and then she was trying to grab me by the hair and strangle me and bite me all at the same time. Then the road crew, uniformly burly, uniformly imperturbable, were pulling us apart. She'd scratched my arm hard enough that bright crimson blood began to trickle down my skin, lurid on the paleness of flesh that never sees sunlight. And she said, "You ungrateful bitch! Without me you'd still be rotting on your ass in moondust! You'll never be anything more than a second-rate fill-in back-up stringer!"

I was gone before I heard any more—I didn't need to. Fact is without her I'd never have been in this band or for that matter ever made it away from suburban Luna. Fact is I mostly believed the rest, too. Sometimes she told me I only had that one good song in me, and sometimes I believed her. We never recorded another one of mine after "Tears," that's true. Huiper, the paparazzi, the fansites, were always making up stories about us. Sometimes it was hard even for me to tell truth from fiction. The legend they tell about me is that I sneaked backstage at a Seekers show on Luna with a demo in my back pocket, which when she heard it, she fell in love with me. In some versions she is heartbroken over Saffron leaving, and that's why she swore off men, and fell for me.

The true story is not like that. First of all, Glory's heart never broke. And second, although I did go to that show on Luna, it hadn't been my intention to meet her. My own band had just broken up from the force of apathy and neglect. I'd been ready to sell the guitar, maybe move to Earth where my parents wouldn't have any more say about me, but I decided to spend at least one night forgetting all of that, suped up and dancing like a banshee at their show. It was at the Dome, huge crowd, thousands at the biggest gathering space on all of Luna. It was being simulcast all over Earth, a big event. I was in the general admission section down front where I elbowed my way to the stage. I can only speculate that she saw me then, and liked what she saw. Halfway through their final encore one of their road crew pulled me out of the crush at the front, over the security wall into the tech pit. I couldn't make out what he was saying but I got the vague idea that I wasn't being busted but invited to some kind of party. There were some others there, dressed like fans, looking lost too, so I figured we were all either equally safe or equally endangered.

It was a party. A tremendous party at the Lunar Grand Hotel. We were all a part of the entourage and never before had I felt so welcome wearing ragged black denim in the retro-look of the times. We were ushered into a grand ballroom where food and swirling lights were already in attendance as if the inanimate party had already begun. And at some point I recall being near her, Glory, and wanting to tell her something about how much I had enjoyed the show. Maybe I did tell her. Anyway, she led me to the true party within the party, an inner sanctum penthouse where the band members and all manner of miscellaneous wildlings were lounging, boozing, orgying, and so on. And eventually she pulled me even deeper into things, and we were in her own room, and in her own bed, in the dimness, as I traced the curve of her stomach by the shine of the glitter there and she breathed hot on my sex and we did not sleep until well into the next morning.

I only remember that night in snatches now. I remember lavender lips and the way she closed her eyes when she kissed me. I kept mine open to watch the way her mouth moved, then closed them as her hand sought deep into my jeans. I remember her left hand seeking between my legs and I imagine that I even felt the calluses on her fingers as she dragged them over my slick clit. I remember being on my back on the expanse of her bed, her body pressing mine down as her tongue hunted in the forest of my bush and I stared at the cleft of her ass, her cunt, pistoning above my face until I reached out with my own tongue. I remember what seemed like hours with my legs over the edge of the bed, and her quick fingers playing over my clit again and again, and sinking her hand into me, first the cone of her fingers, and eventually her entire hand, balled inside. There was probably more, but it has been obliterated by time and drugs and overlayers of bad memories.

It wasn't until after we woke up that afternoon that she began to ask me about myself. Or maybe I should say tell me about myself. I played guitar, right? And I sang. And I wrote about what was black and dripping in the human soul. How do you know? I must have asked, my jaw flapping as she ran her fingers through my straight black hair and remarked how even my lips were moondust pale. And she started calling me Luna right then. She hinted that she was very good at reading people through sex, though of course now I know it could have been the Spark.

Then she told me she wanted to hear me play. She forced the Walker into my hands and made me play. I was too nervous to sing, but I let my fingers go by themselves, through riffs I'd fought with Derel over before we'd both begun to act like we didn't care about the band or each other. And at the end of the song, the one that would later become "Tears" when I wrote words for it, she did have tears in her eyes and she told me she knew just how it was with me.

There is nothing like making love with your lover's tears wetting your face. She kissed me then, and laid the guitar aside, and pushed me back on the bed, and it is not like we were wearing clothes anyway. She dragged her cunt along my thigh, hot and slick like her tearstained face, until she came, and then I flipped her over and fucked her with my fingers and ate her at the same time, until I don't know how many times she came, piling orgasm on top of orgasm, until she turned the tables and did the same back to me.

That was probably the last time I had been in charge at any time in our relationship. Because when her fingers were still inside me, after my third or fourth orgasm, as she sank her other hand into my hair, she asked me if I was interested in leaving Luna, and joining her as rhythm guitarist.

That's the real story of how I got whisked away. Because of course I said yes. Had she already passed the Spark to me? I think she had. I think it happened when she fucked me right after I had played. What would have happened if I had said no? Would the Spark have died and me with it? I just didn't know. There was too much we didn't know. I know that through the fire and heat of music and sex and losing ourselves in both she passed it to me, but even ten years later, I knew very little more than that.

Calla and Basil had not had such an initiation from her. They were still waiting.

I should have realized when Saffron died that I might be in over my head. But I was so caught up in her, and in music, in finally devoting my life to someone and something that I enjoyed, that I felt I was born to do, that I didn't worry about how the Spark worked. It was just the lifeblood that fed us, that kept each of us going; writing, composing, playing. Some nights, when we'd played to a fever pitch, it boiled over, and there were always wildlings around to party with, to soak up that energy and go home both tired and exhilarated in the morning. Groupies don't know it, but it's the Spark they are attracted to, addicted to. Maybe they figure it's just the drugs, or the excitement, they feel it during the sex we have, that thrill singing in their veins. But unless they have music in their souls, it can't hurt them. It passes through them just like the drugs. It's only people like me that it takes hold of and doesn't let go. And Saffron. And Nura and Rose, who were both gone now for years, replaced by a string of studio musicians of Glory's choosing, until now Calla and Basil....

I had started to shiver, there in the doorway, as if the coldness of her flesh were making me chilly. There was also the fact that I was wearing just an old show T-shirt and underwear. I felt cold and empty, and the shaking became worse.

Calla was there, then, dressed in show clothes. Anticipating a press conference, I guess. She wrapped her arms around my shoulders. "Oh, Luna..." she started. "Be strong."

But I wasn't shaking with sobs. Glory had told me once that the Spark runs its course like a fever—oh sure, it could be years and years, but the hotter it burns the more likely it is to burn you up. At some point it burns out and leaves you high and dry and unable to function.

She had waited until after I'd accepted her offer to spell all that out for me. When she told me, it felt almost like it wasn't anything that I didn't already know. Some hacks can go on forever because they never had it in the first place. But those who really had it.... I didn't have to hear her name out the others. The agonizing slow death of Elvis, who staggered on long after the Spark had abandoned him, trying to replace it with amphetamines and sycophants until both failed him. Janis Joplin, whose own insecurities about her talent strangled it and forced her into drugs also. Kurt Cobain. The murderous rampage of the octogenerian Paul McCartney outside Buckingham Palace.

My body was wracked with spasms. And suddenly it made sense to me. The Spark was going to go out for me, if I didn't do something about it. The flame needed to be fed, stoked, with music and sex with other people who had it. Was that what killed Saffron, ultimately? Being cut off from her, and being unwilling to share it with others for his own survival? I wished I had known him better. Had he been losing it already, starting to burn out, when he left the Seekers? Had Glory and I been killing each other with the fighting and "creative differences?" The passion had turned to anger long ago, is that what made her burn up or gutter out?

"What happens now?" I asked Calla, who was squeezing me harder now, as I clenched my jaw to keep my teeth from chattering.

I hadn't meant her to answer, but she did. "Luna, you're sick. We have to get you to medical."

"No!" What would they find? The Spark was a secret not even Huiper knew about. Who could I turn to? I had met very few others who I knew beyond any doubt had it. Bowie, still going in his thirteenth decade, re-invented once again. But I didn't know how to reach him and couldn't imagine the conversation we would have.

Looking at Glory there on the table, I considered the traditional ways out for a moment. But I couldn't see myself drowning my "sorrows" in chemicals or crashing my flyer while "under the influence." I took a deep breath and got the shivering under control for a few moments.

There was really only one choice. Pass the Spark on to Calla or Basil, or die. "Calla," I said, trying to work up the nerve to say something.

But then Basil was there. "Huiper's not reachable. We can try him again at four, though." I looked up to see Calla take her hand, and I suddenly knew the two of them had slept together last night.

No, they were about to. They had each been waiting, hoping, to be the one that Glory took up with when she took up with someone again. Now she was gone, and they could see each other clearly for the first time. They looked into each other's eyes, a kind of wordless connection strung between them.

They looked up at the first sound of the guitar. I had crawled over to where Glory lay, and slid the Walker from her hands to cradle it in my lap. I had no pick and just used my fingernails to strike a chord, the first of a descending series starting up on the neck and working my way down until it felt right. From there, I fell naturally into a minor key riff, alternating the strum with finger picking.

I could almost hear the parts that would go along with it, a cello, with a deep, rich bowed voice, and hand drums, a doumbek maybe. I kept playing. There were no words. I didn't know what to tell them, what I wanted to say about her or me or my life. I just kept playing.

But eventually the song came to a close, as it cycled down and my energy flagged. When I finished, I saw they were both crying. I laid the guitar aside and went to them, and hugged them.

Exactly how that turned into me kissing Calla, I'm not sure. Her mouth was hot in mine, her cheeks wet and scarlet. Her breath came fast and hard. My hands traveled down her sides, over her hips. I felt her weight shift, as she reached out to Basil. Then she was kissing her, too, and in the back of my head I tried to pause. I had done many wild sexual things since leaving my quiet life on the moon. Some of them had been with Glory, some not. But I did not know what Basil had under her jeans and to some part of me that mattered.

The Spark did not much care for my squeamishness. The pang of fear I felt transmuted into thrill, and then my attention went back to Calla and I felt desire flare. I pulled her toward me, Basil trailing along like the caboose, onto the smooth, hospital-cornered bed. I began peeling off the clothes she had just put on. Basil took her other side, and very shortly Calla was naked there on the coverlet between us. Basil and I exchanged a look, then each of us took a nipple in our mouths and Calla gasped. In perfect harmony, we each slid a hand up the inside of her legs, teasing her. Then Basil's fingers cupped over her mons, her labia, and then spread, opening her for me. I used the tip of my index finger to skim the cream from the edge of her vaginal opening, spreading it liberally around her clit. She moaned. I continued to move gently, my touch light, until she ground her hips upward toward my hand. But she could not move much, as Basil and I kept sucking her nipples, and I lifted my hand away from her.

She whimpered and Basil chuckled low in her throat in response. I played with her lightly until she bucked again and this time I let her impale herself on my fingers, my index and middle fingers curving into her, my thumb extended over Basil's hand and then sliding between her fingers to where her clit swelled. One of her hands clutched at Basil's jeans and I gave her a little nod. I had her cunt to myself then, and I took the opportunity to position myself there, my cheeks between her thighs. But as I licked her with long strokes, at first softly but then with urgent energy as her voice rose to a wail, I had one eye fixed on Basil. Under the jeans she had plain white briefs, with a noticeable bulge. My stomach tightened. Then she slipped those off, too, and I almost laughed with my tongue plastered in Calla's cunt. Basil's protuberance was a technocock of some sort, form-fitted and wired to her nervous system, rising rapidly in response to the arousal signals her brain was sending. The skin was imbedded not only with millions of nanosensors, but with accompanying lightglow effects. Right now the base was a deep red but the tip was glowing white like an iron left in the fire.

Calla tugged at Basil's brightly colored cock then and

silenced herself as she pulled the slender machine into her mouth.

Baz gasped and steadied herself on the bed with one hand as Calla's tongue worked. It felt to me like I was licking her, too, as if somehow, through Calla, Basil's cock and my tongue were connecting. "Kee-rist..." she breathed, the only one of the three of us whose mouth was not busy, and yet she could barely speak. "Wow... it's...."

Calla paused to grin up at her. "Is it as good as they say?"

Basil nodded, then must have read the questions in my eyes. "It's new. She... paid for it...." and that was all she could say as Calla's mouth went back to work. It made sense now, the way she kept expecting Glory to invite her to bed. I felt Calla's clit spasm under my tongue and knew she was close to coming. I increased my pressure and she came while Basil thrust into her mouth, into the fleshy side of her cheek where I saw it bulge. Then I closed my eyes and concentrated on making her come once more, two fingers spiraling in and out of her while my mouth drew her clit in and I clicked my tongue on it. She rewarded me quickly, wailing again as Basil popped free.

I sat up and Calla looked at me, pleadingly, both of them did, and it was easy to see she wanted more of the technocock. Basil and she giggled a bit as we swapped positions, and I shifted around until Calla was sitting up, her back against my chest like two kids on a gravity toboggan. I reached around with my hands to brush her nipples and she arched just as Basil thrust in. Soon she had established a rhythm, and I let the waves of sensation come through her body and into my own cunt. I had tucked my head next to hers and she could turn her head to kiss me on the lips. I closed my eyes and kissed her and rode the wave of Basil's backbeat for a while. Then she broke away and kissed her, too.

I was startled out of my reverie then by Baz's lips on mine, her tongue searching urgently for something in my mouth. The Spark flared up to meet her hungrily. And then somehow she was climbing past Calla, and the two of them together climbed onto me. Calla lay along one side, kissing my neck and stroking me from breast to the top of my bush, while Basil crushed the erect technocock into the crook of my hip with her body.

"Luna," she whispered, her throat tightened by desire. "Luna." I quivered under her, the echo of the shivering fit I'd had before starting again. I knew if I paused too long... I knew I didn't want to pause too long. Glory and I had played with dildos, the low-tech kind, from time to time—she liked sticking things into my cunt as a way to prove she was in charge—but never anything like this, and not in a long time. I crooked one knee up and there was the tool, now glowing blue and green and casting an undersea look on Basil's face, bumping up against the flesh between my legs. It had looked so slim before as she had pumped Calla's mouth, but now I wondered if it would hurt when she put it in. I clutched at her sweaty back with one arm, the one that wasn't trapped by Calla, craving it and fearing it all at the same time, which only stoked the Spark hotter. Calla's free hand then, it had to be, reached between my legs and opened me wide, and Basil thrust upward through the slippery juices, then she adjusted its angle and sank into me.

I cried out, not from physical pain but from the sudden memory of the shape of Glory's hand stuffed into me. Basil's technocock was nothing like that, conveniently shaped for pleasure, but not the rock heart that her fist had been.

Calla moved then, letting Basil push my knees up, and straddled my face. I licked at her between gasps as she dug her fingers between our bodies to get at my clit. She soon had the loose skin of my labia and bush stretched up taut toward my belly with one hand while the other jabbed in double time over the hard nub. Basil's thrusts mashed her hand even harder into me and I thrashed my head from side to side. "Harder," I said through clenched teeth. My body wanted violence, needed it to break through the tense wall of pain that separated me from them. The wall that Glory's death had erected.

No, I realized. The wall that Glory and I had built bit by bit over the last few years. Basil and Calla obliged, fucking me and frigging me as hard as they could, until I felt the edge of her finger claw over my clit. "Yes!" She crooked her finger more and I bucked hard against her, Basil now the one along for the ride. The orgasm seemed to radiate along my skin as well as through my insides, doubling back and cresting for a second time as they continued their motions until I went limp.

I was amazed that Basil had not come, but what did I know about how the technology worked? Maybe she had a way to turn it down. She pulled out of me, the tool glistening wet and now throbbing a deep purple, and Calla nearly leapt upon it. Baz obliged, falling onto her back and letting Calla seat herself with the cock deep inside. She moaned and fell forward for a moment, then sat up erect. Now I could again circle her with my arms and get my fingers onto her clit and nipples.

I don't know how long it was before she succeeded in making Basil come. All sense of time had long since fled. The three of us were just in a groove, where she would peak, then I would, using my own fingers when I had to, until eventually she arched and cried out and gripped her by the hips for two last thrusts that set Basil finally into a spasm, while I thrust my own fingers into my empty vagina, trying to remember what Glory's calluses had felt like.

The two of them were then on me again quickly, Calla burying her face in my muff while Basil hugged me from behind. Then, as Calla drew another orgasm out of me, as I beat my palms on the coverlet, I shouted "Enough, enough!"

They fell away from me as the sensation ebbed. There weren't many cases, but there were a few, where people were fucked to death. The Spark can burn out a host, too. It was time to get it back under control.

I think it was some time later that I began to speak. I'm not sure if I blacked out or not, but when I came to, they were still there. The three of us were lying on top of the bed and I had no way of knowing if we'd been there for a minute or an hour. "We're going to play tonight," I said.

"What?" Basil sat up at the sound of my voice and rubbed her eyes.

"We're going to play tonight. A tribute concert for her. Just like we did here. Improvisational, cooperative." Not like anything we'd done before. As I described it to them, I could see the idea catching fire, the memory of the song I had played stirring faintly. "And there's something else I have to tell you." And I told them, about the Spark, about Saffron, about Glory, Rose and Nura, and all I knew. "I'm sorry," I said as I finished. "I should have told you before. For some it becomes a curse...." I looked at Glory, still lying in state on the low table. "But it is a gift, too."

In response, they came and kissed me, both together. I already had the sound in my head of the music we could make together.

Thanks and acknowledgments

THANKS go first to my partner, corwin, who is far more than a "writer support system" (his words, not mine). My writers' group, commonly known as Bass-fwig, and some of the awesome people in my community of writers, artists, and friends who have helped me, including but not limited to Kelly J. Cooper, Lauren P. Burka, Shariann Lewitt, Rachel Silber, Robert Lawrence and Carol Queen, Midori, M. Christian, Susie Bright, John Davis, Patrick Hughes, John Oakes, Lynne Jamneck, Victor Raymond, Debbie Notkin, and many others over the course of years it took to amass these short stories. My agent Lori Perkins, and my editor Don Weise, without whom the book would not be what you see today. Let's not forget my parents: Dad, you were the one who suggested grad school in the first place. Mom, your unconditional support is what has let me be who I am all along.

REPRINT CREDITS:

Love's Year (from *Hot & Bothered*, Arsenal Pulp Press)

Always (from *Herotica* 6, Plume)

The Hard Sell (from Fatbrain.com)

Thought So (from *Best Women's Erotica 2003*, Cleis Press)

Baseball Fever (from *Starf*cker*, Alyson Publications)

The Little Mermaid (from *Aqua Erotica*, Crown)

Rite of Spring (from *Wet: More Aqua Erotica*, Crown)

Bodies of Water (from the *Big Book of Hot Women's Erotica*)

Dragon's Daughter & Hall of Mirrors (from *To Be Continued*,
  Firebrand Books)

The Lady in Black (not yet published)

Storm Rider (from *The Wildest Ones*, Alyson Publications)

Sleeping Beauty (not yet published)

Just Tell Me the Rules (from *Aqua Erotica 2*, Melcher Media)

Halloween (from *Slave*, Venus Books)

Balancing Act (from *Blithe House Quarterly*, Winter 2000 issue)

A Tale of the Marketplace (from *The Academy*, Mystic Rose Books)

Drumbeat (from *On Our Backs* magazine, also *Uniform Sex*,
  Alyson Publications)

Lip Service (from *Best S/M Erotica*, Black Books)

Gyndroid (not yet published)

Now (from *Viscera*, Venus of Vixen Press)

The Spark (Lethe Press)